T0269649

WHAT WOULD SCOTLAND YARD DO WITHOUT DEAR MRS. JEFFRIES?

The Inspector and Mrs. Jeffries: When a doctor is found dead in his own office, Mrs. Jeffries must scour the premises to find the prescription for murder.

Mrs. Jeffries Dusts for Clues: One case is solved and another is opened when the inspector finds a missing brooch—pinned to a dead woman's gown.

The Ghost and Mrs. Jeffries: When the murder of Mrs. Hodges is foreseen at a spooky séance, Mrs. Jeffries must look into the past for clues.

Mrs. Jeffries Takes Stock: A businessman has been murdered—and the smart money's on Mrs. Jeffries to catch the killer.

Mrs. Jeffries on the Ball: A festive Jubilee celebration turns into a fatal affair—and Mrs. Jeffries must find the guilty party.

Mrs. Jeffries on the Trail: Mrs. Jeffries must sniff out a flower peddler's killer.

Mrs. Jeffries Plays the Cook: Mrs. Jeffries finds herself doing double duty: cooking for the inspector's household and trying to cook a killer's goose.

Mrs. Jeffries and the Missing Alibi: When Inspector Witherspoon is the main suspect in a murder, only Mrs. Jeffries can save him.

Mrs. Jeffries Stands Corrected: When a local publican is murdered and Inspector Witherspoon botches the investigation, trouble starts to brew for Mrs. Jeffries.

Mrs. Jeffries Takes the Stage: After a theater critic is murdered, Mrs. Jeffries uncovers the victim's secret shocking past.

Mrs. Jeffries Questions the Answer: To find the disagreeable Hannah Cameron's killer, Mrs. Jeffries must tread lightly—or it could be a matter of life and death.

Mrs. Jeffries Reveals Her Art: A missing model *and* a killer have Mrs. Jeffries working double time before someone else becomes the next subject.

Mrs. Jeffries Takes the Cake: A dead body, two dessert plates, and a gun. Mrs. Jeffries will have to do some serious snooping around to dish up more clues.

Mrs. Jeffries Rocks the Boat: A murdered woman had recently traveled by boat from Australia. Now Mrs. Jeffries must solve the case—and it's sink or swim.

Mrs. Jeffries Weeds the Plot: Three attempts have been made on Annabeth Gentry's life. Is it because her bloodhound dug up the body of a murdered thief?

Mrs. Jeffries Pinches the Post: Mrs. Jeffries and her staff must root through the sins of a ruthless man's past to catch his killer.

Mrs. Jeffries Pleads Her Case: The inspector is determined to prove a suicide was murder, and with Mrs. Jeffries on his side, he may well succeed.

Mrs. Jeffries Sweeps the Chimney: A vicar has been found murdered and Inspector Witherspoon's only prayer is to seek the divinations of Mrs. Jeffries.

Mrs. Jeffries Stalks the Hunter: When love turns deadly, who better to get to the heart of the matter than Inspector Witherspoon's indomitable companion, Mrs. Jeffries?

Mrs. Jeffries and the Silent Knight: The yuletide murder of an elderly man is complicated by several suspects—none of whom were in the Christmas spirit.

Mrs. Jeffries Appeals the Verdict: Mrs. Jeffries and her belowstairs cohorts have their work cut out for them if they want to save an innocent man from the gallows.

Mrs. Jeffries and the Best Laid Plans: Everyone banker Lawrence Boyd met became his enemy. It will take Mrs. Jeffries' shrewd eye to find who killed him.

Mrs. Jeffries and the Feast of St. Stephen: 'Tis the season for sleuthing when a wealthy man is murdered and Mrs. Jeffries must solve the case in time for Christmas.

Mrs. Jeffries Holds the Trump: A medical magnate is found floating down the river. Now Mrs. Jeffries will have to dive into the mystery.

Mrs. Jeffries in the Nick of Time: Mrs. Jeffries lends her downstairs common sense to this upstairs murder mystery.

Mrs. Jeffries and the Yuletide Weddings: Wedding bells will make this season all the more jolly. Until one humbug sings a carol of murder.

Mrs. Jeffries Speaks Her Mind: Everyone doubts an eccentric old woman who suspects she's going to be murdered—until the prediction comes true.

Mrs. Jeffries Forges Ahead: A free-spirited bride is poisoned, and it's up to Mrs. Jeffries to discover who wanted to make the modern young woman into a postmortem.

Mrs. Jeffries and the Mistletoe Mix-Up: There's murder going on under the mistletoe as Mrs. Jeffries and Inspector Witherspoon hurry to solve the case.

Mrs. Jeffries Defends Her Own: When an unwelcome visitor from her past needs help, Mrs. Jeffries steps into the fray to stop a terrible miscarriage of justice.

Mrs. Jeffries Turns the Tide: When Mrs. Jeffries doubts a suspect's guilt, she must turn the tide of the investigation to save an innocent man.

Mrs. Jeffries and the Merry Gentlemen: When a successful stockbroker is murdered just days before Christmas, Mrs. Jeffries won't rest until justice is served for the holidays.

Mrs. Jeffries and the One Who Got Away: When a woman is found strangled clutching an old newspaper clipping, only Mrs. Jeffries can get to the bottom of the story.

Mrs. Jeffries Wins the Prize: Inspector Witherspoon and Mrs. Jeffries weed out a killer after a body is found in a gentlewoman's conservatory.

Mrs. Jeffries Rights a Wrong: Mrs. Jeffries and Inspector Witherspoon must determine who had the motive to put a duplicitous businessman in the red.

Berkley Prime Crime titles by Emily Brightwell

THE INSPECTOR AND MRS. JEFFRIES
MRS. JEFFRIES DUSTS FOR CLUES
THE GHOST AND MRS. JEFFRIES
MRS. JEFFRIES TAKES STOCK
MRS. JEFFRIES ON THE BALL
MRS. JEFFRIES ON THE TRAIL
MRS. JEFFRIES PLAYS THE COOK
MRS. JEFFRIES AND THE MISSING ALIBI
MRS. JEFFRIES STANDS CORRECTED
MRS. JEFFRIES TAKES THE STAGE
MRS. JEFFRIES QUESTIONS THE ANSWER
MRS. JEFFRIES REVEALS HER ART
MRS. JEFFRIES TAKES THE CAKE
MRS. JEFFRIES ROCKS THE BOAT
MRS. JEFFRIES WEEDS THE PLOT
MRS. JEFFRIES PINCHES THE POST
MRS. JEFFRIES PLEADS HER CASE
MRS. JEFFRIES SWEEPS THE CHIMNEY
MRS. JEFFRIES STALKS THE HUNTER
MRS. JEFFRIES AND THE SILENT KNIGHT
MRS. JEFFRIES APPEALS THE VERDICT
MRS. JEFFRIES AND THE BEST LAID PLANS
MRS. JEFFRIES AND THE FEAST OF ST. STEPHEN
MRS. JEFFRIES HOLDS THE TRUMP
MRS. JEFFRIES IN THE NICK OF TIME
MRS. JEFFRIES AND THE YULETIDE WEDDINGS
MRS. JEFFRIES SPEAKS HER MIND
MRS. JEFFRIES FORGES AHEAD
MRS. JEFFRIES AND THE MISTLETOE MIX-UP
MRS. JEFFRIES DEFENDS HER OWN
MRS. JEFFRIES TURNS THE TIDE
MRS. JEFFRIES AND THE MERRY GENTLEMEN
MRS. JEFFRIES AND THE ONE WHO GOT AWAY
MRS. JEFFRIES WINS THE PRIZE
MRS. JEFFRIES RIGHTS A WRONG
MRS. JEFFRIES AND THE THREE WISE WOMEN

Anthologies

MRS. JEFFRIES LEARNS THE TRADE
MRS. JEFFRIES TAKES A SECOND LOOK
MRS. JEFFRIES TAKES TEA AT THREE
MRS. JEFFRIES SALLIES FORTH
MRS. JEFFRIES PLEADS THE FIFTH
MRS. JEFFRIES SERVES AT SIX

MRS. JEFFRIES
and the
Three Wise Women

Emily Brightwell

BERKLEY PRIME CRIME
NEW YORK

BERKLEY PRIME CRIME
Published by Berkley
An imprint of Penguin Random House LLC
375 Hudson Street, New York, New York 10014

Copyright © 2017 by Cheryl A. Arguile
Penguin Random House supports copyright. Copyright fuels creativity,
encourages diverse voices, promotes free speech, and creates a vibrant culture.
Thank you for buying an authorized edition of this book and for complying with
copyright laws by not reproducing, scanning, or distributing any part of it
in any form without permission. You are supporting writers and allowing
Penguin Random House to continue to publish books for every reader.

BERKLEY is a registered trademark and BERKLEY PRIME CRIME and
the B colophon are trademarks of Penguin Random House LLC.

Berkley Prime Crime trade paperback ISBN: 9780399584244

The Library of Congress has catalogued
the Berkley Prime Crime hardcover edition as follows:

Names: Brightwell, Emily, author.
Title: Mrs. Jeffries and the three wise women / Emily Brightwell.
Description: First edition. | New York, NY : Berkley, 2017. |
Series: A victorian mystery ; 36
Identifiers: LCCN 2017025349 (print) | LCCN 2017027767 (ebook) |
ISBN 9780399584237 (eBook) | ISBN 9780399584220 (hardcover)
Subjects: LCSH: Witherspoon, Gerald (Fictitious character)—Fiction. |
Jeffries, Mrs. (Fictitious character)—Fiction. | Women
detectives—England—Fiction. | Housekeepers—England—Fiction. |
Murder—Investigation—Fiction. | Police—England—Fiction. | BISAC:
FICTION / Mystery & Detective / Women Sleuths. | GSAFD: Mystery fiction.
Classification: LCC PS3552.R46443 (ebook) | LCC PS3552.R46443 M642 2017
(print) | DDC 813/.54—dc23
LC record available at https://lccn.loc.gov/2017025349

Berkley Prime Crime hardcover edition / October 2017
Berkley Prime Crime trade paperback edition / September 2018

Cover art by Jeff Walker

147506545

CHAPTER 1

November 5
Guy Fawkes Night

"That awful man is never going to be welcome in this house again," Abigail Chase muttered to her husband. They stood in the doorway of their elegant Chelsea town house and watched as the man in question disappeared around the corner and into the mews. "He completely ruined my dinner party." She glared at her husband for a moment before turning and flouncing off.

Gordon Chase closed the door and hurried after her. "Darling, it wasn't that bad. Gilhaney's a bit rough around the edges, but he meant no harm."

She stopped at the entrance to the drawing room. "Meant no harm," she sneered. "He insulted every single one of our guests and frankly, it's all your fault. You should never have insisted we include him and don't even think about asking him to our Christmas party. I'll not have that ruined as well."

"But, darling, be reasonable, I had to ask him, I had no choice. Newton's put him on the board and he made it very clear, he expected us to host him tonight." Gordon hurried after her as she continued into the room.

"I don't care how important Newton Walker thinks the man is to his company, he's a boor and a bully and I'll never have him in the house again." She pointed to the carriage clock on the mantel. "It's not even nine o'clock and our guests have gone. Most of them didn't even bother to finish their dessert. That wretched man ruined our Bonfire Night festivities." She grimaced as a loud noise boomed through the house. "Hear that? Fireworks are still going off, people are out having fun and enjoying the evening, but not us. There's no revelry here, there's no November the fifth celebration for us, thanks to that odious fellow." She glared at her husband in exasperation. "You shouldn't have told him about the shortcut through the mews—it would have served him right to go the long way around. Well, I for one hope that Christopher Gilhaney breaks an ankle when he takes that shortcut. It'll be dark enough, that's for certain."

Unlike his host and hostess, the man in question had thoroughly enjoyed himself at the Chase dinner party. He chuckled as he went farther into the mews, squinting just a bit to make his way. Mind you, it had ended a bit early for his taste, but he'd had a fine meal as well as the satisfaction of watching them squirm. He pulled his coat tighter against the chill night air and smiled as he remembered the shocked expressions on each of their faces as he'd quietly attacked them with his carefully scripted comments. God, it had been glorious and it was just the beginning. Before he was finished, the whole lot of them would be sorry.

Another explosion rocked the night, this time from the direction of the river. Shouts and laughter mingled with the faint, acrid scent of smoke and for a brief moment, he was overcome with nostalgia. He wished he were back in the old days, back when he'd have been on the banks of the Thames with his beloved Polly and their friends; drinking beer, watching the bonfires, and setting off the few fireworks they could afford. But those times were long gone. Polly was long gone.

He slowed his steps as he moved farther into the darkness, but his eyesight was excellent and he could easily see his way. Tonight had been far more successful than he'd hoped. When Chase had originally invited him, he'd been going to content himself with firing off a few verbal salvos. But his well-rehearsed comments had hit their individual targets with amazing success and, one after another, they'd fled the battlefield. Silly fools, this war was just beginning. He felt a bit bad about poor Mrs. Chase; she'd looked horrified as her guests disappeared, but she'd get over it.

Another burst of fireworks exploded into the noisy night, rising above the shouts, screams, and laughter now coming from all directions. Bonfire Night was drawing to a close and he, for one, intended to get home to his warm bed. The November night was cold and the dampness was seeping through his shoes and into his feet.

As the fireworks faded, he heard footsteps ahead. He stopped for a moment and listened. Someone had come into the mews from the other end, but he wasn't overly alarmed.

There were a lot of people out and about tonight and he wasn't the only person using this shortcut. It slashed a quarter of a mile off the walk between Chelsea and the railway station. Nonetheless, he put his hand in his pocket and slipped his fingers through the brass knuckles he carried for protection. It paid to be cautious.

Ahead of him, a figure emerged and came steadily toward him. The sky suddenly dimmed as the moon slipped behind the clouds so he couldn't see anything except a human shape, but whoever it was moved to the opposite side of the mews. Apparently, they, too, were wary of meeting strangers in dark places.

Reassured, he picked up his pace and began planning what he'd do tomorrow. Newton had told him the first clerks arrived at eight o'clock. He intended to be there at five past eight. He wanted a few words with the accounts clerks before anyone else was present. Newton had assured him that the management didn't arrive till nine at the earliest.

His companion was now close enough for him to make out some details. His steps faltered as he realized whoever it was wore a shapeless, hooded cloak, a garment that looked like it should be hanging around the figure of one of the Old Guy effigies along the riverbank. The cloak covered whoever it was from head to toe, making it impossible to determine if it was a male or female. Surprised, he stared as they came level and then passed each other on opposite sides of the mews. Suddenly uneasy, because there was something about the figure that simply wasn't right, he sucked in a deep breath of air and hurried toward the gas lamp at the far end.

A rash of fireworks went off, along with cheering and shouting from the throngs near the Thames. But despite the noise, his sharp hearing caught the sound of footsteps racing toward him and he turned, pulling the hand wearing the brass knuckles out of his pocket as he moved.

But he was too late; just as the last of the sound of explosions filled the air, the cloaked figure held out a gun and fired three bullets straight into his heart.

Christopher Gilhaney had barely hit the ground before his assailant knelt down and pulled the brass knuckles off his cold, dead hand.

Inspector Nigel Nivens stood in Chief Superintendent Barrows' third-floor office at Scotland Yard and argued that he was the right man for the task. "This isn't a murder, it is a robbery gone wrong. According to his landlady, when he left his lodging house last night, Mr. Gilhaney was wearing a diamond stickpin on his cravat and a gold ring with a black stone in the center. Neither of those items was found on his body."

Nivens was a man of medium height with dark blond hair graying at the temples, bulbous blue eyes, cheeks that were turning to jowls, and a thick mustache. He wore a gray pinstriped suit tailored to disguise the fact that he was running too fat around his middle.

Chief Superintendent Barrows stared at him impassively. He now wished he'd gone with his first instinct when he'd been informed of the murder last night and called in Inspector Witherspoon. But he'd hesitated and now, given the politics of the Home Office and Nivens' family's influence, he was probably stuck with the fellow. Drat. "The landlady is prepared to swear at the inquest that he had those items on his person when he left her premises?"

"She is, sir. This crime was most definitely a robbery, and as such, I believe I'm the most qualified to handle the case, not Inspector Witherspoon. What's more, Kilbane Mews is well within my district, not Witherspoon's."

"When it comes to murder, you know good and well that the spot where the corpse was found isn't the most important factor. Catching the killer is." Barrows pushed his glasses up his nose and leaned back in his chair. He toyed with the idea of giving the case to Witherspoon simply because he didn't like Nivens, but at this juncture, that might cause more trouble than it was worth. The fellow was from a family that had both money and aristocratic connections. Nivens wasn't a bad copper, but he wasn't a brilliant one, either, and they needed this crime solved. On the other hand, if the killing of Christopher Gilhaney was the result of a botched robbery and not murder, then perhaps he was more qualified to handle the case; he was actually quite good at solving burglaries and catching robbers.

But Barrows wanted to ensure that justice was done properly as well. He might be in administration now, but he was still a policeman at heart. "What's more, I'm not as certain as you seem to be that the crime was a robbery. Gilhaney died from three gunshots to his chest. Robbers and ruffians don't use guns. If they get violent at all, they cosh their victim over the head or knock the wind out of him."

Nivens was ready for that question. "What about the Ogden case? Harry Ogden was killed by a gun when he was robbed. He was shot twice."

"Yes, but it was his own pistol," Barrows reminded him. "Ogden carried it for protection, remember? He was only shot with it because Jack Rayley, his assailant, grabbed it when Ogden pulled it out of his pocket."

"I know that, Chief Superintendent, but nonetheless, it was a case of a firearm used during the course of a robbery, which means that regardless of the circumstances, it's likely this is merely a case of a botched robbery, not a murder." Nivens' gaze flicked to the window. He stared at the busy boat and barge traffic on the Thames. He needed to make a compelling argument to keep this case away from Inspector Witherspoon. He was sick and tired of Gerald Witherspoon always being the one the Yard called upon when there was a newsworthy case to be solved. "Furthermore, there was the case in Brighton last month of another gun being used in a robbery. That young hotel clerk who was taking the day's receipts to the bank. If you'll recall, sir, that resulted in a shooting as well. The clerk was wounded in the leg and the perpetrators managed to get away."

"Brighton isn't London," Barrows said.

"But it isn't that far from London, sir. What's more, the criminals that committed the Brighton robbery could have easily come here. My point is this, sir: We've seen a steady rise in the number of cases involving firearms. There was also that shooting in Stepney, sir, and the victim claimed he was being robbed."

"The victim was a Whitechapel thug that was involved in a fight for territory with the Stepney gang. He only came up with that story to keep from being arrested himself." Barrows sighed inwardly. "But in one sense, you're right. There is some evidence that points to the increased use of firearms. So you can take this case."

Nivens nodded smartly. "Thank you, sir."

"Don't thank me, Inspector—I expect you to find the person or persons that did this dreadful crime."

"Of course, sir. I've got constables out questioning the locals, just in case someone might have seen something, and I've got the word out to my network of informers so we should have something from that quarter soon."

"Good, we've already got the Home Office sticking their oar in so I'll expect you to take care of this quickly and efficiently."

"I assure you, sir"—Nivens gave him a tight smile—"I've every confidence I shall have it solved in just a few days."

But the case wasn't solved in a few days or, for that matter, weeks later. It was as if the assailant had simply vanished into thin air.

Nivens stood outside of Barrows' office and took a deep, calming breath. He knew why he'd been summoned here and it wasn't so that the chief superintendent could compliment him on a job well done. He was at his wits' end, but blast it, it wasn't his fault. No one, not even the great Witherspoon, could have solved this case.

None of the neighbors in the mews had paid any attention to loud noises. After all, it was Bonfire Night and half the city was letting off fireworks, drinking like sailors, and screaming as the "Old Guy" burned. A few gunshots wouldn't have stood out. Nor had anyone seen a suspicious figure in the area—again, it was November the fifth and half of London was out roaming the streets.

His network of informers had also drawn a blank. No diamond stickpins or gold rings had shown up at any of the dodgy pawnshops suspected of fencing stolen goods. No matter how much pressure he applied, no one, not even his most reliable informers, had heard anything about a botched robbery.

It was now December eighteenth and Nivens knew he had to come up with a way to deflect the blame off himself or, failing that, make sure that Witherspoon took over the case. That was the only way he could rebound from this failure. This crime wasn't going to be solved by anyone, but if he tried to make that argument right now, Barrows wouldn't believe it. Their glorious inspector, the one who'd solved more crimes than anyone in the history of the Metropolitan Police Force, needed to fail as well.

Now he just had to make certain that Barrows handed the case to the right person. Getting rid of this case was the wisest course; if anyone was to have a black mark against his record, let it be Gerald Witherspoon. Nivens smiled in satisfaction. He'd go ahead and enjoy the holidays by accepting Lord Ballinger's invitation to spend Christmas at his estate in Scotland. He chuckled as he lifted his hand and knocked on the door.

"Come in."

He stepped inside. "Good morning, sir. I understand you wish to see me."

Barrows looked up from the open file on his desk. "I'd like you to explain yourself, Inspector. I've gone through your reports on the Gilhaney case and there's not so much as a hint that you're close to an arrest. For God's sake, Nivens, what's going on here? You insisted that you'd be able to solve this case easily, but it's been six weeks!"

"I'm afraid we've hit a number of false leads, sir."

"False leads? What the devil does that mean? Does it mean you're close to making an arrest? Does it mean you've some idea who murdered Gilhaney?"

"No, sir, none of my usual sources have been very useful, sir."

Barrows sighed heavily and closed his eyes. "As I told you when I let you have this case, the Home Office wanted it solved quickly. They are not happy, Inspector, and neither am I. I assured them you'd take care of the matter promptly."

"At the time, I was sure I could, sir, but unfortunately, none of my informants have any information whatsoever. We've hit one dead end after another." He tried to look embarrassed. "I'm afraid this one might have been a murder, not a robbery."

Barrows gaped at him. "For God's sake, man, six weeks ago you insisted that this was a robbery, not a murder. I took you at your word because I thought you knew what you were talking about. Now I've got the Home Secretary breathing down my neck, not to mention the nasty little digs from the gutter press claiming we're too incompetent to know our elbows from our arses."

"My apologies, sir. At the time, the evidence clearly indicated it wasn't murder but robbery. I was mistaken."

"That's obvious." Barrows took a deep, controlling breath. "You're off the case, Inspector. We need this one solved as soon as possible. I'm calling in Inspector Witherspoon."

This was precisely what Nivens wanted, but nonetheless, he felt a fast rush of resentment that he could be so easily discarded. "I understand, sir. Shall I send my case files to the Ladbroke Road Police Station?"

*   *   *

Inspector Gerald Witherspoon clutched the huge, brown-paper-wrapped parcel to his chest and stepped out of the brightly decorated toy shop and onto the pavement. He turned and glanced at the window. Dolls, clockwork dogs and cats, green, red, and yellow blocks, a brilliantly painted Regency dollhouse, and a dozen other toys were spread against a white cotton field. He shifted his package tighter against his chest. He couldn't wait to show it to Ruth. The other presents were going to be delivered to the house, but he'd taken this one because he wanted her opinion. If she didn't like the toy he'd chosen for Amanda, he'd have her come with him to pick another one.

A cold wind had blown in, threatening rain, and he debated whether to walk home or find a hansom cab. From behind him the shop door opened and he moved closer to the busy road as two matrons, both of whom had shared their opinion about what to buy for his godchild, stepped outside. He nodded respectfully. "Thank you again for your assistance."

"It was our pleasure. Good day, sir," one of them called out as they hurried off.

He wished Ruth had been with him, but she'd had a previous engagement so he'd taken the bull by the horns and gone shopping on his own. All in all, it had been a very good day and he was quite pleased with himself. Just then a hansom rounded the corner, slowed down, and then stopped at the curb. He grinned, told himself that fate had made the decision for him, and started toward the cab, moving slowly so the person inside could step onto the pavement without being crowded. He stopped, blinking in surprise as Constable Barnes—dressed in his uniform—got out. The constable was a tall, ruddy-faced man with ramrod-straight posture and a head full of curly gray hair beneath his helmet.

He smiled apologetically at Witherspoon and then glanced at the driver. "Wait, please. We'll be just a minute."

"Gracious, Constable, what are you doing here?" The inspector's good mood began to disappear. "You're supposed to be on leave."

"As are you, sir." Barnes winced. "Something has come up and Chief Superintendent Barrows wants to see us both immediately."

Witherspoon, who wasn't one to ever complain, felt like complaining now. "But we're both on leave. He's the one who authorized our leaves. We're not due back until January third. What can he possibly want?"

Barnes had heard the talk at the station and had a very good idea what Chief Superintendent Barrows wanted, but he hated to be the one to break it to Witherspoon. The poor fellow had been looking forward to this Christmas holiday. He had big plans and had talked of nothing else for weeks now. The constable wasn't happy about the situation, either. He and his wife had plans of their own and now, if the gossip at the station had been correct, he'd have to cancel their holiday travels, too. But until he actually heard it from the horse's mouth, so to speak, he'd hold his tongue. "We'll have to see, sir. Come along, now. If we hurry, we can get across town before the traffic is too bad."

Looking slightly dazed, Witherspoon stepped into the cab. "But I've just bought some toys for my godchild. The rest of her presents are being delivered to Lady Cannonberry's tomorrow along with some lovely colored paper. We had it all planned, and we were going to wrap them while drinking her father's special mulled toddy recipe."

"New Scotland Yard," Barnes yelled as he swung into the cab behind the inspector and took his seat.

"This will not do, Constable. We've both worked very hard and every time we try to take time off, time we're allowed to have, we get a difficult case." Witherspoon frowned heavily. "This is the first Christmas that Amanda will really understand what it's all about and I wanted to make it special for her. Blast, I've a feeling that whatever Barrows wants with us, it's going to greatly interfere with all our holiday plans."

Barnes nodded and tried to think of something hopeful to say, but he needn't have bothered, the inspector was still talking.

Witherspoon tapped the top of the parcel. "I've found the most wonderful present for Amanda. It's unique. It's a beautiful model of a French shop, a *parfumerie régence*. It's all done up in lovely lavender and pink colors and there are paper dolls with matching dresses for the customers. I know she'll love it. Plus, I've got her a soldier doll along with his lady and I've ordered an enormous dollhouse. Ruth and I were so looking forward to our day tomorrow."

Barnes smiled sympathetically. "Regardless of why the chief superintendent wants to see us, sir, at least we'll have Christmas Day. You'll be there to see the little one opening her presents and enjoying them, sir."

Witherspoon's expression was glum. "Yes, that's true, but we'd plans for a lovely party on Christmas Eve. You know that—you and Mrs. Barnes were invited—and if, as I suspect, we're being called to the Yard because of a murder, you and I won't be able to be there. Which means the only time I'm going to get to be with my godchild is a few hours on Christmas Day. What's more, as you know, Lady Cannonberry and I had plans to leave for the country on Boxing Day. Her friends are expecting us and I was so looking forward to meeting them. But if we've a murder, that's gone right out the window." He sighed. "I'm sorry, I know you're disappointed as well. You and Mrs. Barnes had plans to go to Portsmouth to visit her brothers."

"We can always go later. Mrs. Barnes is usually very understanding about these sorts of changes," Barnes said. In truth, she was, but this time, he had a feeling she'd be quite put out and he didn't much blame her.

"I hope Lady Cannonberry will understand," Witherspoon murmured, his expression now worried. "As a matter of fact, I'm glad to have a few private moments with you. Uh, er, I hope you won't think me overly familiar, but I'd like your advice about something."

Barnes eyed him warily. "What about, sir?"

"Well, you see, Lady Cannonberry and I have gotten very close and, well, last year at Christmas, I bought her a pair of kid gloves. Nice ones, and she liked them very much. She wears them whenever we go out. But this year, I was thinking I'd like to get her something a bit more personal, a bit more in keeping with the closer nature of our relationship. I'm not sure what that would be and it's not the sort of thing I can ask Mrs. Jeffries or Mrs. Goodge, though both of them agreed that the gloves were a good idea."

Relieved, the constable let out the breath he'd been holding. For one brief, horrible moment, he was afraid his superior was going to ask him for advice on that most intimate of moments between a man and a woman. "Let me think, sir. Oh, I know, get her some jewelry. When I was courting Mrs. Barnes and I wanted to let her know without actually saying the words that she was special, I got her a lovely brooch. She wears it to this day."

"That's a wonderful idea." Witherspoon smiled broadly. "As soon as I've a free moment, I'll go to a jeweler's. Would you recommend a brooch, or perhaps a bracelet? No, no, I know, I'll buy her a necklace. What do you think, Constable? What do women like the best?"

By the time the hansom pulled up in front of the New Scotland Yard, they'd debated the merits of bracelets, necklaces, brooches, stickpins, and even rings. Yet Witherspoon still hadn't made up his mind. As they went inside and mounted the stairs to Barrows' office, the one thing the constable was certain about was that he was glad he'd not been the one to completely ruin both their Christmas holidays. He'd leave that up to the chief superintendent.

"It's not fair." Wiggins, the footman, yanked the top off a tin of brass polish and put it on the open newspaper he'd spread on the table. "We should be in the football league. We've done enough to be there. But no, those northern clubs don't want anything to do with us. Southern clubs aren't considered good enough for the likes of that bunch."

Mrs. Goodge, the cook, looked up from her worktable where she was peeling turnips and gazed at him sympathetically. She and the footman were in the kitchen of Inspector Gerald Witherspoon's large house. Outside, a cold rain had begun to fall, but inside it was warm and cozy. "Now, Wiggins, stop feelin' miserable about this. There's nothing you can do to change anything so you might as well make up your mind to look past it. Besides, you told me that while the inspector and Lady Cannonberry are in the country, you're going to two or three football games and all your mates are going to be there as well. You're even going to be staying overnight with one of them so you lads can get up to all sorts of mischief."

Wiggins smeared some polish on the cloth, bent over, and picked up one of the andirons he'd set next to his chair. He laid it on top of the paper. "I know that, but it still rankles. I hate them northern clubs, especially Burnley." He glanced at the cook. "Mrs. Goodge, are you goin' to be alright here on your own? With the inspector gone, we're all goin' to be out and about. Phyllis will be visitin' with her friend and goin' to all them plays. Mind you, I was a bit put out that Phyllis didn't think to ask me to go with 'er. I like plays as well."

Mrs. Goodge winced inwardly. She didn't want to see the lad hurt and she could see that his feelings for Phyllis had grown stronger since they'd ironed out their differences. The trouble was, she wasn't sure that Phyllis saw Wiggins in the same light. The maid seemed to still see him as a brother rather than a potential sweetheart. "Phyllis knows you've got the football."

"I know, and she doesn't get a chance to see her friend that often." Wiggins nodded. "But will you be alright here? Mrs. Jeffries will be out and about, too. She's goin' to all those lectures at the British Museum and she said she might even try to get up to Yorkshire."

The cook, who'd been looking forward to having the place to herself, was touched by the lad's thoughtfulness. "Of course I'll be alright." She grinned. "Even if Mrs. Jeffries goes to Yorkshire for a few days, Phyllis and I will be here the night you're gone, and between us, we'll be right safe."

"I wasn't worried about that." He smeared the polish on the top of the brass. "Even Betsy and Smythe will be gone. They're takin' the little one to France for a few days and you'll be alone for a lot of the time. Won't you get lonely?"

"I've lots to do," she assured him. "Luty and I have plans to go to a restaurant for dinner on the twenty-seventh and I've letters to write to my friends, and if any of you lot have been listening to my hints on what to get me for Christmas, I should have at least one nice cookbook to read."

"But still, I don't like to think of you 'ere on your own." He picked up the polishing cloth and rubbed it against the metal. "I'm glad you and Luty are goin' out together. Hatchet's got that friend comin' from the Far East so he'll be out and busy as well."

"And they'll both be at Luty's at night," Mrs. Goodge reminded him. "Hatchet's friend is staying with them. Now stop your frettin'. Luty and I will be right as rain."

"This is the first time where we've all got plans for the holidays," he mused. "Even the inspector won't be back from the country till after the New Year."

"We'll be together at Christmas and that's what's important." Mrs. Goodge headed for the cooker. "I'm goin' to put the kettle on. It's getting cold and I hear Mrs. Jeffries comin' down the stairs."

Mrs. Jeffries, the middle-aged, auburn-haired housekeeper, hurried into the kitchen. She carried a huge ledger. "Bless you, Mrs. Goodge. I'm dying for a cup of tea and I've finally got these wretched household accounts finished."

"I'm almost done polishin' the andirons," Wiggins said.

"And Mrs. Goodge and I was just chattin' about the holidays, how it's the first time we can recall that all of us have plans."

She opened the bottom drawer of the pine sideboard, dumped the heavy account book inside, and used her foot to close it. "It's rather exciting, isn't it?" She slipped into her spot at the head of the table. "I'm so looking forward to those lectures at the British Museum. Dr. Furness is a leading authority on ancient Egypt and he's giving three of them."

"When did you get interested in Egypt?" Wiggins went to work on the second andiron.

Mrs. Jeffries' eyes sparkled with excitement. "I've always been interested in the subject. I've read as much as I could on my own. But this is the first opportunity I've had to really learn anything from a genuine expert."

"Looks like we're all ready to really enjoy ourselves this Christmas," Wiggins said. "Let's just hope it's not all ruined at the last minute."

The kettle whistled and Mrs. Goodge yanked it off the cooker and poured the boiling water into the big brown teapot. "How could it be ruined?"

"You know what I mean," Wiggins replied. "We could get us a murder, that's how."

Witherspoon stared at Chief Superintendent Barrows, his expression incredulous. "Let me make certain I understand, sir. You want us to investigate a murder that happened six weeks ago."

"That's correct." Barrows looked down at the open file on his desk and pretended to read from it. He was Wither-

spoon's superior, but that didn't mean he wasn't embarrassed by what he had to do now. He'd made a dreadful
mistake in giving the case to Nivens. "Christopher Gilhaney
was shot on November the fifth, Guy Fawkes Night. Since
then, Inspector Nivens has been investigating the case as a
robbery gone bad"—he looked up—"but we've finally come
to the conclusion it was actually a premeditated murder."

Witherspoon's heart sank as his worst fear was confirmed. "Do we have any witnesses, sir?"

"He was leaving a dinner party in Chelsea when he was
shot, so we do have some idea of how he spent his last few
hours. But we've no witnesses to the murder itself, nor does
anyone from the neighborhood recall hearing anything at
the time we think the killing took place."

"Where was he murdered, sir?"

"In Kilbane Mews. It's near the river." Barrows leaned
back in his chair and studied the two policemen's glum expressions. Witherspoon sat across from him in a chair while
the constable stood at attention by the door. "Look, I understand this isn't an ideal situation." He smiled apologetically.
"The truth is, Inspector Nivens made a bit of a mess of
things. Now we've got the Home Office breathing down our
necks and we've got to get this case solved."

"That might be rather difficult, sir," Witherspoon protested. "The killer has had six weeks to destroy any evidence
linking him or her to the crime, witnesses will have forgotten anything useful they might have seen or heard the night
of the murder, and I didn't have a chance to examine the
body at the crime scene."

"Yes, yes, I'm aware of all that and I know that with the
murder having taken place so long ago you won't be able to

employ many of your 'special methods,' but you have solved more murders than anyone in the history of the Metropolitan Police, Inspector, so I want you to give this one your best effort."

"Of course, sir," Witherspoon muttered. "That goes without saying."

"The Home Secretary himself is nagging us about it," Barrows explained. "This morning I got a telegram from him demanding I put you on the case."

"I take it the victim was prominent?" Witherspoon's spirits plummeted as he saw his hopes for the holidays vanish. If the Home Secretary was putting his oar in, the pressure to catch the killer would be immense.

Barrows shook his head. "Not really. Gilhaney was an accountant. He'd come down from Manchester to join a large firm of builders as their head of finance and he'd taken a seat on their board. But he himself wasn't particularly prominent nor was he well connected. As a matter of fact, he's more an example of working-class boy makes good. It's the press coverage, you see—that's what is so disturbing to the H.O."

"The press coverage, sir?" Witherspoon didn't recall there being a lot of negative articles about this case.

"That's what I've been told." Barrows frowned slightly. "But I've not seen it. However, the H.O. is particularly sensitive to criticism of the police and apparently, there are some in the gutter press that won't let this story alone. It's the usual story; the police are being called incompetent at best and elitist at worst."

"Elitist, sir?" The inspector had no idea what that could possibly mean.

"We're being accused of ignoring murders that don't involve the rich or aristocratic."

The inspector was genuinely outraged. "That's ridiculous, sir. We work hard to solve each and every murder regardless of who the victim might be."

"Of course it's ridiculous, but the secretary is very upset about it." He closed the file and handed it to Witherspoon. "This is the main file. There's not much to it—as I said, Nivens made a bit of a mess of things. I've had the postmortem report, and what other few reports there were, sent to the Ladbroke Road Police Station. I'd appreciate it if you and Constable Barnes would start investigating immediately."

"What about our leave, sir?" Witherspoon faced him squarely.

"You can go back on leave as soon as you've solved this one, Inspector." Barrows glanced at Barnes. "Both of you. Now do get on with it. We're counting on you to take care of this matter as soon as possible. Perhaps then we can all enjoy our Christmas holiday."

Mrs. Jeffries met the inspector as he came in the front door. "Goodness, sir, you must have spent hours shopping. We were starting to get worried." She watched his face as he handed her his parcel. He didn't resemble the happy, carefree fellow who'd left earlier in the day to buy presents for a beloved godchild. He looked positively grim.

Witherspoon swept off his bowler. "I'm afraid my shopping excursion was cut short. We got called to the Yard."

Mrs. Jeffries put the parcel on the table next to the umbrella stand and reached for his hat. "The Yard? But how did they know where to find you? You were shopping."

"I'd told Constable Barnes I planned to go to the toy shop on Regent Street."

"Gracious, sir, is something wrong?"

He unbuttoned his overcoat and slipped it off. "You could say that." He gave her the garment. "Chief Superintendent Barrows has canceled our leave. Constable Barnes and I now have to investigate a murder."

Mrs. Jeffries, who would usually be thrilled by such an announcement, had a decidedly different reaction this time. She was bitterly disappointed. "But . . . but you were promised this Christmas off."

"I know." He sighed wearily and trudged down the hall toward his study. "And that's not the worst of it. If Mrs. Goodge can hold dinner for a few more minutes, we'll have a glass of sherry while I tell you the details."

Mrs. Jeffries dashed after him. "We've plenty of time, sir. Mrs. Goodge said dinner won't be ready for another half hour." She tried not to panic. Perhaps it wouldn't be as awful as it seemed. But it was difficult to stay calm.

Inspector Gerald Witherspoon had solved more homicides than anyone in the history of the Metropolitan Police Force and there was a very good reason for his success. He had lots of help.

His entire household and several of their special friends secretly investigated his cases. He had no idea that they used their considerable resources on his behalf; they chatted with witnesses, talked to servants, tracked down clues, followed suspects, and generally engaged in activities forbidden to the police. They fed him the information they learned through a variety of sources, the main ones being herself and Constable Barnes.

When they reached his study, she went straight across the room to the liquor cabinet while he settled in his favorite chair.

"Give us a generous pour," he instructed as she pulled out a bottle of Harvey's Bristol Cream sherry.

He didn't speak until she'd handed him his glass and took her spot across from him. "Now, sir, please tell me what is happening. From your expression, I can see you're dreadfully upset."

He took a quick sip and then gave her a wan smile. "Don't mind me, Mrs. Jeffries, but as usually happens, I've been given a murder. I wouldn't mind, except that I was so looking forward to our Christmas party on Christmas Eve; all of the people who are so very dear to me would be here and we were going to have such a jolly time. As I was growing up, you see, it was just my mother and myself . . . I didn't even really get to know my late aunt Euphemia until I was an adult. Don't misunderstand, my mother did a wonderful job, but we always lived very modestly. Christmas was always a simple affair. It was just the two of us."

"Yes, sir, I understand." Mrs. Jeffries' mind worked furiously. Even with a murder to solve, perhaps it wouldn't be impossible to attend at least one of Dr. Furness' lectures. There were three of them and the last one was in the evening; surely she'd be able to get to that one. Gracious, she'd already bought the subscription and had the tickets.

He gave her another sad smile and took a quick gulp. "Of course you do. I'll admit I'm very disappointed, but still, one must do one's duty. I was also looking forward to going to the country to visit Lady Cannonberry's friends. I was thrilled when she asked me to accompany her on the trip."

The invitation seemed to herald a new and important step in our relationship."

"I thought so as well," she murmured. She had to force herself to pay attention. "But you and Lady Cannonberry weren't scheduled to leave for the country until Boxing Day, so perhaps you'll still be able to go."

"I doubt that." He grimaced. "The case files are a mess."

"A mess? What are you talking about, sir? Why would there be case files when you just got the murder?"

"Because this murder happened six weeks ago." He sighed again.

"Six weeks?" If possible, her spirits sank even lower. "Who has been in charge of it since then?"

"Inspector Nivens, apparently. When the victim was shot, he managed to convince Chief Superintendent Barrows the crime was a robbery. But now the view is that Gilhaney was deliberately murdered."

"And I take it he couldn't solve it," Mrs. Jeffries commented. She and the rest of the household loathed Nivens. He was jealous of Witherspoon, and for years he'd been trying to prove the inspector had "outside help" on his cases. The fact that it was true didn't make the man any more likeable. He was a disgusting snob of a man, disliked by the rank-and-file officers serving beneath him and feared by his peers as well as his superiors. Nivens had aristocratic connections and used them mercilessly in dealing with others. But to the household's way of thinking, Nivens' worst fault was that he was simply a bad policeman. Justice meant nothing to him. "Oh dear, that will make it difficult, sir, but not impossible."

"True, it isn't impossible, but on my other cases, I was

able to use my methods. This time, I can't examine the body at the scene of the crime and we've no witnesses to speak of." He drained his glass and held it out to her. "I think I need another."

She got up and poured him another sherry. "Now, don't despair, sir, it's only the eighteenth and our party isn't until Christmas Eve. That's six days. You've solved other cases in less time than that." But even as she said the words, she didn't believe them.

"I know, but I'm going to have to start from the beginning. You know I don't like speaking ill of another police officer, but Inspector Nivens ought to be ashamed. He had six weeks and he's done very little. He didn't even take proper statements from the people at the dinner party. That's where the victim was prior to being murdered."

"Who was the victim, sir?" Mrs. Jeffries took a sip from her glass. She might as well learn a few facts to share with the others tomorrow.

"A man named Christopher Gilhaney. He'd come to London to join a firm of builders and as I said, right before he was murdered, he'd attended a dinner party in Chelsea. The other guests were the executive members of the firm and some large shareholders. Apparently, the dinner had ended rather early. At least that's what we deduced from reading Nivens' less-than-extensive notes on the case."

"He didn't take proper statements, sir?"

"No, his entire investigation is borderline incompetent." Witherspoon shrugged. "Except, of course, for the ones that deal with his 'sources' when the case was considered a robbery. But there's not much we can do about that aspect of the investigation. The hosts that night were Gordon and

Abigail Chase. Mr. Chase is an employee and a board member of Walker and Company, Builders and Architects."

"And the other guests who were there, do you have their names?"

Witherspoon nodded. "Yes, at least that gives us a place to start. Gilhaney had just moved to London from Manchester, so other than the people at the dinner party, we've no idea if he had any connections to anyone else."

"I take it Nivens didn't inquire into the victim's past in Manchester," she guessed.

"He did not. I've already sent off some telegrams to the Manchester police asking for their assistance, so perhaps we'll learn something useful from that quarter."

"Mr. Gilhaney was shot?" she clarified.

"The poor fellow had been shot through the heart three times."

"Three times?" she repeated. "And no one reported hearing a gunshot?"

"It was Guy Fawkes Night," he told her. "And loud noises were expected."

"Guy Fawkes Night," she repeated, her expression thoughtful. "Perhaps, sir, that's the very reason the killer picked that night to do the deed."

CHAPTER 2

Mrs. Jeffries waited until breakfast the next morning to tell Wiggins and Phyllis that they now had a murder case.

"A murder!" Wiggins protested. He put down his fork. "Cor blimey, I knew this was goin' to 'appen. Why do people keep killin' each other durin' the 'olidays? If they 'ad any decency, they'd wait till after the New Year to do their evil deeds."

"What about all our Christmas plans?" Phyllis asked. "Does this mean the inspector won't be going to the country? Or that we're not getting our party?"

"At this point we don't know what it means," Mrs. Jeffries answered honestly. She'd spent a restless night and hadn't fallen asleep until the wee hours of the morning.

"But we all know what our duty is." Mrs. Goodge looked at Phyllis and Wiggins. She'd found out about the murder early that morning. "So you two hurry and eat. We've much to do if we're going to have our morning meeting."

"I'll go to Luty's." The footman gave an exaggerated sigh. "But Hatchet's not goin' to be 'appy about this."

"None of us are pleased at this development." Mrs. Jeffries picked up her mug and took a sip.

"Should I go to Betsy and Smythe's?" Phyllis asked, her expression glum.

"Yes, see if everyone can be here by ten o'clock," Mrs. Jeffries said.

Wiggins finished first, pushed away from the table, and then looked at Phyllis. "Do ya want me to wait for you? We can walk together. The omnibus stop is just round the corner from Betsy and Smythe."

"But I need to help clear up," she began, only to be interrupted by the cook.

"I'll take care of that. You two get going."

As soon as they'd left, Mrs. Goodge rose to her feet and began picking up the dirty plates. She glanced at the housekeeper, who was staring off into space. "Look, Hepzibah, these things happen and there's naught we can do about it unless we decide we're not going to help on this one."

Mrs. Jeffries caught herself. The cook used her Christian name only when they were alone or when she wanted to make a point. "I know and we'll do our best—we always do—but Phyllis and Wiggins both seemed so upset. It's so sad that they're going to have to change all their plans."

"Nonsense," the cook replied. "Phyllis' plays are in the evening and Wiggins' football games only take a few hours out of his day. Even if the worst happens and we're still on the hunt come Christmas, I think the investigation can get along without the both of them for a few hours . . ." She broke off as they heard a faint knock at the back door.

"Who on earth is that?" Mrs. Jeffries got up.

"Constable Barnes, I imagine." Mrs. Goodge chuckled. "He always comes to accompany the inspector when there is a murder case. There's enough tea in the pot for us all. I'll pour if you'll go to the door."

But before going upstairs for the inspector, Constable Barnes always stopped in the kitchen to see the two women. Years earlier, he'd realized that Witherspoon had help on his cases and, being the clever copper that he was, it hadn't taken long before he'd known exactly where that assistance originated. For a time, he'd held his tongue while he watched them and saw how competent and clever they were. They had another advantage over him; people who usually wouldn't be caught dead cooperating with the police would talk to them.

Mrs. Jeffries led Constable Barnes into the kitchen and a few minutes later, the three of them were settled around the kitchen table. Barnes spoke first. "I'm not sure we're going to solve this one. The truth is, I'm not sure anyone can catch this killer. It'll be a black mark on the inspector's record."

"It would be a black mark on your record as well," Mrs. Jeffries said. "You don't deserve that."

"Why do you think you won't catch him or her?" Mrs. Goodge asked. "Surely Inspector Nivens couldn't have mucked it up that badly."

"He did his best." Barnes put down his mug.

Mrs. Jeffries took a sip of her tea, her expression thoughtful. "Do you think it's possible that Nivens was deliberately incompetent? That once he had the case, he realized he'd not be able to solve it and that it would eventually come to Inspector Witherspoon, so he did as little as possible."

"So that he could make our inspector look bad."

Mrs. Goodge nodded eagerly. "That sounds like something Nivens would do."

Barnes looked amused. "He isn't that clever and this isn't the first case he's bungled. Unfortunately, given his connections, it won't be the last. But he's not our problem now. This murder is six weeks old and we have very little to go on."

"What are you going to do?" Mrs. Jeffries asked. "Where are you going to start?"

"The only place we can, with the dinner party he attended on the night he died." Barnes shrugged. "He was a guest at the home of Gordon and Abigail Chase; they live in a posh part of Chelsea. There were ten people altogether at the Chase home that night: the victim, of course, and the Chases, Theodore and Hazel Bruce—he's the managing director of Walker and Company—Mrs. Bruce's father, Newton Walker—he established the company—a man named Leon Webster . . ." He paused, his brow wrinkled in thought. "And two other ladies, Ann Holter and Florence Bruce—she's Theodore Bruce's sister. Both are shareholders in the company. The last person is one of the company directors, Robert Longworth." He reached into his pocket and pulled out a sheet of paper. "I wrote out their addresses for you." He handed her the list. "I know it's not much, but it's all we have." He pointed at the last line on the bottom of the page. "That's the address of the victim's lodging house, but he'd only been there a few weeks before he was killed."

"The inspector said he came from Manchester," Mrs. Jeffries said, "and that he's sent off telegrams asking for their assistance. Perhaps you'll find something useful from that quarter."

Barnes looked skeptical. "I hope so, but I'm not holding my breath. We don't know how long Gilhaney even worked in Manchester. He's not originally from there; his origins are right here in London. He was raised in Clapham and possibly still has connections there, but Nivens didn't bother sending anyone to his old neighborhood."

"Does the victim still have family there?" Mrs. Jeffries asked.

"We don't know. All we know for sure is that his parents are dead. Nivens didn't go to Gilhaney's funeral, so we've no idea who might have shown up and been a useful witness."

"How did Gilhaney get the position at Walker and Company?" Mrs. Goodge asked.

"We don't know that, either." He got up. "I'd best get moving. We're going to start taking statements this morning, but memories fade when so much time has passed so I've not much hope."

"Cheer up, Constable." The cook got up as well. "You're both very clever policemen and I'm certain you'll do just fine. Who are you seeing first?"

"The Chases, and then we'll decide who to see next after we speak to them."

"Are you going to the murder scene?" Mrs. Jeffries rose to her feet.

"Not right away. What would be the point? The killer is long gone." He nodded respectfully and then headed up the back stairs.

Mrs. Goodge picked up the teapot and took it to the sink. "Are you going to go have a word with Ruth this morning?" she asked.

"About the murder?" Mrs. Jeffries winced. "Gracious, I

suppose I ought to—she'll want to be here this afternoon for the meeting. I hate being the one to break the bad news to her. She was so looking forward to taking the inspector to meet her friends."

"And she can still do it." The cook put the pot in the sink and bent down to pick up Samson's food dish. Her big, old orange tabby had licked it clean. "We've plenty of time to get this one sorted out, Hepzibah. It's only the nineteenth. Now, you put your cloak on and get across the garden to Ruth's. I'm going to send off a few notes to some of my sources and then we'll get cracking. This case isn't going to solve itself."

"Yes, of course." Mrs. Jeffries forced herself to move to the coat tree. She grabbed her cloak and draped it over her shoulders but didn't bother with her hat. "But I'm not so sure we've got much of a chance with this one."

It might have been six weeks since her dinner guest was murdered after leaving her home, but there was nothing wrong with Abigail Chase's memory, Witherspoon thought to himself. She'd been talking nonstop from the moment he and the constable had arrived.

He sat across from her in an elegantly furnished drawing room. The three tall windows facing the garden were draped by turquoise and pink curtains topped with intricately intertwined valances and tied back with silver cording. A large blue and cream rug patterned with silver fleur-de-lis covered the floor, and the French Empire–style furniture draped with pale-blue-and-silver-striped satin was lovely to look at but very uncomfortable. Witherspoon shifted his weight slightly and glanced at Barnes. The constable was sitting in an armchair. He'd planted one of his feet up against a heavy cabinet, probably to keep from sliding off the slippery material. He had his little brown notebook at the ready.

"Yes, I was sorry Mr. Gilhaney was killed—I am, after all, a decent Christian woman—but I must be honest, that awful man ruined my Bonfire Night party," Abigail Chase declared. She was a plump, attractive woman with a few strands of gray in her brown hair, a lovely ivory complexion, and dark brown eyes that flashed angrily with every word out of her mouth.

"Exactly how did he ruin your party?" Witherspoon asked.

"He spent the entire evening insulting everyone. He started the moment he walked into the house. Of course, he wasn't overt about it, but he managed to imply something dreadful about each and every one of my dinner guests." She gave a delicate, ladylike snort. "It was almost as if he'd prepared a script for the evening."

"Could you be more specific, Mrs. Chase?"

"Well, I can't remember every word he said, but it started almost as soon as he entered the drawing room. After the pleasantries were observed, Mr. Gilhaney began to make very odd remarks." She frowned. "I wish I could recall exactly what he said . . . well, I can't, so I'll just have to do my best."

"Yes, ma'am." Witherspoon nodded in encouragement. "We understand it's been six weeks and we don't expect you to give a verbatim accounting of the evening."

"Gilhaney started with Leon Webster. He's an old friend of my husband as well as a board member at Walker's—or is he a shareholder?" She tapped her finger against her chin. "I don't suppose it matters in this regard. Gilhaney asked Leon how he was enjoying his current position—he works for his family's company, Webster's Metals. Leon looked a bit embarrassed, but said that he enjoyed his work."

Witherspoon interrupted. "Why would Mr. Webster look embarrassed?"

"He shouldn't have, but men are sensitive about these things. Leon had some health problems last year and had to step down as the managing director."

"So he no longer works at his family firm?"

"He still works there, but he's really no more than a clerk. Gilhaney seemed to take great pleasure in pointing that out to everyone. Yet, Leon didn't seem to get really upset until Gilhaney started making comments about Leon's family."

"What kind of comments?" Barnes asked.

"As I said before, very odd ones. Gilhaney went on and on about the sanctity of family ties and how they could protect one in a cold, heartless world. Poor Leon turned absolutely white. I swear, he'd have left right then if my husband hadn't stepped in and changed the subject. But Gilhaney didn't stop there. Before we'd even finished the second course, he'd managed to insult half my guests. He implied that Ann Holter had been left at the altar years earlier, that the Bruces loathed one another, and that Theodore Bruce had only married Hazel so he could run Walker and Company. I can't recall what else he said, but before dessert was served, he'd insulted nearly everyone, except for Newton Walker, and of course, that's to be expected."

"Why didn't he insult him?" Witherspoon would sort out who was who later.

"Because Newton had just hired Gilhaney, that's why. He'd given the man carte blanche over the company finances."

*   *   *

Luty Belle Crookshank and her butler, Hatchet, were the first to arrive for the meeting. Luty, an elderly American with a generous heart, a love of flashy clothes, and almost as much money as the Queen, had noticed the household asking questions on one of their very early cases. As smart as she was kindhearted, she'd come to them with a problem of her own and since then had insisted on helping. Her resources were substantial; she knew every banker in London, had a half dozen law firms at her beck and call, and had the knack of getting people to confide in her. Additionally, she was equally at home dining with a street lad or an aristocrat. Hatchet, her butler, was a tall, white-haired man with the bearing of an admiral and a number of resources of his own.

The others arrived shortly afterward and Mrs. Jeffries waited till everyone was at their usual spot before she spoke. "I'm sorry to get everyone here on such short notice, but I had no choice. Not if we want to get this case solved before Christmas. Unfortunately, we're at a disadvantage because the murder was done six weeks ago, on Bonfire Night."

"This just gets better and better," Hatchet muttered. "Six weeks. The killer is probably long gone."

Mrs. Jeffries ignored him as she surveyed the faces around the table, but she could tell by their expressions that most of the others agreed with him. Hatchet was frowning, Betsy and Smythe both looked irritated, Phyllis' mouth was set in a flat, grim line, and Wiggins was sulking like a three-year-old. The only exceptions were Luty, who was holding Amanda on her lap and playing patty-cake and who looked downright cheerful, and Mrs. Goodge, who, while not at the table, smiled enthusiastically as she put a cup of tea in front of the housekeeper before taking her own seat.

"*If* we get it solved," Wiggins muttered.

Mrs. Jeffries ignored him and kept on speaking. "Ruth won't be able to join us. She had a prior engagement but she'll be here for our afternoon meeting."

"It might be a waste of 'er time." Smythe nodded his thanks as the cook handed him a mug. "I doubt we'll learn much today."

"Now, don't say that, Smythe," Mrs. Goodge said as she poured Betsy a cup of tea. "There's no reason we'll not make a bit of progress on this case. We've already got a nice list of names and addresses to start with."

"Constable Barnes has been very helpful." Mrs. Jeffries could see that none of them were particularly enthusiastic. "He pointed out that Christopher Gilhaney hadn't been in London very long, so he probably hadn't had time to make many enemies."

"Where was he from?" Phyllis asked.

"Originally he was from London, but he'd been working for years in Manchester. On the night he was killed he'd been at a dinner party in Chelsea. So the other guests were the last ones to see him alive. That gives us a place to start."

"The killer could have followed him here from Manchester," Wiggins muttered. "And I don't see how we can be expected to 'elp solve this one. Hatchet's right, the fella was murdered weeks ago and the killer is long gone."

Mrs. Jeffries nodded. "That's true, but we can at least try."

"I don't think it's fair," Phyllis protested. "Poor Inspector Witherspoon was looking forward to his trip with Lady

Cannonberry and now he's stuck investigating an old murder that's going to be impossible to solve."

"He wasn't the only one with travel plans," Betsy murmured. "But let's get on with it. What do we know about the victim?" She looked at Mrs. Jeffries expectantly.

But the housekeeper was staring off into space with a slight frown on her face.

Mrs. Goodge cleared her throat and, when that didn't get Mrs. Jeffries' attention, plunged in herself. "Constable Barnes was able to supply a few details. The victim came to London to take a position at Walker and Company; they're a firm of builders. According to the constable, it's a large firm and Christopher Gilhaney had just been appointed as head of finance and been given a seat on the board."

"Where did he live?" Hatchet asked.

"At a lodging house in Putney. We've got the address."

Hatchet looked puzzled. "That seems strange. You'd think someone like that would be staying at one of London's best hotels."

"Maybe he had a reason for keeping his head down a bit," Wiggins suggested. "After all, someone killed 'im."

Mrs. Jeffries gave a small shake of her head. "Yes, well, I'm sure we could speculate, but I think it much more useful for us to get out and about. We need to gather some real facts. But the first thing we should do is find out what we can about the victim."

"But he'd only been in London a few weeks, so are ya wantin' one of us to go to Manchester?" Wiggins demanded.

"Of course not, but he'd not lived his whole life in Manchester. He was originally from London, from Clapham, to be precise. But first, I think you ought to nip around to his lodging house in Putney."

Wiggins took a sip of tea. "That sounds easy enough. Maybe Phyllis can talk to the local merchants there as well." He gave the maid a hopeful smile. "We could take the omnibus or even a hansom cab since there's two of us."

"I'd rather she concentrate on the guests who were at the dinner party the night of the murder." Mrs. Jeffries turned her attention to the maid. "Theodore and Hazel Bruce live less than a quarter mile away, on Seldon Place. Florence Bruce—she's Theodore's sister and was also at the dinner party—lives with them."

Phyllis said, "I'll start there."

"There were seven guests, the Chases, and the victim at the dinner party that night. So we're going to be spread a bit thin on this one."

"And we don't even know if one of them is the killer," Smythe pointed out. "As Wiggins said, someone could have followed Gilhaney here from Manchester. But this lot is as good a place to start as any. Who d'ya want me to start with?"

Mrs. Jeffries noticed he didn't mention tapping his own sources, one of which was most reliable but quite expensive. Apparently, Smythe had so little faith in their ability to catch this killer that he didn't want to waste his money on a visit to Blimpey Groggins, a buyer and seller of information. The others in the household didn't realize that Smythe used his own money on their cases, and he could well afford it, but she'd figured it out long ago. But, wealthy as he was, he wasn't one to pour money into a case he considered a lost cause. She didn't blame him. She had very little confidence in their ability to solve this one. The clues were as cold as the brass knob on the attic door. What was more, from the dour expression on both his and Betsy's faces, it was obvious they were both put out over the thought that they'd miss their trip to Paris. "Why don't you go to the local pubs, ask about, and pick up what you can?"

"And me?" Betsy asked. "Should I find out what I can about Ann Holter?"

"That's a good idea." Mrs. Jeffries glanced at the note-paper on the table. "Her address is number seven Abbington Road in Chelsea."

Smythe frowned at his wife. "What about Amanda? I don't want her out in this cold."

"Our neighbor can watch her," Betsy said. "Elinor's a good lass and she needs the extra money. She's saving to go to secretarial college."

"I'll spend the morning sending out notes to my sources," Mrs. Goodge said. "And the butcher's boy is coming today. He might know something, though I doubt it, as the poor lad is thick as two short planks. Still, we've got to ask."

"Who would you like me to investigate?" Hatchet asked. He looked gloomier than an undertaker.

"Leon Webster. He works in his family business, Webster's Metals. They're one of Walker and Company's suppliers and he's also on the Walker and Company board. He lives at number eighteen Nolan Court, West Brompton." She turned her attention to Luty. "And if I give you the list of names, can you find out whatever you can about their finances? See what you can learn about Newton Walker as well; he might have had his own reasons for bringing Gilhaney into his company."

"Sure will." Luty grinned. "And I'll find out about Gil-haney's finances, too. If I've got to sweet-talk a bunch of boring bankers, I might as well kill as many birds as I can with one stone."

"Goodness, it appears we've got a bit of work ahead of ourselves." Mrs. Jeffries tried to summon a cheerful smile. "So let's get on with it."

"What about Robert Longworth?" Wiggins asked. "You want me to find out what I can about 'im after I've finished with Gilhaney's lodgin' 'ouse?"

"That won't be necessary, Wiggins." Mrs. Jeffries stood up. "I'll take care of Longworth."

Everyone stared at her with shock, and in one case a hor-rified expression, on their faces. Finally, Betsy said what they were all thinking. "But, Mrs. Jeffries, you don't do things like that. You do the thinking, we do the investigating."

"I know." She straightened her spine. She didn't know if she ought to feel very flattered or extremely insulted. "But this is a special circumstance. We're spread very thin and we want to get it solved as quickly as possible."

"I'm not sure it's possible at all," Hatchet muttered darkly.   •

Luty poked him in the arm and gave him a good glare. "Quit bein' such a crepe draper. Of course it's possible. We're goin' to catch this killer. Now, let's git movin' so we have something useful to report at our afternoon meetin'."

"What time did Mr. Gilhaney leave that night?" Wither-spoon asked. He generally had a lot of faith in the impor-tance of what he termed "time lines," but he feared that in this case, it might be a pointless exercise. However, he knew his duty and this was pertinent information. Besides, he or Barnes would verify her statements with the servants.

"It was fairly early—" She broke off with a frown. "No, no, I tell a lie, he was one of the last to leave. The only person who left after he'd gone was Newton Walker . . ." Her voice trailed off. "No, again I tell a lie, they left at the same time. Newton had to wait for his carriage to be brought to the front of the house and it came just as Mr. Gilhaney left."

"And this was at what time?" the inspector reminded her gently.

"Gilhaney left at eight forty-seven," a deep male voice said.

They turned to see a middle-aged man with graying brown hair and spectacles coming toward them. "Good day, gentlemen, I'm Gordon Chase. You must be the police."

Witherspoon rose to his feet. "That's correct, sir. I'm Inspector Gerald Witherspoon and this is my colleague Constable Barnes."

Barnes nodded respectfully and put his notebook on the table so he could get up, but Chase waved him back into his seat.

"Please stay where you are, Constable," Chase said. He extended his hand to the inspector and the two men shook. "Do be seated, Inspector. This is a dreadful business and I'm sure you want to get it cleared up as quickly as possible."

"How did you know the police were going to be here this morning?" Abigail Chase eyed her husband curiously as he sat down next to her.

He laughed. "There was a message from John Denby waiting for me when I got to the office today."

"That man that works at the Home Office, the odd-looking gentleman with the protruding teeth and the lazy eye?"

"That's not his fault, Abigail, but yes, that's him."

"Goodness, he must have really been upset about Gilhaney's death to send you a telegram first thing in the morning," Abigail replied.

"He didn't send me a telegram, we spoke on the telephone. Newton had one installed at the office last year and John's had one for several years now. Each time the wretched contraption rings it scares Newton's secretary so badly the poor fellow almost faints. But nonetheless, that's how I learned there had been a substantial change in the investigation. But I'm sure the police have more important things to worry about than how I happened to come home to speak with them." He patted his wife's hand and then looked at the inspector.

"You were very precise in your answer as to the time Gilhaney left," Witherspoon said. "You must have a very good memory."

"Not especially, Inspector, but his departure stuck in my mind because my wife very kindly pointed to the clock just after we'd seen everyone out the door." He looked amused.

"That's right, I did." Abigail Chase smiled approvingly. "I should have remembered the time myself. It was almost ten minutes to nine and our Bonfire Night was over. I was furious. Normally, one wouldn't even dine until eight o'clock, but Newton had made it obvious that eating after half seven gave him indigestion so for his sake, dinner was served early. But still, one shouldn't have a completely empty drawing room before nine o'clock when one has a dinner party. Of course that wasn't our fault, it was that wretched

Christopher Gilhaney. His insults were so awful it's no wonder everyone left."

"Now, now, dear." Gordon Chase patted his wife's hand again. "It isn't right to speak ill of the dead."

"Why not—he spoke ill of the living and ruined our party!"

"Mr. Chase, can you recall the order in which your guests left?" Barnes asked.

He thought for a moment. "Well, the first one to go was Ann Holter—she claimed a headache and then bolted as soon as she'd finished her meal. She didn't withdraw with the ladies while the gentlemen had their port."

"Do you recall the exact time?" Witherspoon asked. Perhaps he still might have a chance at getting a reasonable time line after all.

"Not really." Gordon looked at his wife but she shook her head. "Then they began to leave in quick succession. Leon Webster went next—he left before the port was served—and then I believe it was Robert Longworth and then the three Bruces." He frowned. "Or was it Gilhaney?"

"No, no, Gilhaney left with Newton Walker," Abigail declared. "Everyone else had gone by then. Remember, Newton had to wait for his carriage."

"That's right, Newton offered Gilhaney a ride home, but he refused and claimed he wanted to walk."

"Humph." Abigail snorted delicately. "If the fool had gotten into the carriage, he might still be alive."

Wiggins grimaced as he stared at the tall redbrick building that had once housed Christopher Gilhaney. The lodging house was at the end of a short road in Putney. A cold misty rain fell and he was chilled to the bone. He'd been up and down the street several times and hadn't seen anyone so much as stick a nose out. "Blast a Spaniard," he muttered as he started down the street again. "How can I find out anything if there's no one to talk to?" It wasn't fair, it just wasn't fair. For the first time ever, he had big plans for the holidays and now they were ruined because Inspector Nivens couldn't be bothered to investigate properly. Why should their inspector have to clean up Nivens' mess? That's what he wanted to know.

He shoved his cold hands in his pockets and trudged to the end of the road. This was a stupid, pointless exercise. No one was going to come out in this misery of a day, and if they did, they'd probably not know a thing about the late Christopher Gilhaney. He turned the corner, intending to go around the block and up the other side of the street, when he spotted a sign on the side of a wooden fence across the road. It read CRAVEN COTTAGE – FULHAM and had an arrow pointing toward Bishop's Walk.

Nell's bells, as Luty would say, Craven Cottage was Fulham Football Club's new grounds and it was just up the road. He wasn't a real Fulham supporter, but if he saw the place, he'd have something to tell Tommy. Tommy loved Fulham. It was his favorite team and Wiggins knew Tommy hadn't been here yet.

Cor blimey, it was Saturday so the players might actually be at the grounds practicing for this afternoon's game. Tommy would be green with envy if Wiggins saw the grounds, or even better, some of the players, before he did.

Wiggins hesitated and then came to a full stop. He glanced at the sign again and then in the direction of the lodging house. He was supposed to be getting a bit of information for their meeting. But from what little they knew, Gilhaney hadn't even been in London very long so even if he could find someone to chat with, odds were they'd not know very much. Besides, it was blooming cold today and no one in their right mind was going to take it into their head to go for a stroll. It couldn't hurt just to nip past the football grounds. If for no other reason than to see if Tommy had been exaggerating about how big he'd heard the grounds were.

He made up his mind and headed toward Bishop's Walk. Craven Cottage was less than a mile away. He could nip there, have a good look, and then get back for their afternoon meeting with time to spare. Mrs. Jeffries couldn't expect him to find out something useful if there wasn't anyone about to speak to, could she?

"Are you here for Miss Bruce's laudanum?" The elderly man behind the counter stared at Phyllis suspiciously. He wore a heavy black apron over his neatly pressed white shirt. "I've never seen you before. When did you start working for them? Miss Bruce always gets her medicine herself."

"I don't—" Phyllis began, only to be interrupted.

"Then why are you in my shop asking questions about them?" he demanded. "This is a respectable chemist's shop; we don't give out information about our clients. What's wrong with you, girl, have you no decency?"

"But I just wanted to know how . . ." Phyllis tried again. She felt tears well up and blinked hard to hold them back. For a moment, she felt like she was fourteen years old again and facing Mrs. Lassiter, her old mistress, over some mistake she'd made.

"She just wanted to know how to get to Seldon Place," the woman who'd come into the chemist's shop right behind her said. "For goodness' sake, Mr. Conway, the girl is simply asking for directions."

"Don't be absurd, that's not all she was asking." He shot Phyllis another accusing glare. "She was asking about them, about how often they come in here and what they buy."

As that was exactly what Phyllis had wanted to ask, but hadn't, she wondered for a brief moment if the old man could read minds.

"Mr. Conway, I came in right behind her. All she said was that she had a note to deliver to the Bruce family on Seldon Place but she couldn't find that street. Now, come along, where's your daughter? You're not supposed to be out here on your own. You know that. Call her, now, I've not got all day." The woman held up an empty shopping basket. "I've all my shopping to do yet and I must be home in time to give Leopold his tea."

Phyllis gave her a grateful smile. "Thank you, ma'am. The directions my mistress gave me weren't very clear."

"Humph, I'll bet they were clear as the church bells, but you probably weren't listening, were you." The chemist snorted in derision. "That's the trouble with you young people, you've no sense at all."

"Father, your lunch is ready." A young woman stepped out from a set of curtains behind the counter. She sighed heavily when she saw there were customers. "Father, I told you to call me if anyone came into the shop."

"Don't be ridiculous, I'm perfectly capable of taking care of our customers."

"I know you are, Father, but I'll serve them and Mr.

Bingley will be here in a few moments to take care of the afternoon's prescriptions. Hurry along, Father, your food is getting cold."

He looked confused for a moment and then retreated behind the curtains.

"I'm sorry if he was rude to you." She smiled at Phyllis. "He's elderly and shouldn't really be working, but he insists. He gets very upset if we don't let him come into the shop."

"That's alright." Phyllis edged toward the door. She felt sorry for the elderly man, but she felt sorrier for herself. This was the way her entire morning had gone. She'd not found out a ruddy thing and every single person she'd spoken to had been either too busy to chat or downright mean. "I didn't mean to upset him. I was just so lost and hoped that one of the local shops could help me."

"She wanted to know how to get to Seldon Place," the woman said. "I know it's nearby, but I can't think where it is."

"I'm not certain where it is, either," the young woman behind the counter replied. "I think it might be one of those small streets near the river."

"Thank you." Phyllis smiled brightly. "I'll go in that direction. Good day, then." She hurried out of the shop and started walking down the busy pavement. Thus far, she'd been to the butcher's, the greengrocer's, the chemist's, and even the ironmonger's shop and the only thing she'd learned was that Florence Bruce took laudanum. Fat lot of good that would do her—from what she'd heard, half the population of London took the stuff. Her footsteps slowed as she reached the last shop on the block, a tobacconist and newsagent's shop.

Phyllis climbed onto the top stair and stared through the

window. A sour-faced woman stood behind the counter folding newspapers. She felt like crying. Could it get any worse? She'd been hoping for a friendly girl or lad, someone who wouldn't be in a rush to get rid of her and who might know something about the Bruce household.

She sighed in self-pity. It wasn't fair, it just wasn't right. Why did they have to get a murder now? For the first time since she could remember, she had a bit of money and something wonderful to do during the Christmas holidays. Her plans might not seem all that grand to anyone else, but to her, they were a sign she'd come up in the world, that she, too, could do things she'd only dreamed of when she was a young girl worrying that she might be tossed into the street for making the slightest mistake.

She was just going to the theater and the music hall. All the three performances she had tickets for were at night, so even with the investigation, she could still go. But it wouldn't be the way she'd hoped it would be. It wasn't just the performances she'd looked forward to, it was going to the theater hours before the performance and seeing the brightly colored playbills and then going to have a cup of tea or perhaps even a light meal before the show itself. Now she'd be lucky if she could get there before the curtain opened.

Suddenly, she was bumped from behind.

She whirled around just as a man stumbled backward. "Oh dear, I'm terribly sorry, it's my fault completely. I was so lost in my thoughts I wasn't paying attention. I didn't mean to bump into you."

Phyllis stared at him for a moment and then gave him an apologetic smile. He was an incredibly handsome young chap. He was tall, with dark blond hair beneath his bowler hat, a broad forehead, high cheekbones, and the lightest, most beautiful blue eyes she'd ever seen. "It's alright; it was my fault as much as yours. I shouldn't have been standing in the doorway."

He returned her smile with one of his own. "Are you going inside, miss?"

"No, I've changed my mind. I was only going to ask for directions." She moved to one side and stepped past him onto the pavement.

"Directions? Perhaps I can help? I work for an estate agent and I know the area very well."

Phyllis hesitated for a moment. After all, she, like most young women, had spent most of her life being warned about "strange men." But then she realized she had no reason to worry. It was broad daylight and he was nicely dressed in a decent gray overcoat open enough to reveal he wore a proper navy blue business suit beneath it. "Actually, I'm dreadfully lost and I've a note that needs to be delivered. You wouldn't by any chance happen to know where Seldon Place might be?"

"I do." He pointed straight ahead. "It's that way, but you need to cross over the road at the first junction, turn left, and then turn right at the next street."

"Oh dear, it sounds dreadfully complicated." She understood his directions, but she wanted to prolong this encounter as long as possible.

"Only if you don't know the neighborhood." He took off his hat and she was thrilled to see he had wavy hair. "I don't wish to seem forward, miss, but if you can wait for just a moment, I'm going in that direction."

"I don't want to inconvenience you," she replied. "But

truth to tell, I've a terrible sense of direction." That, of course, was a bold-faced lie. But it served to give her a bit more time with the young gentleman and find out if he knew anything about the Bruce family.

"It's no trouble at all. Let me get my newspaper and I'll be right back." He disappeared inside the shop.

Phyllis ignored the wave of guilt that swept over her as an image of Wiggins' earnest face flashed through her mind. She had a perfect right to smile and be nice to a handsome young gent who might be able to help with this case. She wasn't being deceitful or disloyal to anyone else; it wasn't as if she and Wiggins had an understanding. Far from it—until recently they'd been sniping at one another and had barely spoken. They'd cleared the air and she was glad of that; she was genuinely fond of the lad. But she wasn't sure she wanted their relationship to move any further. Not at the moment.

The young man returned. He had a newspaper tucked under his arm. He swept off his bowler again. "I'm Jonathan Talmadge."

"I'm Phyllis Thompson." She could have bitten her tongue when she realized she'd given him her real name. When she was on the hunt, she always used a false name. It wouldn't do to leave a trail back to the Witherspoon household. But then again, they weren't likely to solve this one anyway so what was the harm. What's more, if she ever saw him again, it would be awkward trying to explain why she'd lied about her name. "This is ever so kind of you."

"Not really, I'm delighted to be able to assist you. It's this way. Do you live nearby?" he asked as they started walking.

"I live near Shepherd's Bush," she replied, hedging just a bit because the Witherspoon household was actually in the Holland Park neighborhood. "I work there, I'm a housemaid."

"And I'm a clerk," he said. "But I'm hoping one day to have my own estate agency."

She almost told him she hoped one day to have her own detective agency, but she wisely realized that would probably frighten him. She didn't know a lot about men, but she had learned that most of them didn't like the idea of a woman doing what she liked with her life. "It's nice to have ambition," she murmured.

"What's the address on Seldon Place?" He took her arm as they crossed the road and made a sharp left onto a quiet street.

"Number twelve. I'm taking Mr. and Mrs. Bruce a note from my household."

"Ah, the Bruces'." He nodded. "Interesting family. Their house is lovely. Of course, it's been in the family for years. We often get inquiries from people about it."

"What kind of inquiries?"

"Mostly people want to know if it is for sale. It's a freehold property and that increases its value. But Mr. Newton Walker is no fool and he isn't going to let it go at the current level of prices in that area."

"Mr. Newton Walker?" she repeated. "I thought it belonged to the Bruces."

He shook his head. "No, Mrs. Bruce's father owns it and upon his death, it will go directly to her. But I doubt she'll ever be interested in selling. She's lived there all her life. Of course, if she does sell, she'll give us the business. She went to school with our owner's wife and she often recommends our firm to people."

"That's very good of her." Phyllis knew she was on very thin ice here. She'd no idea what to ask next, but she wanted to keep him talking.

"It is. Of course, in all fairness, we do our very best for our clients. We work hard to get the full amount of worth out of a property when our customers are selling while at the same time, making sure our clients are getting value for money when they're buying."

"I'll remember that if I ever buy or sell some property," she said.

He gave an embarrassed laugh. "Sorry, I didn't mean to sound as if I were bragging."

"No, no, you're just proud of your firm." She smiled. "I think that's very admirable."

By this time, they'd reached the junction. He pointed at a street farther down the block. "That's Seldon Place. The Walker house is easy to find. It's the biggest one."

She couldn't think of anything to say that didn't sound ridiculous, but she'd learned one thing. The house belonged to Mrs. Bruce. "Thanks so much for your assistance, Mr. Talmadge."

"It was my pleasure, miss." He doffed his bowler for the third time. "Now I must go. I'm meeting a client nearby. Perhaps one day we'll meet again."

She sincerely hoped so.

CHAPTER 3

"Let's hope that Mr. Newton Walker's memory is as good as Mr. and Mrs. Chase's," Witherspoon said as the hansom came to a stop. "Their recollection of the evening Gilhaney died was excellent."

"I'm not surprised, sir. I'll warrant that Mrs. Chase has reminded Mr. Chase of it on more than one occasion these past weeks." Barnes chuckled. "She did tell us that she only invited Gilhaney because her husband insisted."

They stepped out of the cab and Witherspoon stood on the pavement while the constable paid the driver.

"From the looks of this place, he's not hurting for money," Barnes muttered as he joined the inspector. They stared at the home for a moment. The house was a five-story, made of pale gray stone with immaculate white trim around every window and a freshly painted peacock blue front door topped with an ornate half-circle transom window.

"Well, he is a builder, so I suppose a beautifully maintained house is to be expected. If Mr. Chase was right, Mr. Walker should be home by now," Witherspoon said as he and Barnes started up the short paved walkway.

"I'm amazed that a man his age even works half days," Barnes said. They climbed the broad stairs and he banged the polished brass doorknocker against the wood. "Mrs. Chase claimed he was at least seventy-five. I wonder why he came out of retirement to go back to work. Do you think we should ask him?"

Before the inspector could reply, the door opened, revealing a tall, black-clad butler. If he was surprised to see a uniformed policeman on the doorstep, he didn't show it. "Good day."

Witherspoon stepped forward. "We'd like to speak with Mr. Newton Walker."

The butler opened the door wider and motioned them inside. "Mr. Walker is waiting for you in his study. It's this way."

Barnes gave the inspector a quizzical look as they moved inside and followed the butler down a long corridor. The inspector shrugged, indicating he, too, had no idea how Walker knew they were coming. They'd only decided to come here instead of going to the Bruce house when they climbed into the hansom cab after leaving the Chases.

"The police are here, sir," the butler announced as they stepped through the double doors.

Shelves filled with books lined two of the walls, a fire crackled in the fireplace, and a calico cat was curled on a soft rug next to the hearth. The cat lifted its head, gazed at them for a moment, and then went back to sleep.

Newton Walker sat behind a massive desk in front of three long windows. He had a thick thatch of unruly gray hair, bushy eyebrows, and a prominent nose above his mustache.

He stared at Witherspoon for a long moment. "You're the policeman who's caught so many murderers, aren't you? I told Denby at the Home Office to make sure to get you. I'm disgusted with how that other chap made a right mess of this case. I told him right off it wasn't a ruddy robbery, but the fellow wouldn't listen. Now the case is weeks old and the killer could be in Timbuktu. Please, please, both of you sit down. Would you like tea? Or perhaps coffee?"

"Nothing, sir, but thank you," Witherspoon said as he took one of the two leather wing-back chairs in front of the desk. He was pleasantly surprised. Often, the upper class had no qualms about treating the police as if they'd brought plague into their house. "And to answer your question, Constable Barnes and I, along with the hard work of many other police officers, have solved a number of murders. All of us will do our very best to solve this one as well."

Walker said to the butler, "Thank you, Banfrey, that'll be all. I'll ring if I need anything else." He turned his attention back to the inspector. "A wise leader always gives credit where credit is due. Denby said you were a modest fellow. Let's just hope this one hasn't been left too late even for your substantial talents. Now, what do you need to know from me?"

He glanced at Barnes to see if he was at the ready and saw that the constable was comfortably seated with pencil in hand and notebook open.

"Mr. Walker, we understand that you left the Chase home at approximately the same time as Mr. Gilhaney, is that correct?"

"That's right. I had to wait while the footman fetched my carriage. I offered Gilhaney a lift, but he insisted on walking, he didn't want to take me out of my way."

Barnes looked up from his notebook. "As you were leaving, did you see anyone hanging about the immediate area?"

Walker frowned slightly. "Not really, but I can't say that I would have noticed. It was a very peculiar evening, Constable. The dinner party hadn't gone well and the other guests had already left. I had a terrible case of indigestion. All I wanted to do was to get home to my bed."

"Do you know if anyone had a grudge against Mr. Gilhaney?" Witherspoon asked. "I know that seems a strange question—someone obviously wanted him dead—but it would be helpful if we knew of anyone who might have a reason for hating the man."

"I've thought about that, Inspector, and I honestly can't give you a useful answer. I didn't really know the man well at all. I'd hired him based on several recommendations from a business associate in Manchester. Gilhaney had established quite a reputation there and I'd mentioned to a number of colleagues, other men that I did business with, that I was looking for someone with a specific set of talents. Christopher Gilhaney fit my requirements perfectly."

"What were those requirements, sir?" Witherspoon asked.

"I needed a genius, Inspector, someone brilliant with numbers but also able to look at the whole company and help me determine its worth. I took the company public last year and, as it has turned out, I'm not sure that was a wise decision. I'm still the majority shareholder, but I needed some expert advice on the best course of action for the future. When I met with Gilhaney in Manchester, we had a lengthy discussion and it was obvious to me that he was the right person. The only trouble was, he had two other employment offers. Both of which I thought were more generous than mine, so I was surprised when he accepted my terms. The only thing he insisted upon was that he report only to me, not the managing director or the board. That seemed a reasonable request. As a matter of fact, I was quite pleased that he instinctively seemed to understand what it was I needed from him."

"Which was?"

"Impartiality and honesty, Inspector. I wanted the truth about my company's finances and prospects."

"Did Mr. Gilhaney make it a habit to change employment often?" Witherspoon asked.

"He never stayed long at any firm and that was his choice. He made it perfectly clear to me that he'd examine my books, ensure that everything was in decent order, and then give me his best advice on whether or not to sell the company. After that, he'd leave for another position. He was unorthodox, Inspector, but a man of his genius could get away with such behavior."

Barnes stared at him skeptically. "In what way was he a genius?"

"Gilhaney could take one look at the ledgers and know if something was off or not."

The constable cocked his head to one side. "With all due respect, sir, that's a bit hard to believe."

Walker, instead of being offended, laughed. "Of course it is. I didn't believe it myself until I saw it with my very own eyes. I'm afraid I haven't been as clear as I should have been.

Gilhaney wasn't a magician—he couldn't tell at first glance
if there was something amiss with the finances. His talent
was that he could remember what he saw. All he had to do
was look at something once and he could recall it as if it was
still in front of him. I don't know whether that was an in-
born skill or a talent he'd cultivated over the years, but I do
know he had it. As I said, I took the company public last
year and we've an enormous amount of activity at the moment. We're building an office block, and we've several gov-
ernment contracts and overseas tenders in the works and
half a dozen private residences. I needed someone who could
look at everything and give me the best possible advice."

"How did the board of directors feel about bringing Mr.
Gilhaney into the company?" The inspector felt something
bump his leg. Looking down, he was surprised to see the cat
rubbing against his trousers. He reached down and stroked
the animal's head.

"They were fine with it." Walker grinned. "Sheba, be-
have yourself. He's not here to pet you. I'm sorry, Inspector,
she's very friendly."

Witherspoon chuckled as he ran his hands over her soft
fur. "She's fine, Mr. Walker. I like animals. What did Mr.
Chase and Mr. Bruce and your other managers think
about it?"

"Gordon Chase was fine with it. He's set to retire again
next summer."

"Retire again," Barnes interrupted. "What does that
mean? Had he retired previously?"

"Not from our firm—from another company of builders," Walker explained. "We belong to the same club and
he'd been retired for a year or so when I talked him into

joining us. He's an excellent manager. He was quite happy when I told him that Gilhaney was coming on board."

"And Mr. Bruce, he's your managing director, how did he feel about an outsider coming in?" Witherspoon straightened up as Sheba trotted back to her bed by the fire.

"He wasn't quite as enthusiastic about it as Gordon had been," Walker admitted. "He, of course, doesn't want to see me sell the firm. But I'm getting old and he and my daughter haven't been blessed with children. At least if I sell the company, I can make certain my daughter will never want for anything as long as she lives."

"Mr. Walker, you stated that you tried to tell Inspector Nivens that Gilhaney's death hadn't been a robbery and he wouldn't listen," Barnes began.

"That's right, the fellow wouldn't listen to anything I said. I got the distinct impression he thought I was senile." Walker snorted. "I may be old, Constable, but there's nothing wrong with my mind."

"Of course, sir," Barnes agreed, "but what I need to know is what made you think it hadn't been a robbery? His landlady testified at the coroner's inquest that Gilhaney had on a diamond stickpin and gold ring when he left for the Chase home that night. They were missing when he was found dead."

"I understand that, Constable." Walker folded his hands together and leaned back. "And I've no proof for what I think, but my instincts told me that poor fellow was murdered for some other reason than robbery. I've learned to trust my feelings over the years. Gilhaney was a working-class lad who wasn't in the least ashamed of where he came from, nor was he intimidated by the upper classes or anyone

else. He knew how to take care of himself and he wasn't a
fool. I'm certain if he thought someone was following him,
he'd have taken steps to evade his assailant. What's more, no
one but the members of the dinner party could have possibly
known he was wearing valuable jewelry. He was never os-
tentatious. During our interviews, he wore good-quality but
very plain clothing. I'd met with him several times and I only
saw him wear the stickpin and the ring that night."

"Someone may have seen him coming to the Chase
house," Barnes argued.

Walker shook his head. "No, he came by hansom. My
carriage pulled up right behind his cab and we went into the
house together."

"Mr. Gilhaney was originally from London," Witherspoon said. "Had you ever met him prior to meeting him in
Manchester?"

Walker smiled slightly. "It's odd that you should ask me
that, Inspector. When I met Gilhaney for the first time, I
thought I'd seen him somewhere before, but for the life of
me, I couldn't recall where it would have been."

"Did you ask him if you'd ever met?"

"I did and he assured me we hadn't." Walker shrugged.
"He had no reason to lie about such a matter, Inspector, and
as my late wife used to say, I'm quite bad at recalling faces.
I tend to get people mixed up."

Smythe took a sip of his beer and tried not to grimace as it
hit the back of his throat. What was he doing here? The
place was empty save for a grizzled old man drinking gin by
the fireplace. He was tired, his stomach was soured from the
beer he'd drunk, and this was his third ruddy pub. The

White Hart was a working-class place on a small street off the river and the farthest from the spot where Gilhaney drew his last breath. But this pub, just like the others, might as well be on the moon. He'd learned nothing and he was wasting his time here.

Blast a Spaniard, this wasn't right. He and Betsy ought to be out shopping and picking up last-minute bits and pieces for their trip to Paris. The tickets were booked, the hotel was waiting for them, and for the first time since they'd been married, he'd be able to give his wife anything money could buy. He was a wealthy man but because of their circumstances he'd had to hide it.

Years ago, he'd made a fortune in Australia. But because he'd promised his old employer, Euphemia Witherspoon, the inspector's aunt, he'd watch out for him and not let him be taken advantage of by greedy people, he'd found himself in a situation where only a few friends and, of course, Betsy knew that he could afford anything he wanted. Most of the time he and Betsy didn't mind the pretense; after all, they were doing something important. They were serving justice.

But a trip to Paris was different. It would let them do what they wanted, spend what they liked, with no one the wiser. They could eat, drink, and be merry. If Betsy was of a mind to, she could bathe in champagne. The thought made him smile and then, just as quickly, he sobered. But now, because they'd got stuck with a ruddy case that was so cold the clues were covered in frost, they might have to cancel their trip. He put his beer on the counter and pushed it away.

"That not sittin' well with you?" the publican, a ruddy-faced man with slightly bulging hazel eyes, asked. "The beer's decent here, sir."

Smythe stood up straighter and tapped his glass. "The beer's fine, it's me stomach that's acting up."

The publican nodded and pulled a clean rag out from beneath the counter. "I've not seen you in here before."

"That's because I've never set foot in the place." Smythe made a quick decision. "That's probably why my gut's gone sour. My guv sent me here to do the impossible." He was suddenly glad he'd worn a decent coat and jacket and not his usual coachman's attire.

"And what would that be?" The publican moved a few feet down the counter and began wiping up spills.

"I work for a newspaper"—Smythe was making it up as he went along—"and the guv wants me to find out what I can about that murder that happened on Bonfire Night."

"You mean the man that was shot in the mews?" The publican stopped cleaning. "I thought that was a robbery."

Smythe shook his head. "Guv has a source at the Yard—now they think it was just a straight old murder and the killer just took a few bits and pieces off the dead man to make it look like a robbery." He grimaced in disgust. "I don't know what my guv is thinking. Gilhaney—he's the victim—was at a dinner party the night it happened and none of those toffs is goin' to open their door to me or anyone else who works for a newspaper that isn't the *Telegraph* or the *Times*."

"That's hard luck." The barman gave him a quick, sympathetic smile. "One of the advantages of ownin' your own place is you get to be your own boss. The only thing I 'ave to worry about is people losin' their taste for beer or gin and I don't think that's goin' to happen soon."

Smythe knew this had all been a waste of time. This fellow didn't know anything, either. If he did, he'd be puffed up like a self-important bullfrog and talking his ruddy head off. "I'd better get moving. I can't go back empty-handed. There must be someone around here that saw or heard something that night that fellow was shot."

"Everyone heard something!" The publican laughed heartily. "It was Bonfire Night."

"I know something."

Smythe turned to see the old man by the fireplace watching him. "You do?"

"If you'll buy me a gin, I'll tell you."

Smythe hesitated. This could be just a ruse to get another drink. He glanced at the publican, but even though he'd heard everything, he kept his gaze averted as he continued cleaning the bar. Smythe suspected he didn't want to miss out on another sale. "Two gins, please," he ordered. "And make it your best."

"Coming right up." He stopped wiping and grabbed two glasses from beneath the counter. He poured the drinks as Smythe slapped some coins on the bar.

Picking up their gins, he crossed the room and gave the old fellow a friendly smile. "What do you have to say?"

Nodding his thanks, the old man grabbed the glass and took a fast sip. "One of the people who was at that party with the murdered man, he was here that night. Bonfire Night."

"And who would that be?" Smythe found it interesting that the locals knew Gilhaney had been killed after leaving a dinner party.

"Leon Webster. He was at the Chase house that night and he was here later."

Smythe looked behind him at the barman. He was watching them with a skeptical but interested expression. "Is he tellin' the truth?"

"Could be. Sometimes he does. But I don't know this Webster person from Adam and I'm not sure that old Hamish there does, either. He does like his gin so it's a safe bet that he'll say anything to get a drink."

"Yeah, and you'll do anything to sell one. You held your tongue until after I'd paid," Smythe shot back.

"That's not true—Leon Webster was here that night," Hamish insisted. "I know because my nephew was with me and he used to work at Webster's. Mr. Leon Webster bought us both a couple of drinks." He jabbed his finger at the barman. "You ought to remember, he paid you properly."

The publican frowned in concentration. "Was he that nervous rabbit of a fellow in the black suit? The one that kept spilling his drink every time the fireworks exploded?"

"That's right—we was sitting right over there." He pointed to an empty table by the end of the bar. "And Mr. Webster bought us both two drinks—good stuff, too, not that swill you pour and then pretend it's decent."

The barman shrugged and pulled a tray of glasses out from beneath the counter.

Smythe had heard enough to believe the man was telling the truth. He yanked a stool away from the nearest table and sat down. "Tell me everything you remember," he instructed. "And I'll buy you another drink."

"I'm sorry to be such a nuisance, but I've lost the paper that had Mr. Longworth's address on it," Mrs. Jeffries explained to the butcher. He was a young man and rather nice looking.

"I'm sorry, I've never heard of him. I don't think he shops here, but let me ask my brother. He does the accounts." He turned to a man in a bloodstained apron cutting at a rack of ribs on the worktable behind the meat counter. "Hey, Syd, you ever heard of this Robert Longworth? This lady is lookin' for his house and he's supposed to live in this neighborhood. Does he have an account with us?"

Syd didn't look up from his task. "No Longworths on our books."

The butcher gave her an apologetic smile. "Sorry, ma'am."

"That's quite alright." She smiled as she backed away from the counter. "I appreciate your efforts." She whirled about and almost ran for the door. How on earth did the others do it? This was a disaster. After all her big talk about getting out and about, she'd have to be at their meeting this afternoon with nothing to show for her efforts.

She dodged to one side to avoid crashing into a matronly woman coming in the front door. As soon as she was safely outside she took a deep breath and tried to get her wits about her. She had no idea what she was doing wrong. This was the right neighborhood—it had to be. It was the closest to the Longworth home. The other street of shops was over a mile away so she couldn't imagine their household did their shopping there.

Before coming here, she'd done what she'd heard the others did; she'd had a good look at the Longworth residence. It was a four-story brown brick town house with a neatly fenced front garden and nicely painted white trim around the windows. A home like that would need several servants to maintain it properly, and servants, because they were smart, didn't waste time going miles away to do their shopping.

She reached the corner, turned, and looked back the way she'd just come. Was she using the wrong approach? She'd heard Wiggins, Betsy, and Phyllis talk about their methods and she'd duplicated them to some extent. But she'd been to the grocer's, the chemist's, the greengrocer's and even the haberdashery. None of them had ever heard of Robert Longworth. Or if they had, they certainly weren't going to share any information with her.

Sighing, she started to cross the road and then stopped. She refused to show up at the meeting with nothing. This case was irritating enough without her having to endure the smug expressions on everyone's faces. Perhaps she wasn't as good as they were at getting merchants and clerks to talk, but there was something she could do. She glanced up and down the busy road until she spotted a hansom and waved it down.

"Where to, ma'am?" the driver asked as he pulled up next to the curb.

"St. Thomas' Hospital," she replied before stepping inside. With any luck, she could find out what she needed to know and still get back to Upper Edmonton Gardens by four o'clock.

The Bruce home was as carefully maintained as the Walker house, both inside and out. Witherspoon and Barnes stood in the elegantly appointed drawing room waiting for the arrival of the lady of the house.

The double doors opened and a tall, blonde-haired woman stepped into the room. She moved gracefully and wore a maroon and white dress. An ornate diamond ring and a pair of pearl earrings were her only jewelry. "I'm Mrs. Theodore Bruce," she announced as she took a seat on the sofa. "I understand you wish to speak to me about the late Mr. Gilhaney."

"I'm Inspector Witherspoon and this is Constable Barnes," he replied. He hoped she'd ask them to sit down. "You're correct, ma'am, we are here to ask you some questions."

She gestured toward the two balloon-back chairs across from her. "You may sit down if you like, but I doubt you'll be staying very long. I've already made a statement about that evening. Surely you know that."

Witherspoon didn't reply until he and Barnes were seated. "We understand that, ma'am, but we still need to ask you a few questions."

She shrugged. "You may ask what you like. My father seems to think you might be able to solve this puzzling crime, but frankly, I doubt it. Mr. Gilhaney was killed weeks ago. I hardly think you'll find out anything new about the matter."

"Nonetheless, ma'am, we must do our duty," Witherspoon murmured.

"Was the Chases' Bonfire Night party the first time you'd met Mr. Gilhaney?" Barnes asked.

"No, I had met him on a previous occasion."

"When was that?" Witherspoon asked.

"In Manchester. He worked for my friend's husband and I met him at a dinner party. He expressed his desire to come to London, which was where he was originally from, and as he was highly regarded, I was the one who recommended him to my father."

Witherspoon hoped his surprise didn't show on his face. Newton Walker hadn't mentioned this fact. He'd specifically said that several of his business acquaintances had recommended Gilhaney. "You knew your father was looking for someone like Mr. Gilhaney? We understand he was well known for his financial abilities."

"He was excellent at his work," she replied. "And yes, I did know that my father was looking for someone. He wanted the finances of Walker and Company vetted properly. It's now a public company and Father wanted to ensure the shareholders were getting true value for their money."

Witherspoon nodded but made a mental note that she hadn't mentioned the fact that her father hired Gilhaney for advice on selling the company, not on ensuring the shareholders made a profit. "We understand that Mr. Gilhaney was rather rude to people at Mrs. Chase's dinner party—was that your impression?"

"Did Abigail Chase tell you that?" She smiled mirthlessly. "I imagine she's still smarting over having her dinner party ruined."

"Yes, ma'am, we got that information from Mrs. Chase, and Mr. Chase confirmed it as well," Witherspoon replied. "Can you tell us about the evening?"

"It was awkward from the very beginning. As I said, I'd met Christopher Gilhaney several times and on those occasions, his behavior was exemplary. It was obvious he was from a rougher background than what one would expect to find at a social occasion such as the Chases' Bonfire Night party; nonetheless, despite his background, I was quite surprised by the way he acted."

"What do you mean by that?" Barnes asked.

"He was very working class, Constable," she replied. "He was obviously self-educated and well-read and perhaps could have behaved as a gentleman, but I don't think he particularly cared about what we thought of him. His behavior that night was shocking."

"Can you be more specific, ma'am?" Witherspoon pressed.

"Gilhaney was already in the drawing room when we arrived"—her brows drew together and she frowned slightly—"Abigail was serving sherry, and after we greeted everyone, I went to speak with Mr. Longworth. I was surprised to see him there. He didn't look well; he was very pale. We started chatting, and suddenly he looked over at Leon Webster. Gilhaney was talking with him. He was standing close to him, his face was only inches away from Leon, and there was a strange expression on his face."

"What kind of expression?" the inspector asked.

She cocked her head to one side as she thought back. "Victorious, Inspector, that's the only way I can describe it. Christopher Gilhaney looked as if he'd just triumphed over the whole world. Leon's eyes were big as saucers and he was obviously very upset."

"Upset how?" Barnes looked up from his notebook.

"I've tried to forget that dreadful evening, Constable, so my recollection isn't perfect, but I do remember seeing poor Leon turn red and gulp his sherry."

"What did Mr. Gilhaney do?" the inspector asked.

"Nothing, he just smiled and then he turned and looked at us."

"Us?"

"Robert and I. He started towards us, but just then, dinner was announced and we went into the dining room." She closed her eyes and a small shudder wracked her body. "That's when the insults really started. I don't remember exactly how he said it, but he made a comment to Ann Holter about how it was better to be a spinster than to be left at the altar." She shook her head in remembered disbelief. "We were all shocked. But Ann, to her credit, simply stared at him and then she said something odd. I can't recall exactly what it was."

"You don't need to remember her exact words," Witherspoon urged. "Just tell us what she might have meant."

"That's just it, Inspector, I don't know. Her comment made little sense. She said something to the effect that an intelligent ape was nothing more than an animal with a bag of tricks, but in the end, it was still just an animal. After that, she said very little, but she left the party early. She didn't withdraw with the ladies while the gentlemen had their port."

"What happened then?" Witherspoon wondered if concentrating on the dinner party guests was the best course of action. Mrs. Bruce was essentially giving the same account as both the Chases and, to some extent, even her own father. Albeit, with a very different point of view. He was afraid he was going around in circles. None of this was new information. Perhaps the killer was an old enemy from Manchester or someone who resented Gilhaney coming into the firm and usurping their authority or even someone from his distant past.

"He started making strange comments again. This time I think they were directed toward Robert Longworth." She clasped her hands together. "But I don't recall what it was he actually said. I'm sorry."

Witherspoon made a mental note to ask Longworth.

Surely the man would remember a disparaging remark directed to him. "Anything else, ma'am?"

"Isn't this enough, Inspector? He insulted people left and right, so much so that the party was over before nine o'clock. Poor Abigail was at her wits' end. Even Gordon was upset. Before the dessert was served he interrupted the meal to drag everyone out to the terrace to watch the fireworks." She gave a short, denigrating laugh. "That did nothing to improve the situation. The fireworks were barely visible over the trees, but oddly enough, Gilhaney said nothing derogatory at that point. We all trooped back inside. Oh yes, now I remember, it was then that Ann Holter left and then Leon Webster bolted as soon as he'd eaten two bites of his charlotte russe. That's really all I can recall, Inspector." She got to her feet. "I'm sorry, I know this isn't very helpful. You've probably already heard most of this from the Chases. But that's really all I can tell you. Now, if you'll excuse me, I've an appointment."

Barnes glanced at Witherspoon. He nodded and the two men got up. But the constable had one more question to ask. "Mrs. Bruce, wasn't it odd that with Mr. Gilhaney insulting everyone he didn't insult you or your husband?" He watched her closely. He wanted to see how she would respond. Mrs. Chase had made some very interesting comments about both Theodore and Hazel Bruce. According to her, Gilhaney claimed the Bruce marriage was a sham and that Theodore Bruce had married his wife so he could run Walker and Company.

She stared at him impassively. "Don't be absurd, Constable. Gilhaney was bold, but he wasn't a fool—he'd not make that kind of mistake. My husband is his superior. He reports to him directly. He'd make sure not to offend either of us."

Barnes looked at the inspector. This, too, was a lie. Walker had specifically said that Gilhaney would report only to him.

"I'm sorry to barge in like this, Doctor, but we're in a bit of a muddle," Mrs. Jeffries explained as she followed her friend Dr. Bosworth into his small, cluttered office. She'd been lucky upon arriving at St. Thomas' Hospital that Bosworth was not only on duty, but able to see her.

He was a tall man with dark red hair, a longish nose, and very pale skin. He smiled and pulled a stack of medical periodicals off the chair opposite his desk. He popped the magazines onto the floor and gestured for her to sit down. "No apology is needed, Mrs. Jeffries, you're always welcome here."

Dr. Bosworth was one of their "special friends." After completing medical school in Scotland, he'd gone to San Francisco, where he became somewhat of an expert on bullet wounds and, more importantly, on the type of gun that had inflicted a wound. Apparently, there was no shortage of bodies in that part of the world. Mrs. Jeffries frequently relied on his expertise when they had a difficult case. He firmly believed that much could be ascertained about a crime by a thorough study of the body and the surrounding environment.

Bosworth was not only a physician at St. Thomas' Hospital, he was currently the police surgeon for both K and W districts of the Metropolitan Police. He went behind his desk and sat down. "Now, what can I do for you? I haven't seen the inspector's name mentioned lately in the press. Does he have a new case?"

"If only it were a new one." She gave him a rueful smile. "But unfortunately, it's an old one, I'm afraid."

"An old case?" Bosworth repeated.

"The victim was killed some weeks ago," she began.

He interrupted. "And they've just now discovered the body? That's dreadful. I know I've told you before, but depending on the environment, once a corpse gets past rigor mortis it decays quickly and then it's hard to ascertain anything useful from either the location or the flesh itself."

"No, no, they discovered the body at the time of the murder. Oh dear, I'm not explaining this very well. Forgive me, but I've had a dreadful day. I'm apparently not very good at getting information out of people, but that's neither here nor there." She broke off and sighed. "Let me start over. The victim was a man named Christopher Gilhaney and he was shot on Guy Fawkes Night."

"Guy Fawkes Night!" he exclaimed.

"I know. The problem is that the crime was mistakenly assumed to be a robbery gone wrong rather than a premeditated murder. Unfortunately, the inspector in charge of the case handled it badly and now our inspector has been tasked to find the killer."

"A rather thankless task, I'll wager." Bosworth shook his head. "That was weeks ago—it's nearly Christmas."

Mrs. Jeffries nodded. "That's one of the reasons I've come to see you. I'm hoping you can help. At least if we knew what kind of gun killed the fellow, we'd have a bit more information to work with."

Bosworth put his elbows on the desk and leaned forward.

"What about the original postmortem report? Surely it contained some useful facts."

She shook her head. "No, from what the inspector said the postmortem merely stated cause of death." She stared at him curiously. "I was surprised. Dr. Procash is the police surgeon for the division that includes Chelsea and he's done a number of postmortems on the inspector's cases. He's usually very good, almost as detailed as you are in his reports."

"Dr. Procash retired at the end of October and I'm afraid the man who replaced him got the position through his connections and not his abilities. Dr. Spicer is a very old man and frankly, he should have been struck off the medical register years ago, but as I said, he has some very powerful connections." Bosworth smiled sympathetically. "What's more, like many incompetent people, Spicer doesn't like to share his reports. He doesn't want anyone competent to know what he's done. I'll do anything I can to help, but if the postmortem report merely states cause of death, I doubt there's much I can learn."

Mrs. Jeffries sagged against the chair. Her day just went from bad to worse. She'd been counting on Bosworth even though she'd known before she came that the original report was very brief. The inspector had complained about it before dinner last night, but somehow, she'd expected the good doctor to be able to provide some assistance. She was annoyed at herself for being so foolish. She'd come here because her vanity was bruised and she hadn't wanted to admit she was terrible at getting people to talk. Gracious, this investigation really was going to Hades in a handbasket. She'd no idea what to do now.

"The victim was murdered in Chelsea," he murmured. "Close to the river?"

"Yes, in Kilbane Mews."

"Then the postmortem was probably done at Belgrave Hospital. I've a colleague there, a young doctor who is very interested in pathology. There's a chance he might have observed Dr. Spicer's postmortem. I'll contact him and see if he did, and if we get lucky, he might remember what he saw."

"Thank you, Dr. Bosworth, that would be wonderful." She smiled gratefully.

"I don't want to raise your hopes, Mrs. Jeffries. Even if he observed the autopsy, he might not remember anything useful."

"That sounds to me like someone was pullin' your leg," Luty said to the young clerk. She was in the outer office of Widdowes and Walthrop, Merchant Bankers. She was waiting to see one of her sources, John Widdowes. But as she had a few minutes to kill, she'd decided to try her luck with the only person left in the room, a young man diligently laboring over a huge, open ledger.

His eyes widened at the mention of the word "leg" and he hastily looked away as a blush spread up his cheeks. "Er, no, ma'am," he stammered. "That's what I've heard."

"You tellin' me that this Gilhaney fella could see something once and remember it even weeks later?"

The lad smiled gratefully as the inner office door opened and John Widdowes appeared. "Now, Luty, stop tormenting the poor boy. You'll scare him to death with all your questions."

John Widdowes was a middle-aged man with dark, honey-colored hair and a precisely groomed beard, a burly build that was muscle, not fat, and a ready grin. He was half the owner of Widdowes and Walthrop. Luty had never met his partner.

"Scare him? Hogswaller. I'm a sweet little old lady and most of your staff like me."

"That's true, they do, they love it when you come by—so much so that Byron went to fetch the tea the moment you arrived." John nodded toward the clerk. "But he's new and quite talented, so I'd appreciate it if you didn't scare the devil out of the lad. Let's go into my office and have tea."

Luty winked at the young man as she moved through the wooden barrier that surrounded the clerks' desks and followed her friend into his inner sanctum.

John motioned her toward the wing-back chair in front of his massive desk. The wall next to the door was lined with boxes and ledgers, two windows looked out upon the Thames, and on the wall opposite the desk hung a series of lovely paintings of the ocean.

Luty pointed at them. "Those are new."

John grinned. "Yes, they are. I saw them at a gallery recently and a friend of mine suggested they'd look lovely here."

Luty chuckled. "I betcha I know who the friend is. How is Chloe?"

"She's very well. As a matter of fact, I'm glad you're here. Chloe and I were just talking about you—she hopes you'll be free for dinner sometime soon." He sat down behind his desk.

"I'd love to, just name the date and I'll be there with bells on," she replied. Chloe Attwater had been involved in one of their previous cases and then had provided some very pertinent information in the inspector's last investigation. Luty was the one who introduced her to John and she was now delighted that two of her favorite people seemed to be happy together. He was a good man who'd come from rough beginnings and made a success of his life. But he wasn't one of those that looked down on the less fortunate because he'd pulled himself up by his bootstraps. She knew that he gave more to charity than most of the aristocrats in London put together.

"Excellent. Now, how can I help you? Did the inspector get another case?"

"It's an old case, I'm afraid. Do you remember a few weeks back when a man named Christopher Gilhaney was shot? It was on Bonfire Night."

"Of course. I knew Gilhaney," John replied. "He was a decent man. Like me, he'd come up the hard way. But he was very successful. I went to his funeral. It was a sad affair, not many people there at all, but some of his old mates from Clapham came and that was nice."

"Did he have a family?" Luty asked.

"No, like me, he grew up in a workhouse. But wasn't he killed during a robbery?"

Luty was amazed at the lack of bitterness in John's voice. But either he'd gotten over any misery of having been raised in one of those hellholes or he'd learned to hide his feelings. "No one rightly knows, and now the inspector has got stuck with the case. Can you tell me what you know about him?"

"What I know . . . Well, to begin with, he was a genius. Secondly, I was shocked when I heard he'd come back to London to work for Newton Walker."

"Why?"

"He had some sort of grudge against the company. Something happened years ago. I never heard what it was. We had a business relationship. We weren't close friends. Gilhaney had a strange life. After leaving the workhouse, he did carpentry work on the docks for a few years and then, about twenty years ago, he decided to use his brains." He looked toward the door as it opened and a young clerk carrying a loaded tea tray stepped inside. He grinned at Luty as he put the tray down on the edge of John's desk. She gave him a wink and a wave as he retreated.

John poured their tea and handed Luty a cup. "That's how I met Gilhaney. He came to see me to obtain seed money for a new product. One of his friends had invented a new process for waterproofing wood. Gilhaney talked the man into manufacturing the item instead of selling it or licensing it to an existing company. We both made a lot of money off the deal and that was the beginning of Gilhaney's business career."

"But how do you know he hated Walker's firm?" Luty asked.

"He told me. The item was a huge success. A year or so later, I happened to run into Gilhaney one night. He insisted on buying me a drink and we went to a nearby pub. He got very drunk—it was the anniversary of something for him, he wouldn't say what, but it wasn't a nice memory—and he began talking about Walker and Company. He hated them. I could see he was in his cups, so I put him in a hansom and went on my way."

"Then why would he go to work for Newton Walker?" Luty demanded. "That don't make any sense."

John shrugged. "Perhaps Walker offered him a huge amount of money. I know that Walker was looking for someone with Gilhaney's talent."

"How do you know that?"

"It was no secret. Walker wanted someone to examine his finances. His company had gone public and he claimed he wanted to attract more investors."

Luty cocked her head to one side. "You sound like you don't believe that."

"What I believe and what I know are two different things," he replied. "But in my experience, you only get someone like Gilhaney in when you're looking to see if someone has cooked the books."

CHAPTER 4

Lady Cannonberry, or Ruth, as the household knew her, was the first to arrive for their afternoon meeting. "Am I too early?" she asked as she glanced around the empty kitchen.

"No, they're late." Mrs. Goodge put a pot of tea on the table next to the plate of brown bread and mince tarts. "But as you're here and they're not, we'll have a cup of tea and I'll tell you what we know so far."

"Good, the only thing Hepzibah told me was that the victim had been murdered on Bonfire Night and that his name was Christopher Gilhaney."

"That's right, and we don't know much more than that except that on the night he was killed, he'd been at a dinner party in Chelsea." Mrs. Goodge told her what they'd learned thus far. When she was finished, she took a deep breath and tried to think of the best way to say what needed to be said. "I'm not sure how to say this," she finally admitted.

Ruth stared at her curiously. "What is it? You can tell me anything, we're good friends."

"I know, and I know you'll understand what I'm sayin', it's just I don't want you thinkin' ill of Hepzibah."

Alarmed now, Ruth grabbed the cook's hand. "What are you saying? What's wrong?"

"Nothing's wrong. Oh dear, I'm not telling it right." Mrs. Goodge smiled ruefully as she extracted her fingers. "I know you would never think badly of her, it's just that she seems very different on this case. I know she really wanted to go to those lectures, but it's not like her to be so . . . I don't know . . . so . . . so . . ."

"Detached." Ruth supplied the very word the cook needed.

"You noticed it, too? Thank goodness, I was afraid it was my imagination. And it's not just her, it's all of them. They've got their noses out of joint because they're scared this murder will mean they have to cancel their Christmas plans—" She caught herself. "Oh dear, I did it again. You and the inspector were going to go to your friends' in—"

Ruth interrupted. "Stop fretting, now, the inspector and I can visit my friends anytime we like. I don't know about the rest of the inspector's household, but you're right about Hepzibah. She was very distant when she was telling me about the Gilhaney murder. Not at all like her usual self."

"Like I said, it's not just her, it's all of 'em." Mrs. Goodge thought for a moment. "No, Luty's fine, but the rest of them acted like gettin' out and about today was a right interruption to their day. I don't know what we'll do if they keep this up."

"Perhaps we won't have to do anything," Ruth suggested. "Perhaps they'll come to realize that justice is more important than a few holiday plans." She stopped as they heard the back door open and then light footsteps coming up the hall.

Phyllis, her cheeks flushed from the cold, hurried into the room. Before she'd even reached the coat tree, the door opened again, and within five minutes, most of the others had arrived and taken their places around the table.

Mrs. Goodge kept glancing at the carriage clock on the pine sideboard as she poured mugs of tea and handed them around the table. The others said little as they filled their plates with buttered brown bread and mince tarts.

"It's a quarter past four," Wiggins exclaimed. "Where's Mrs. Jeffries? Cor blimey, I hope she hasn't run into trouble. She's not like the rest of us—she's not used to being out and askin' questions."

"Don't be silly." Mrs. Goodge took her seat. "She's quite capable of asking a few questions about Robert Longworth. She's very clever."

"We know she's clever"—he helped himself to a second slice of bread—"but askin' questions is different from puttin' all the bits and pieces together like she does."

"It's not that different." Luty cast a worried glance at the clock. "But it's gettin' late and Hatchet and I need to git moving before too long. I want to go to the Rucklands' dinner party. Old Harry Ruckland has business interests all over the south of England and might know something useful."

"We've plenty of time, madam," Hatchet said. "You're not expected until half seven. You just want to get the meeting started because you've found out something and you can't wait to tell us."

Luty grinned. "Danged right, and from that long, sour face of yours, I can tell you didn't learn anything."

Hatchet snorted faintly but said nothing.

"You don't think Mrs. Jeffries is in real trouble, do you?" Phyllis looked at Wiggins, her expression anxious. "We were all late back today and it's not a quarter past, it's twenty past. That clock is five minutes slow."

"She'll be here soon." Betsy smiled reassuringly. "You know how it is, sometimes when you're on the hunt, time gets away from you. But I agree with Luty, if she isn't here soon, we'll have to start. Amanda will be wanting her supper and poor Elinor isn't much of a cook."

"It's not like Mrs. Jeffries to be this late," Phyllis muttered.

Wiggins reached over and patted her hand. "Don't fret, now, I'm sure she's on her way."

"You're the one that thought she might be in trouble," Phyllis protested.

"She's not in trouble, but her bein' this late is a bit worryin'," Smythe said. "Some people don't like to answer questions and they can be right nasty about it."

"Don't be daft," Mrs. Goodge cried. "She can take care of herself. For goodness' sake, she knows what she's about. She knows what she's doing."

"Does she?" Hatchet asked. "She's brilliant at putting the clues together, but we've no idea how skilled she might be in extracting information in a subtle manner and, as Smythe just pointed out, some individuals take offense quite easily."

They all started discussing the matter, their voices rising as they each tried to make their point. The conversation became so loud that none of them heard the back door open.

"Mrs. Jeffries knows what's what and she's just fine," Mrs. Goodge shouted over the others. "She'll be here soon, so stop your worrying."

"Why, thank you, Mrs. Goodge." Mrs. Jeffries took off her hat and cloak as she crossed the floor. "I'm so sorry to be late, but there was horrible traffic on the Westminster Bridge. I was stuck in a hansom cab and, frankly, could have gotten home faster if I'd walked." She hung up her garments and took her seat. "Now, what have I missed?" As she'd stopped in the corridor and eavesdropped, she'd overheard some of what had been said about her. She wasn't sure if she ought to be insulted that they had little faith in her interrogation skills or flattered that they cared about her enough to fret when she was late.

"Nothing," Mrs. Goodge said firmly. "We were discussing whether or not to start without you. But as you're here now, it's not important."

"Good, who would like to go first?"

"I will," Luty volunteered. "I wasn't able to find out too much about Walker and Company or even the name of the firm in Manchester where Gilhaney worked before he came here, but I did learn that he's supposed to be one of those people that is brilliant at finances. He ain't just good with numbers, he's got one of those brains that can remember something after only seein' it one time."

"How is that possible?" Hatchet asked. "Honestly, madam, sometimes you're very naive. You believe the most ridiculous nonsense."

"It ain't nonsense." She shot him a glare. "And I heard it from two different sources. Now, if you'll wait your turn, I'll finish with my report." She told them the rest of what she learned from both John Widdowes and his young clerk. "Accordin' to my source, Gilhaney was a real decent man, a good man. So I sure would like to know what it was that made him hate Walker, but more importantly, I'd like to know why he then went to work for the fellow." She glanced at the faces around the table. Except for Ruth and Mrs. Goodge, none of them seemed overly excited about what she thought was a very significant bit of information.

"Yes, well, we'll do our best to find out." Mrs. Jeffries took a sip of tea. "Who'd like to go next?"

"Mrs. Bruce, this is an awkward question, but it must be asked." Witherspoon hesitated. He couldn't recall Abigail Chase's exact words, but he was sure she'd mentioned that the Bruces, and Mrs. Bruce specifically, had been Gilhaney's victims as well. "If Mr. Gilhaney didn't insult you, why did you and your husband leave so early?"

She stared at him coldly. "Because I was very, very sleepy, Inspector. Frankly, after we ate dessert, I could barely stay awake. What's more, it had become apparent to me that, socially, it was much better to leave rather than stay and be the only ones to remain. That would have been humiliating for Mrs. Chase. So my husband put myself and my sister-in-law into a hansom and we went home."

"Your husband didn't go with you?"

"No, the Chase house is less than half a mile away and he wanted some fresh air. Besides, the only vehicle available was a hansom and they're not very comfortable if there are more than two people. Now I really must go." She started for the door.

"Is Miss Florence Bruce at home?" Barnes asked.

"Yes, she's probably in the library. I'll send the maid to fetch her. Good day."

Witherspoon waited till the door closed behind her. "What do you think, Constable?"

"I think she's lying about not being insulted." Barnes flipped through his notebook. "Abigail Chase specifically said that Gilhaney implied that the Bruces loathed one another and that Theodore Bruce had only married his wife to run Walker and Company."

"I agree." Witherspoon nodded. "Mrs. Bruce isn't telling the truth, but is she lying to hide something or is it simply that she didn't wish to admit she'd been the victim of the same public humiliation as the others?"

"Perhaps we'll know more when we speak with Miss Bruce," Barnes replied just as the door opened and a tall, middle-aged woman with brown hair and thick eyebrows stepped into the room. She was dressed in a simple gray skirt, a high-necked white blouse with puffy sleeves, and a forest green velvet cummerbund that fitted perfectly around her waist.

"I'm Florence Bruce. I understand you wish to speak to me?" She crossed the room and took the spot her sister-in-law had just vacated.

Witherspoon said, "Yes, we're here—"

"I know why you're here," she interrupted. "I'm sorry, that was rude of me. But I've an appointment soon and I've not much time so can we get on with it?"

"I'll be as quick as possible. When you were going into the Chases' dinner party on Bonfire Night, did you notice anyone in the immediate neighborhood that appeared suspicious?" Witherspoon asked.

"It's been weeks, Inspector. I'm sorry, but I'm not going to be much help to your investigation. I can't remember anything about that night except that it was a dreadful dinner party and Mrs. Bruce was terribly sleepy."

"She mentioned that as well." Witherspoon tried another tactic. "Miss Bruce, had you ever met Mr. Gilhaney prior to that night?"

"No. I believe that Hazel and he were acquainted at one time. He worked for a firm in Manchester owned by one of her friends."

"Yes, Mrs. Bruce told us she knew him." Witherspoon tried to think of something useful to ask the woman. Once again, he had the feeling he was going around in circles.

"Only as an acquaintance. On the way to the Chase home, she mentioned she'd met him socially."

"Would you please give us your impressions of the evening." Witherspoon noticed she kept glancing at the clock on the marble mantel.

"I'm not sure I understand what you're asking." She frowned irritably. "I've told you, I don't recall the events all that well. It was such a miserable party all I wanted to do was leave."

"We understand that, Miss Bruce, but a man has been murdered and you may have seen or heard something that will help us catch his killer," Barnes interjected. "All the inspector wants to know is what happened that night, according to how you saw the events. We've been told that Mr. Gilhaney was rude to everyone. Do you think that's true or were Mrs. Chase and Mrs. Bruce being overly sensitive?"

"Overly sensitive!" She laughed. "Constable, take my word for it, my sister-in-law is most certainly not sensitive about anything and Abigail Chase is one of the most practical women I've ever met. No, Christopher Gilhaney was a rude boor." She paused and her expression grew thoughtful. "I can't recall if he was already there or if he came in right after us, but that doesn't matter. He was horrible the entire evening, short as it was."

"We understand he started with Leon Webster."

"He did. I'm sure you already know what was said in these exchanges. Frankly, Gilhaney's comments were most understood by the people he was speaking with, while at the same time, they were obvious enough for the rest of us to know that he was being insulting." She glanced at the clock again. "Is this going to take much longer?"

"Just a few more minutes," Witherspoon promised. "You said Mrs. Bruce had met Mr. Gilhaney in Manchester? Correct?"

She nodded impatiently.

"How long ago was this?"

"I'm not sure. She often goes to visit Mr. and Mrs. Ormand. She merely mentioned she'd met him socially but she didn't give us any details."

"Us?"

"My brother and I," she explained. "She told us she'd met him when we were going to the Chase home. Ted was very surprised."

"Was Mr. Bruce happy that Mr. Walker had engaged Gilhaney?"

"I've no idea, Inspector. He doesn't discuss his business with me." She got to her feet. "Now, if there's nothing else . . ."

"How long have you lived here?" Barnes asked.

She seemed surprised by the question. "What kind of a question is that? My living arrangements have nothing to do with Mr. Gilhaney's murder."

"Of course not," Witherspoon said quickly. "We merely like to know as much as possible about the background of our witnesses. We never know who might be called to testify in the event of a trial. I'm sorry if the question offended you, but the constable is simply doing his job." He'd thought the question odd, too, but he'd learned to trust Barnes.

"I am offended and I can think of no reason for me to have to testify on this matter. I didn't know the man and, except for meeting him at a dreadful dinner party, he's nothing to do with me. Now, if you'll excuse me, I must go." She got up and hurried out of the room.

The inspector didn't try to detain her; he merely nodded as she flounced out of the room.

"Sorry, sir, perhaps I shouldn't have asked her," Barnes began, but the inspector cut him off.

"Nonsense, Constable, you've excellent instincts. When we leave, you should have a quick word with the young lady that took our coats. If Miss Bruce won't answer a simple question like how long she's lived here, we'll ask the maid."

"You don't want to talk to all of the servants, sir?"

"We've no real reason to speak to all of them," he replied. "Not yet anyway."

"I'll have a go now," Wiggins offered. "Mine won't take much time—there's not much to tell. I went to Putney and hung about the place for ages, but I didn't have any luck finding someone from Gilhaney's lodging house." He grabbed his tea and took a quick drink to avoid making eye contact with anyone. He felt miserably guilty. He shouldn't have gone to Craven Cottage. Unlike the stories he'd heard, what little he could see of the pitch was empty.

"Did you try speaking to the local merchants?" Phyllis asked. She silently hoped he had, because if he'd already done it, that meant she'd not have to troop down to Putney tomorrow. She'd much rather go back to the Bruce neighborhood. Perhaps she'd run into that handsome Jonathan Talmadge again.

"I didn't have time," he lied. He put his cup down, looked at his empty plate, and then reached for another tart, even though he was no longer hungry. "I mean, I hung about all afternoon because I know it's important for us to find out what we can about the victim." He glanced up at their faces and saw nothing unusual in their expressions. Relieved that they believed him, he slumped back in his chair. No need to worry now—they couldn't possibly know he'd shirked his duty. "I'll try again tomorrow."

"Don't look so gloomy." Betsy gave him a cheerful smile. "I didn't find out anything today, either. Maybe we'll both have better luck tomorrow. No one I spoke to knew anything about Ann Holter." She didn't add that she'd only spoken to two shop assistants in the Holter neighborhood. But neither of them knew anything about the woman so she'd given up and just done a bit of shopping for her own family. She still had hopes of getting to Paris.

"I found out a little bit," Phyllis volunteered. "It isn't much, but it was the best I could do. Florence Bruce takes laudanum. I don't know why she takes it or for how long— my source didn't say—but she's got a standing prescription for it." That comment was a bit of a stretch, but she thought it reasonable, considering the way the old man at the chemist's had behaved. "And the Bruce home is owned by Newton Walker, Mrs. Bruce's father. The locals refer to it as 'the Walker house.' When he dies, the property is going to her."

"I thought you claimed you'd not found out a lot." Mrs. Goodge gave her an encouraging smile. "You've learned two facts we didn't know and, as Mrs. Jeffries always says, we've no idea what might or might not turn out to be important."

"Who would like to go next?" Mrs. Jeffries said.

"I will." Smythe put his cup down. "I didn't have much luck, either. The only thing I found out was that Leon Webster was at a pub near the Chase house on Bonfire Night. Accordin' to the fellow I talked to, Webster was as nervous as a kitten in a roomful of bulldogs. He jumped every time the fireworks exploded." He repeated everything he'd learned from old Hamish. "My source was lucky he had his nephew with 'im. Webster recognized him as a former employee and bought them both a couple of drinks."

Mrs. Jeffries nodded, but she'd only been half listening. She tried to think of a question, but nothing popped into her head.

"What time did he get to the pub?" Luty asked.

Smythe grinned. "Ten minutes before last call, and the place closes at half ten. And Webster didn't just buy drinks for the others, he downed two whiskeys himself."

"Why is that important?" Mrs. Goodge asked. "Oh, silly me, of course it's important." She glanced at Mrs. Jeffries. "The inspector told you the dinner party ended early the night Gilhaney was killed." She waited for Mrs. Jeffries to make a comment, but she simply sat there, staring off into space. The cook surveyed the faces around the table. Ruth and Luty looked like they were listening, but the rest of them appeared to be bored or daydreaming.

Mrs. Jeffries finally came out of her daze. "Yes, yes, he did. Now I guess it's time for my report. Actually, I've nothing of substance to say. I didn't have much luck today. The truth is, I learned nothing."

"I don't think this will take long, Constable. Miss Holter was the first to leave the night Mr. Gilhaney was murdered," Witherspoon said as he and Barnes hovered in the foyer of the Holter house.

She lived in a large town house at the end of the street. The exterior was slightly shabby and needed a bit of paint and a good scrub. The inside wasn't much better; the black and white floor was missing several tiles, the gold-patterned wallpaper had dulled with age, and there was a thin layer of dust on both the cabriole-legged side table and the blue ceramic umbrella stand.

"Let's hope not, sir. I'd really like for us to have time to get to Putney. We need to speak to Gilhaney's landlady. Nivens' report didn't even tell us what had happened to his belongings. Surely the man had more to his name than just the clothes he was wearing that night."

Witherspoon pulled out his watch and frowned. "We'll not have time, Constable. It's past four and with the traffic on Putney Bridge we'd not get there before dark. I'd prefer to do it in daylight. I want to have a good look at his last residence." He tucked the watch back in his vest pocket. "After we speak to Miss Holter, I'd like you to have a word with her servants and confirm the time she arrived home that night." He pursed his lips and shook his head. "What was I thinking? No wonder it feels like we've been going in circles. We've every right to confirm their statements and we don't need their permission to speak to their household." He looked down the gloomy corridor. "I wonder what's taking them so long."

"It's been a good five minutes, sir." Barnes could tell that the inspector was aggravated. He was, too, but whether it was because of Ann Holter's tardiness in receiving them or the case in general was hard to tell. "I don't think the housemaid will lie for her mistress. I don't think the girl likes Miss Holter very much, sir. She was grinning from ear to ear when we told her why we were here."

The maid was still smiling when she returned. "This way, gentlemen." A few moments later they were led into the Holter drawing room. Witherspoon noted the windows were draped in heavy, old-fashioned gray velvet curtains, the furniture was upholstered in green horsehair and had thick, claw-footed legs and feet, and the pattern on the carpet was so threadbare as to be unrecognizable.

"You wish to speak with me?" Ann Holter stood in front of the unlighted fireplace and glared at them.

"Yes, ma'am, we do. I'm Inspector Gerald Witherspoon and this is Constable Barnes . . ." he began.

"I don't care what your names are," she interrupted. "Just ask your questions and then leave my house."

She was a tall, bony woman of early middle age. Her hair was dark blonde streaked with gray, parted in the center and fitted into a disheveled knot on top of her head. Several tendrils had escaped and hung limply behind her ears. She had a long horse face with small eyes so deeply set that in the subdued light he couldn't even tell what color they might be.

She was dressed in a high-necked yellow blouse that appeared too large for her thin frame and a brown skirt.

The inspector knew she wasn't going to ask them to sit down. "Miss Holter, I understand you were at a dinner party at the home of Gordon and Abigail Chase on Bonfire Night, is that correct?"

"Yes."

"What time did you leave the Chase home?" Barnes asked.

Her beady eyes shifted to the constable. "Since when do underlings speak in front of their betters?"

"Constable Barnes is an essential part of this investigation," Witherspoon said softly. "Please answer his questions."

"Yes, I was at the Chase home the night that Christopher Gilhaney was killed."

"What time did you leave?" Barnes asked.

"I don't know the exact time, but it was before the dessert was served. It was probably half past eight or thereabouts."

"How did you get home?" Barnes asked again, just to irritate her.

She said nothing for a moment. "I took a hansom cab."

"What time did you get here?" Witherspoon asked.

"Not everyone watches the clock, Inspector," she replied. "But as it's only a quarter mile or so, I imagine it was about a quarter to nine. The fireworks were still going off—I could hear them. I don't know why people waste their time and money on such frivolities. It's just an excuse for the lower classes to indulge in drunkenness."

Witherspoon ignored her comment. "When you were

leaving the Chase home, did you notice if there was anyone suspicious hanging about the neighborhood?"

"I had a headache, Inspector. My only desire was to get home as quickly as possible."

"Of course. I understand now," the inspector replied. But it had suddenly occurred to him that Gilhaney had been very disrespectful to her. Why? Why go out of your way to be rude to someone you'd never met before? That simply didn't make sense and if he'd learned one thing about the victim, it was that he wasn't foolish. He was extremely intelligent. So why had he made himself out to be a boorish lout to a roomful of strangers? "Miss Holter, was the Bonfire Night dinner party the first time you'd met Mr. Gilhaney?"

"I'd never seen the man prior to that," she said quickly, but a flush had crept up her cheeks and Witherspoon noted that the constable was staring at her with a hard, knowing expression on his face.

"Are you sure of that, Miss Holter?" he pressed. His gentlemanly instincts decreed that he give her a chance to tell the truth.

"How dare you," she snapped. "I've told you that I'd never met the man."

"We understand Mr. Gilhaney was quite insulting to you that night." Barnes watched her carefully as he spoke. "Why would he do that if you hadn't been previously acquainted?"

"How should I know? He was a disgusting boor." She pushed away from the fireplace, stalked to the settee, and sat down. "That is what comes of letting the lower classes into a decent person's home. Give them an inch and they'll take a mile. Gilhaney was like that: a stupid little upstart that thought he could mingle with his betters."

Witherspoon interrupted her tirade. "Are you saying he deserved to be murdered?"

She caught herself. "Certainly not. I'm a good Christian woman and I'd never condone murder. Please, just get on with your questions. I've an engagement this evening and I've not much time."

"I've no wish to be indelicate," Witherspoon said, "but can you tell us specifically what Mr. Gilhaney said to you that night?"

Her eyes narrowed. "I don't remember."

Witherspoon knew she was lying. She'd been grossly insulted and humiliated; that was the sort of thing that people, especially women, remembered. His mother had once told him that she recalled every single detail of the moment she'd realized his father's family thought he'd married beneath him. She hadn't shared the specifics of the memory with him, but he'd known she remembered it vividly. He suspected that no matter how hard he pressed, Ann Holter would never tell him Gilhaney's exact words. "If you do happen to recall what he said, please let us know. Do you know if Mr. Gilhaney had any enemies?"

"How would I know that, Inspector? As I've already told you, I'd never met the man prior to the Chases' dinner party."

"Are the Chases friends of yours?" Barnes asked. "The reason I'm asking is because the guests at the dinner party were all involved in some way with Walker and Company."

"They're not particularly close friends," she admitted. "Abigail Chase's father was a bank clerk, but Gordon is from a decent enough background. The reason I went was because my mother and I are shareholders in the firm. My late father was on the board of directors."

"Your mother lives here as well?" Witherspoon asked.

"She does, but she didn't go with me to the Chases'. She was invited, of course, but her eyesight is failing and she's not comfortable going out at night. She limits her social engagements to the daylight hours."

Barnes gave her a bland smile. "May we speak to her, Miss Holter? Perhaps she can verify the time you arrived home that night."

"You may not. My mother has nothing to do with this matter and I'll not have her disturbed." She glared at him. "She retires right after dinner and was sound asleep when I arrived home. Now, if there is nothing else, I'd like you to leave."

Witherspoon glanced at Barnes, who gave a barely imperceptible nod indicating he had no more questions for her. "Thank you for your time, Miss Holter," he said.

She said nothing as they left the drawing room. The housemaid was waiting in the hallway to see them out.

Barnes held his questions until they were almost to the front door. He wanted to make sure they were out of earshot. "Excuse me, Miss . . . uh . . . I'm afraid I don't know your name."

"Kemp, sir, Joy Kemp." She gave him a mischievous grin. "And I imagine you'd like to speak to me, wouldn't you?"

"You seem a very bright young woman." The constable couldn't help but smile back. "I know it might be difficult, but can you recall what time Miss Holter arrived home on Guy Fawkes Night?"

"Of course I can." She laughed. "The mistress came in at half ten. I know because I saw her going up the front walkway just as I got home that night. I had to duck behind a bush so she'd not see that I was late in myself. Lucky for me the servants' entrance is so far from the front, she didn't hear me."

*   *   *

Mrs. Jeffries put the brochure down and sighed heavily. She'd dreamed of these lectures at the British Museum. She'd been fascinated with Egypt for many, many years. Truth to tell, one of the reasons she'd left Yorkshire when David died was so she could come to London and spend as much time as she liked staring at the exhibits to her heart's content.

She had a feeling that if she'd been born in a different time, perhaps years from now, she'd be the one sifting through the warm desert sands and uncovering the secrets of one of the greatest civilizations the world had ever known. Archaeology was a new science, but one she thought might just change the world.

She stared at the picture on the front of the brochure she'd just put down, her attention focused on one of the figures: a woman wearing a wide jeweled collar, a diaphanous white skirt, and not much else. She couldn't help but think that if women dressed like that in ancient Egypt, surely they must have been the equal of men; surely they must have had more rights and privileges than women in this time and place.

Closing her eyes, she tried to ignore the anger that pierced through her as she remembered the unfairness of being a female. It was a memory she'd tried hard to forget; it was the moment she'd decided to leave it all and come to London. It was the moment David's odious little cousin, the ginger-haired half-wit, had shown up on her doorstep and claimed that the cottage, her home with her beloved husband, now belonged to him. He was a man and family property went to males.

She could have taken him to court—there had been cases

where the old laws had been ignored—but she'd been weary and not up for a battle. She and David had been estranged from his sister, who'd married up and might have been in a position to help, but pride wouldn't let her ask for assistance from that quarter, so she'd taken his pension and come to London.

Mrs. Jeffries caught herself—she'd not thought of this in years. Why on earth she was thinking of it now was a mystery. She glanced out her window and saw that the gas lamp across the road was lighted. It was getting late and Witherspoon would be home soon.

Ten minutes later, she forced herself to smile as the inspector came through the front door. "Good evening, sir." She reached for his bowler and his heavy black overcoat. "How was your day?"

"Very confusing," he admitted. "Let's have a sherry and I'll tell you all about it. Honestly, Mrs. Jeffries, I do believe that this case is going to be the one that I cannot solve."

"Nonsense, sir." She forced herself to laugh. But in truth, she was of the same opinion. The murder was too old. "You're far too clever a detective to give in to such thoughts. You'll solve this one just like you've solved all the rest."

He gave her a rueful smile. "I appreciate your encouragement, Mrs. Jeffries, but I'm afraid that this time, it's simply too late. What few clues there might have been have been swept away by the sands of time and what few witnesses there were either can't or won't remember anything important."

Witherspoon trudged down the hall and into his study. Mrs. Jeffries, who felt the way he looked, followed him in and went straight to the liquor cabinet. She poured two glasses of Harvey's all the way to the brim and without spilling a drop crossed the room. "Perhaps this will help a little, sir." She handed him his drink and took her seat.

He took a quick sip. "Today was very, very tiring. We took statements from a number of people, most of whom were at the dinner party with the victim the night he died. But I'm not certain we've made any progress to finding Gilhaney's killer. Honestly, we heard the same information repeatedly and I had the distinct impression we were going in circles. But as Constable Barnes pointed out, hearing several people give an account of the same circumstances does show that not everyone has been truthful."

"You mean they gave different versions of the same event?"

"Yes, frankly, it became obvious that at least two people lied to us. The trouble is, they were both so humiliated by Gilhaney, I can understand why they'd avoid telling the truth."

"Why don't you tell me about it, sir," she suggested.

"We went to the Chase home first. I thought that might be a good place to start and, as it turns out, indeed it was. Mr. Gordon Chase knew exactly when Gilhaney left their home that night. It was at eight forty-seven. That might come in useful."

"That's early for a dinner party to end," she murmured. An image from ancient Egypt flashed into her head and she realized how badly she wanted to go to those lectures. It wasn't just about women being better treated in that society—though, to be honest, she wasn't absolutely certain that was altogether true—it was because the place itself was so very fascinating. Why, even their art was filled with brilliant colors as though they contained the sunlight itself.

"There's a reason it ended so early. You'll not believe the way the victim behaved that night." He took another drink. "And I must say, Newton Walker was rather a surprise. Not at all as I imagined he'd be. He's the one who insisted I get the case."

Mrs. Jeffries realized she'd not heard a word he'd said. She blinked and shook her head. This wouldn't do, it simply wouldn't do. The inspector was doing his duty and she would do hers. "Really, sir?"

She forced herself to pay attention as he told her the details of his day. When he'd finished, she said, "Goodness, no wonder you're exhausted, sir. It sounds as if you've taken statements from half of London."

"It feels as if we did," he agreed. "But you do see my point about taking statements from a number of people about the same event. Constable Barnes and I are certain that Hazel Bruce and Ann Holter lied to us. Gilhaney said awful things to both of them. Honestly, I don't condone murder, but he was certainly no gentleman; his behavior was indecent. But the question is, did the ladies lie to save themselves the humiliation of repeating what Gilhaney said, or did they lie for another reason?"

"You mean to cover up the fact that either of them might be involved in the murder?" She knew there was something here she ought to remember, something someone had said at today's meeting, something about Gilhaney's character. But for the life of her, she couldn't recall what it was.

"That's right. It's too early to make any assumptions yet, but in my experience, when people lie to the police, they're often, but not always, guilty. It's a difficult situation, Mrs. Jeffries."

"I'm sure it is, sir. But you'll keep digging until you get to the truth, you always do. What is on your plate tomorrow?"

"We've still to speak with Theodore Bruce, Leon Webster, and Robert Longworth." He looked at his empty glass. "Do we have time for another before dinner?"

"Of course, sir." Mrs. Jeffries drained her own drink before getting up. She could use another one herself. She poured seconds for both of them. "After you speak to those three men, what will you do next?"

"We'll look deeper into Gilhaney's background."

"Have you had any response from the police in Manchester?"

"I don't know—we didn't go back to the station before coming home. I'm hoping they can tell us something about the fellow. We're going to his lodging house in Putney tomorrow."

Again, Mrs. Jeffries had the sensation that there was something she ought to recall, some bit of useful information that she'd heard today and that should be passed along. But the feeling disappeared before she could examine it properly. Instead, she said, "What if it was simply a robbery gone bad?" She handed him his glass and took her seat. "I know Chief Superintendent Barrows has gone off that idea, as did Inspector Nivens, but that doesn't mean the victim wasn't simply in the wrong place at the wrong time. It does happen, sir."

"I know," he agreed. "But Inspector Nivens has excellent sources amongst the criminal classes; he's got a veritable army of fences and informants, and he keeps a list of pawnshops that have been known to move stolen goods. He put an enormous amount of pressure on these sources and none of them knew anything about the crime."

"Perhaps none of them wanted to speak up because Gilhaney was killed, something which rarely happens," she suggested. "Murder is a hanging offense."

"We thought of that, and of course it is a possibility." He sighed. "We have no way of knowing what really went on that night, so we must assume his death was a deliberate murder. A murder I'm afraid I won't be able to solve."

Downstairs, Mrs. Goodge was in her cozy quarters trying to decide what to do. She sat in her rocker petting Samson, who was draped across her lap. "It's very discouraging, Samson. I've no idea what, if anything, I can do about the situation. At first I thought I must be imagining it, but I'm not. None of them are interested in solving this case. It's as if justice has to go on holiday just because it is Christmas. Luckily, Ruth and I think even Luty saw what was going on today."

Samson meowed faintly in agreement. But he always agreed with the cook. They frequently had long and, to her mind, very interesting conversations with one another.

"If Hepzibah and the others don't come to their senses and start doing this investigation properly, they'll be stuck here through Christmas and I, for one, was looking forward to having the place to myself for a bit. Good gracious, it's already the nineteenth and we're running out of time."

He rubbed his head against her.

"There's no help for it, Samson. Ruth and Luty and I will have to do something about this problem. I'm not sure what we can do, but between the three of us, we'll come up with a solution."

He kneaded his claws against her stomach.

"This can't go on. We've all been given a great opportunity, Samson. People like us usually spend their whole life workin' hard to make ends meet and keep a roof over their heads. But because of our circumstances, we've been given a chance to do more with our time on this earth, to do something important and noble. I'll not let them turn their backs on their duty just because it's inconvenient."

He yawned, closed his eyes, and curled into a ball.

"They've no right to ignore justice just because their holiday plans might be ruined. As I said, I was looking forward to having a bit of time to myself, time where I didn't have to cook three huge meals a day and keep everyone fed, but I didn't shirk my duties, did I. No, I've sent out notes to all my colleagues and tried to find out what I could."

Mrs. Goodge stroked his back. "We'll just have to see what the three of us can come up with. We've got to do something, that's all there is to it."

Samson purred loudly.

CHAPTER 5

"You look fit and raring to go this morning," Mrs. Goodge said cheerfully as she put a mug of tea in front of Constable Barnes.

"Appearances can be deceptive." He yawned. "My bones are tellin' me this case is going to be a killer, Mrs. Goodge."

"Don't be silly." She slipped into the chair across from him. "It's no better than the others. You're just down in the mouth because the timing's gone a bit sour. But I understand how you must be feelin'. Yesterday I was sure I'd overcooked the roast beef. The laundry boy arrived at just the wrong moment and truth to tell I quite forgot I had the joint in the oven. By the time I remembered, I was sure it wouldn't be fit to eat—the crust was almost black. So I let it sit a bit and waited, cut the worst patches off the ends, and guess what, it was tasty as any of my other joints."

Barnes and Mrs. Jeffries both stared at her.

"I know what you're thinking, you don't see the connection." The cook laughed. "But it's there. What I'm saying is that sometimes the timing is all wrong, but that doesn't mean we're not capable of doing what needs to be done." She felt much more optimistic since she'd had her chat with Samson.

"But the timing on this one couldn't be worse," Barnes complained. "What's more, you're an excellent cook so you know how to fiddle with a hunk of meat until it's good, but we've got to work with the leftovers from Inspector Nivens' investigation and that's an entirely different cut of meat."

"Thank you for the compliment about my cooking, Constable, but you and the inspector are excellent at your work as well. I have faith in both of you and you should as well. This is the proper season for it. But time is getting on, so I'll let Mrs. Jeffries take over. She's got a lot to say—we learned quite a bit yesterday."

"We did?" Mrs. Jeffries raised an eyebrow. "We didn't find out that much. It was actually disappointing."

Mrs. Goodge shot her a quick frown but said nothing.

"But we did learn one or two pertinent facts," Mrs. Jeffries continued. She gave him a fast, but accurate, report on what the others had found out. "So, that's it. We'll try our best today and see what happens."

"That's what we'll be doing as well. I take it the inspector gave you a full report on our activities yesterday?" He looked at Mrs. Jeffries expectantly, waited a moment, and then said, "You don't have any questions for me or any details you need sorted out?" It was his habit to fill in any bits and pieces the inspector might have neglected to mention during his evening chat with the housekeeper.

"The inspector was quite thorough when we spoke yesterday evening," Mrs. Jeffries murmured.

"I've got something to say." Mrs. Goodge shot the housekeeper a quick, anxious frown. "Everyone you talked to yesterday, except for perhaps Newton Walker, said that Gilhaney was a rude boor or worse. But one of Luty's sources insisted he was a good and decent person. I think that might be worth looking into."

Barnes stared at her with a puzzled frown. "I'm not sure what you mean."

Mrs. Goodge took a moment to assemble her thoughts properly. She knew she would never be as clever as the housekeeper when it came to understanding clues and putting the pieces together, but she had a feeling this discrepancy might be important. "What I mean is, if the way he behaved the night he was murdered wasn't the way he usually behaved with people, then there had to be a reason."

"And the reason might be important, might have something to do with his murder?" Barnes nodded thoughtfully. "It's possible, but opinions about someone's character can vary from person to person. It could well be that Gilhaney was decent to Luty's source because he had to be."

"I still think it's something to look at," she insisted. "What's more, Luty says that some of Gilhaney's old mates were at his funeral. They'd know about his character and you could ask the police in Manchester as well. It wouldn't be hard for them to talk to people who knew him."

"Did she have any names of these old mates?"

"No, but there's usually a remembrance or visitors' book for people to sign when there's a funeral."

"That would be very useful, but the problem might be

tracking it down. It wasn't mentioned in Nivens' reports. That's one of the reasons our first stop this morning will be at Gilhaney's lodging house. We're hoping his landlady can give us some more information about him. Nivens didn't bother with the funeral and we don't even know where his personal belongings ended up. His investigation was a shambles and if I had my way, he'd be run off the force." Barnes shook his head in disbelief, drained his mug, and rose to his feet. "I'll see you ladies tomorrow, then." He disappeared up the back stairs.

"I'm glad you remembered Luty's source having a different view of Gilhaney's character. I'd completely forgotten about that, and you're right, it might be important." The housekeeper gave her a smile and shoved her chair back. "I'm going to dash upstairs to do a bit of cleaning before the others get here for the morning meeting."

Hearing her words, Mrs. Goodge's spirits soared. Perhaps she'd been wrong. Perhaps Hepzibah wasn't as unconcerned as it appeared. "That's a good idea, I'll tidy up the kitchen as well. We'll get the chores out of the way so everyone can concentrate on solving this murder." She smiled confidently. Perhaps today, the others would follow Hepzibah's lead and start taking a real interest in the case.

But the cook's hopes that things might be different were dashed as soon as the meeting got under way. Betsy looked bored, Smythe was grumpy, Wiggins fidgeted, Hatchet yawned eight times, and Phyllis stared off into space. But the worst was Mrs. Jeffries: She repeated what they'd learned from the inspector and Constable Barnes in a flat, monotonous tone of voice. The only two people at the table who showed any genuine interest in the case were Ruth and Luty Belle.

As the meeting broke up, Mrs. Goodge poked Luty on the arm. "Stay back a minute," she whispered.

Luty nodded. "Hatchet, go on out to the carriage, I want to have a quick word with Mrs. Goodge about a joint Christmas present for our baby girl."

"I'll see you outside, madam," Hatchet replied.

"What a lovely idea," Ruth said as she put on her bonnet.

"Stay," Mrs. Goodge hissed softly. "I want to talk to you, too."

Ruth's eyes widened. "Of course."

As the kitchen cleared, the only one left was Mrs. Jeffries. But the cook had already thought of a way to get rid of her. "Mrs. Jeffries, would you do me a great favor? My rheumatism is acting up and I've just remembered that I lent my favorite recipe book, the one I use every Christmas, to Mrs. Ellis. I hate to ask, but could you fetch it for me?"

"Of course. She's the cook at the Tamblyn residence, right?"

"That's right, the last house at the end of the road. I'm so sorry to put you to such trouble." She had lent the other cook her recipe book, but it was an old one she hadn't used in years.

"Don't be silly, a nice walk will do me good."

As soon as the three women were alone, Mrs. Goodge motioned the other two back to the table.

Luty looked at Mrs. Goodge as she sank into her chair. "What's wrong?"

The cook knew they didn't have much time before the housekeeper came back so she got right to the point. "Everything. I don't know what to do about it. But if we don't do something, the person who murdered Gilhaney will get away with it. Ruth and I have already talked about it, but I wanted to know if you'd noticed how the others were acting?"

"You mean actin' like they've all got better things to do than be out on the hunt?" Luty snorted. "Danged right I've noticed it. I jawed Hatchet's ear off on the way home yesterday, but he didn't pay me any mind."

"I kept hoping I was wrong and that Hepzibah was just preoccupied yesterday, but it's worse now. She's totally disinterested and the others are taking their cue from her. I can understand why. Everyone had such lovely plans and now they're worried they'll have to cancel them," Ruth said.

"Nobody will have to cancel anything if they get out and do a proper job of sussing out the truth," Mrs. Goodge muttered. "Honestly, there were half a dozen times today when I wanted to scream. The inspector learned lots of interesting bits and pieces and normally Hepzibah would point them out to us and get everyone talking and making silly assumptions and sharing our ideas, but she didn't."

"Even if we agree that the others ain't wantin' to do their part, what can we do about it?" Luty demanded. "I can't put my Peacemaker to their heads and force them to care." Luty loved her Colt .45 and on several occasions, it had come in useful.

"I know that, but there must be something we can do." Mrs. Goodge wasn't going to give up. "We're three very intelligent women and we must come up with a way to get the others to do their part."

"Not just to do their part," Ruth amended. "But to understand that justice doesn't take a Christmas holiday."

"So you're wantin' us to come up with something, an idea that'll make 'em jump aboard this wagon?"

"I've got one," Ruth replied. "But it is rather negative in scope."

"Let's not be picky here," Luty said. "What is it?"

"Shame." Ruth smiled. "We'll shame them into doing their duty."

Luty drew back and Mrs. Goodge's mouth gaped open. Both women were stunned.

Ruth crossed her arms and faced them squarely. "I know you're both surprised that someone such as myself would come up with such a solution. Playing on negative feelings is not something I would generally countenance, but in this situation I believe it might be our best option. Shame is a terrible thing, but it's also quite useful, and considering the circumstances, it's needed."

Luty chuckled. "You can be real surprisin', Ruth, but like I said, we can't be picky here, we're runnin' out of time."

"Shame could work." Mrs. Goodge grinned. "And along with some shame, we can add a healthy dose of competition."

"I can see how shamin' 'em might work"—Luty eyed the cook warily—"but what kind of competition do you have in mind? You goin' to hand out prizes to the person who brings in the most information?"

"That would work, too, but I was actually thinking that we should just play on what we've got." She looked at Luty. "Hatchet can't stand for you to get one over on him, so regardless of what you've found out, you've always got to outdo him, even if you have to stretch the truth a bit. Ruth and I will do our part. We'll heap praises on you no matter what you say."

Luty chuckled. "That'll be fun. But what about the others?"

"Betsy gets annoyed if she thinks Smythe is doing better than she is," Ruth pointed out. "So if we can make it seem as if one of them has done better than the other, regardless of what either of them actually tells us, we might be able to get both of them doing their best."

"Now you're getting it." The cook nodded in approval. "Phyllis and Wiggins have mended their fences a bit, but she still doesn't like him to get ahead of her. Mind you, there are other problems in that quarter, but that's for another time. Right now, we'll just pit them against each other."

"So let me make sure I understand. We're goin' to shame 'em at the same time we're playing 'em off against one another," Luty said.

Ruth nodded enthusiastically. "When you put it like that, it sounds very devious, but as I said, it's necessary in this instance. We've all been given a great gift; we've been part of something bigger and better than ourselves. Working for justice has made my life more meaningful than anything I've ever done and that includes all my work for equality of the sexes."

"I couldn't have said it better myself." Luty reached over and patted Ruth's hand. "Me and Mr. Crookshank spent our lives amassing a fortune and I enjoyed it. We did it proper like, we didn't cheat or lie or steal, but nothing has made my life more worthwhile than the part I've played in makin' sure justice is done. We've kept the innocent off the gallows and we've made sure the guilty paid the price."

"That's true." Mrs. Goodge smiled at her two friends. "We've found something most people only dream of, a genuine noble purpose for our lives. Now, I know they all wanted to have a wonderful Christmas holiday, but catching a murderer is more important, and if we can get them out on the hunt, maybe we'll be able to have our holidays after all."

Christopher Gilhaney's last known address was a nicely furnished, well-maintained lodging house with a lighted fire in both the common rooms. Imogene Lennox, the plump, red-haired owner of the establishment, led the two policemen up the carpeted staircase.

"I'm very particular about who I accept here. Mr. Gilhaney had a recommendation from his landlady in Manchester and he turned out to be everything she claimed he would be: kind, considerate, and a gentleman. He had the largest suite in the house," she explained as they reached the first-floor landing. "A full sitting room and a bedroom."

"How long did he live here?" the inspector asked.

"He moved in on October fifteenth. Unlike some of my other tenants, he didn't take a full board. He took breakfast here but not the other meals."

"Are his quarters currently occupied?" Witherspoon asked.

"Yes, I'm afraid so." She pointed to the first door in the short corridor. "Those are his former rooms. I'm afraid I can't let you in, but there would be no point in doing so. None of the gentleman's things are still there. As a matter of fact, I'm quite glad you've come here. I've sent several letters to that other police officer, Inspector Nivens, but he's never replied."

Witherspoon rested against the newel post while Barnes caught his breath. "About what, Mrs. Lennox?"

"About Mr. Gilhaney's things." She gave an exasperated sigh. "He told me that the police would try to locate

Mr. Gilhaney's next of kin. But I don't think he's done anything about it."

"You have Mr. Gilhaney's personal items?" Barnes asked, his expression hopeful.

"They're stored in the box room." She pointed up toward the attic. "Surely he had someone who should inherit his things. He was a very good man and I feel terrible that no one has claimed his possessions. It's not right, Inspector. He wasn't here very long, but he was one of the nicest gentlemen I've ever met. He was always offering to help me and the other tenants. We couldn't believe it when he was murdered like that. I know he had friends here in London and if the police can't find his next of kin, I'm going to contact one of them. Someone close to him should have his personal things."

"You know who they are?" Barnes asked quickly.

"I don't know them properly, Constable, but I have met several of them and one of the housemaids knows where one of them lives," she replied. "Oh dear, this is going to sound strange, but do hear me out. Mr. Gilhaney was a very handsome man and Laura, the upstairs maid, was a bit infatuated with him. But he was always a gentleman and treated her most kindly. However, I noticed that Laura always made it a point to be the one who answered the front door when Mr. Gilhaney was expected. People tend to come and go at the same time each day and I suspect she kept watch for him from one of the upstairs windows."

"You keep the front door locked and he didn't have a key?" Barnes asked.

"That's correct. If my tenants are staying out late, I'll give them a front door key so they can come in when they like. I don't approve of the maids having to stay up till all hours of the night. But as I was saying, Laura made it her business to be at the door to take Mr. Gilhaney's coat and hat of an evening. One day, he had a friend with him and, as usual, Laura met him at the door and then took his friend into the parlor to wait while Mr. Gilhaney got something from his room. I came downstairs just as the two of them were leaving for dinner. I overheard Laura telling Gina— she's the downstairs maid—that Mr. Gilhaney's friend lives in Clapham, next door to her sister."

Witherspoon stared at her curiously. "Mrs. Lennox, there's something I don't understand. If you knew the whereabouts of one of Mr. Gilhaney's friends, why didn't you contact him about the next of kin?"

"I did, Inspector. I spoke to him at Mr. Gilhaney's funeral. Three of his old friends were there and they all said the same thing. Mr. Gilhaney had no relations here in London; he'd been raised in a workhouse. One of them thought he might have had some cousins in Manchester or Liverpool. That's why I was so eager for the other policeman to make inquiries. But as I said, he never replied to my letters." She clasped her hands together. "Handing his possessions over to one of his friends is a last resort. It doesn't feel right, not if he has family somewhere. There were several items of value, the sort of objects that should stay in a family rather than go to strangers."

"What kind of items?"

"Rings, Inspector. There were two rings in his room and one of them looked to be an heirloom. It's a lovely sapphire ring set in an old-fashioned heavy gold setting. The other was more modern, just a simple green stone in a very plain setting."

"An emerald?" Barnes guessed.

She shook her head. "No, Constable, this is a very light green stone. I've no idea what it is, but it was obviously important to Mr. Gilhaney. He kept it in a velvet box. The other ring was stored in a red fabric pouch."

"Why are you following me?" The housemaid turned, put her hands on her hips, and glared at Wiggins.

"I'm sorry, miss, but you're mistaken. I'm not following you," Wiggins lied. "I'm just walking to the high street." He pointed toward the busy shopping thoroughfare fifty yards farther up the road. "My guv says there's a hardware store there that sells brass 'andles."

"You're lyin'," she charged. "I saw you hangin' about in front of the master's house. The only reason I came out with the likes of you around was because Cook ran out of salt and without that, none of the food will taste decent. Now, get off with you before I start screaming loud enough to bring the fixed-point constable here. He's just on the corner and I've a fine set of lungs."

She was a petite young woman with dark brown hair tucked up beneath her housemaid's cap, an oval face, deep-set brown eyes, porcelain skin, and a slightly turned-up nose.

"I'm sorry, miss." He gave her a weak smile as he silently cursed himself. He'd been careless and he knew it. He'd been daydreamin' and not payin' proper attention. Now he'd been seen. "You're right, I was following you. But not because I mean you any 'arm," he protested as she quickly stepped back from him. "I was hopin' you could help me. I'm in a bit of a mess." It took less than two seconds to decide which way to go here and he hoped he'd made the right choice.

"I'm a reporter, miss, and if I don't give my guv some information about that murder, I'm getting the sack."

She stared at him suspiciously. "What murder?"

"The one from Guy Fawkes Night." He breathed a bit easier. "That Gilhaney fellow, the one that was shot in the mews just down the road."

"You mean the man that was robbed? Why would the papers care about that now?" Her expression cleared just a bit.

Wiggins realized she probably had reason to be suspicious of strange men. A girl as pretty as her had to be careful. "Because our source at Scotland Yard says the bloke weren't killed by a robber. It was a straight-out murder and your master and mistress were with him that night."

"They were at the Chase house," she replied. "But they already talked to the police." She said nothing for a moment, her expression thoughtful, and then she laughed. "So that's what they were arguin' about this morning at breakfast. I thought I heard the mistress tell the master the police would likely be round again. I wondered what she was on about."

"Probably Gilhaney's murder." He smiled, and this time she smiled back. "Can you tell me what you overheard? Can you remember their exact words?"

Her grin disappeared and was replaced with a worried frown. "I can't and I've already said too much."

"You've not said hardly anything," he protested. He planted himself in front of her. "Come on, tell me something. My guv don't care about what I give 'im but I've got to give 'im something."

She shook her head. "Then you're out of luck, I don't know anything. I don't know what they were talkin' about this morning and even if I did, I'd not say a word. You're not the only one who worries about losing their position. The Bruces would sack me in an instant if they thought I'd been talking about them." She stepped around him and stalked away.

"Look, I don't want to get you into any trouble, but surely, you must 'ave overheard a few bits about the murdered fellow."

She looked back the way they'd just come and he turned to look, too. The Bruce house was out of sight. "Listen, I'm not goin' to say it again, I'll not risk my position by talking to you. I hate the place, but I've nowhere else to go." She started moving again, this time almost at a run.

He raced after her. "But I'll not let on that I heard anything from you, I promise."

She stopped and whirled to face him. "Why should I believe you? You don't know what those people are like. It's a right miserable household. The master and mistress watch each other like hawks, they get angry over the least little thing, and if something is out of place and they can't see it, they'll accuse you of stealing." She stalked off again.

"Something was missing from the house?"

"Lord, you're a determined one, aren't you." She ignored him and kept on going.

He wasn't learning very much, but at least she'd stopped threatening to scream for the police. That would be hard to explain if the inspector caught wind of it. But he wasn't giving up. First of all, he didn't want to leave her with the impression that he was just a nasty reporter, and if he could get her to slow down and listen to him, maybe she would see that he was a decent enough fellow. Secondly, he wanted to have something to say at their meeting this afternoon, even if it was just a bit of silly gossip about the Bruces. "Can you tell me what was taken, at least?"

"Nothing. Nothing was taken." They'd reached the corner. She looked both ways and then dashed into the heavy traffic, dodging between a hansom cab and a slow-moving omnibus. He was right on her heels.

"Nothing," he repeated.

"That's right, nothing. But the mistress thought Anna had taken her ruddy perfume bottle, until Miss Bruce found the stupid thing in the front garden." She snorted faintly. "What use would a housemaid have for an empty little perfume bottle? It's not like Anna could afford to buy something to put in it."

"When was this?" He didn't much care what was being said as long as he could keep her talking.

"How should I know? It was weeks ago, but they're still watching Anna like they think she'll pinch the silver." She weaved around two elderly men walking very slowly. "But that wasn't the worst of it. Miss Bruce—that's the master's sister—told the mistress that someone had taken some of her medicine. The only reason none of us were accused of stealing was because the bottle was still there and the mistress thought Miss Bruce was mistaken about how much was left. Like I said, it's a right miserable place to work."

"I'm sorry, miss, I didn't mean to be rude. I know what it's like to live at the mercy of others." He remembered what his life had been like before he came to the Witherspoon household as a footman for Euphemia Witherspoon.

"Do you?" She laughed harshly. "Then quit following me and asking me all these questions."

In truth, he was being ridiculously persistent. But she was a very pretty girl. He felt guilty as an image of Phyllis flashed through his mind. "You're right, and I'm truly sorry. Let me buy you a cup of tea," he pleaded. "There's a nice tea shop on the high street and I'd like to make up for being so rude."

"You just want to get me to tell you something." She didn't look at him, simply kept on walking. "I've nothing to say and if you think I'm going to lose the roof over my head for a cup of tea and a bun, you're sadly mistaken."

Barnes grabbed the handhold as the hansom swung away from the curb in front of the Ladbroke Road Police Station. The inspector and Barnes had stopped in with Gilhaney's possessions, which consisted of two suitcases and a large, hinged wooden box. They would go through them thoroughly once they'd finished taking statements from the rest of the Bonfire Night dinner guests.

"There's something I don't understand, sir," the constable said. "By all accounts, Gilhaney was a very successful man—he must have had an estate. But none of Inspector Nivens' reports mention finding a post office or bank account or an investment firm that handled his wealth. So where did he keep his money? And if he had money, who is going to inherit it? You'd think that when Nivens realized it was a botched robbery, he'd have found out who benefited financially from Gilhaney's death."

"That is troubling," Witherspoon agreed. "Inspector Nivens didn't follow up obvious areas of inquiry. I suppose the kindest thing one can say is he simply wasn't used to handling murders. Perhaps when we go through the victim's things, we can find some answers. Otherwise, we'll need to contact his previous employer and landlady in Manchester and see if they can help us. Speaking of which, when we stopped in at the station, the duty sergeant said we'd received a reply back from the Manchester police. Gilhaney was highly regarded and no one had a bad word to say about him."

"It's beginning to seem like Gilhaney's behavior the night he was killed was out of character for him," Barnes muttered. "It'll be interesting to see what his old friends from Clapham have to say about him. I've got the address from the housemaid for one of them and he should know where the other two live. We caught a lucky break there, Inspector."

"We did indeed. Let's hope our good fortune continues and Leon Webster can help shed some light on this case."

The two policemen discussed the investigation as the cab made its way to the east end of London. Webster's Metals was located in a two-story brown brick building on a narrow lane off the Commercial Road. The offices were on the first floor. Barnes led the way inside to a huge room filled with three rows of clerks. A man at a desk in the back stood up and came toward them. He didn't look happy. "I'm Leon Webster. I take it you're here to see me."

"That's right." Witherspoon introduced himself and the constable. "We'd like to ask you some questions."

"I've already told that other policeman everything I know," he complained. "I don't know what else you expect to learn."

"Is there someplace we can speak privately, sir?" Witherspoon asked.

"We can use the file room." He led the way down the narrow front hall to an open door at the end of the corridor.

They followed him into a dimly lighted room at the far end. A badly scratched table and six chairs, along with filing cabinets topped with ledgers, file boxes, and stacks of paper, were the only furnishings.

Webster pulled out a chair and flopped down. "Now, do be quick about this. I've work to do."

"May we sit down, sir?" Witherspoon asked politely. "We've a number of questions to ask and this will take a few minutes."

"Sit down, then," he muttered. He was a small rabbit of a man, with a long nose, watery blue eyes behind his spectacles, and thinning brown hair.

"Thank you." Witherspoon took a seat and waited until Barnes was settled with his notebook and pencil out before he spoke. "On the night that Christopher Gilhaney was murdered, you said in your original statement that you left the Chase house and walked straight home. Is that correct?" he asked.

"That's right." Webster shifted in his seat.

"Are you sure, sir?" Barnes asked.

Webster looked away. "Of course I'm sure."

"You'd be prepared to swear to this fact under oath?" he pressed.

"Well, it's been quite a while since that night, let me think for a moment." Webster pulled a handkerchief out of his pocket and wiped his forehead. "Actually, I might have stopped at a pub that night . . . yes, that's right. I did. It was a workingman's pub, not the usual sort of place I'd go to. It was near the river. I wanted a drink."

"You wanted a drink? But hadn't there been plenty of

wine served at the Chase home?" Witherspoon said. "Mrs. Chase said you left the dinner party before the port was served."

"I don't like port, furthermore, the wine they served at dinner was very poor quality," he snapped. "The Chases are a bit like the late Mr. Gilhaney, not really the sort I'd choose to have as social acquaintances, but as Mr. Newton Walker was going, I could hardly refuse."

"You sound as if you didn't like Mr. Gilhaney," Barnes said.

"I had no feelings about him one way or the other." He shrugged. "He was simply a boorish guest of the Chases."

"And you left the party very early. Wasn't that a bit boorish?" the constable said, deliberately keeping the pressure up.

"Do you often speak to your betters in such a manner?" Webster's eyes narrowed.

"Constable Barnes is doing his duty," Witherspoon said firmly. "As I'm sure you must have realized, we've already had a statement from both Mr. and Mrs. Chase as to the events that night."

He sagged a bit. "Then I'm sure Mrs. Chase told you why I left. I was tired of being insulted by Christopher Gilhaney. He was rude to me from the moment he arrived. By the time dessert was served, I'd had enough."

"Do you know the name of the pub you stopped at?" Barnes needed Webster to supply the name. If Webster got there right before closing he'd have had plenty of time to lie in wait for Gilhaney. He could easily have killed him.

"I don't remember the name—no, wait, it was the White Hart and it was on Linndal Road. Why? Do you intend to ask them to verify my account? Don't waste your time. Gilhaney was killed weeks ago. By now no one is going to remember that I was there."

"You don't know that, sir," Witherspoon said. "Furthermore, it's our duty to confirm your movements that night. Why was Mr. Gilhaney so insulting? Had you met him before? Did he have a grudge against you?"

"Of course not," Webster snapped. "I'm sorry the man was killed, but he was a dreadful person, a boor, and most certainly not a gentleman."

"Do you know of anyone who had a grudge against Mr. Gilhaney?" Witherspoon asked.

"Considering his uncouth behavior, I imagine he had a multitude of enemies. He knew he had enemies as well."

"How do you know that, sir?" Witherspoon asked.

"He carried a set of brass knuckles, Inspector. I saw him switch them from one of his coat pockets to another when he was in the cloakroom."

Witherspoon was surprised. "Did you tell Inspector Nivens about this?"

"He never asked, Inspector." Webster gave them a sour smile. "One doesn't like to speak ill of public servants, but Inspector Nivens spent less than two minutes taking my statement. I would have told him what I'd seen, but he was in a hurry to leave."

"I see." Witherspoon nodded. "Let's get back to Mr. Gilhaney's enemies. Is there anyone who might have had reason to dislike him?"

"Ted Bruce didn't like him. As a matter of fact he was quite annoyed when Newton announced he was bringing Gilhaney into the firm. He announced it at our last shareholders' meeting and I could tell that Bruce was furious. Oh, he gave us all that smarmy little smile of his, but I happened to go past his office on my way out and he was still ranting and raving to his secretary about how unfair it was."

"Isn't Mr. Bruce the managing director?" Barnes looked up from his notebook.

"What difference does that make? Newton still has the power. He retains the majority share in the company."

The inspector tried to think of what to ask next, but his mind simply went blank. He took a deep breath and remembered Mrs. Jeffries' words about "trusting his inner voice." He expelled the air in his chest. He'd give his "inner voice" time to work and then he'd be back. He glanced at Barnes, who shook his head.

"Thank you for your time," the inspector said as he and the constable rose to their feet.

Once outside, Witherspoon said, "What did you think, Constable?"

"I think there's something he's not telling us. That's why I asked him about going straight home the night of the murder." The constable chose his words carefully. Of course, he knew from Mrs. Jeffries that Smythe's source at the White Hart claimed Webster had shown up at closing time. But he could hardly admit that to Witherspoon. "There was something about his manner that made me think he was lying, sir. You know, sir, policeman's intuition."

"I thought so as well. I think Webster knows exactly why Gilhaney went out of his way to be rude."

"You think they'd met previous to the dinner party," Barnes said.

"I do." Witherspoon pulled his gloves out of his overcoat

pocket and slipped them on. "We're policemen, Constable, and sometimes we simply have to rely on our 'inner voice,' as Mrs. Jeffries calls it. We both sensed Webster was hiding something pertinent from us. Now we've got to find out what it is. Let's send a constable over to the White Hart in Chelsea. Perhaps someone will remember him."

"Where to now, sir?"

"Let's go to Walker and Company and have a word with Theodore Bruce."

"Oh, there was a bit of a scandal about Webster's Metals." Ida Leahcock grinned at Mrs. Goodge. "But it was hushed up by the family. You remember Gracie Toller."

"The tweeny, the one with curly hair and the blue eyes?" Mrs. Goodge exclaimed. She grinned at her friend. She and Ida had worked together years earlier. Ida had left service and come to London. She and her late husband had opened a tobacconist's shop and done very, very well. Ida, a widow, now owned a half dozen shops throughout the city. But her greatest talent was in gossip. She spent her time chatting with her old associates, who were spread all over London and the southeast of England, listening to her customers' conversations, and generally sticking her nose in where most people would say it didn't belong. She had helped in a number of the inspector's cases with the tidbits of information and gossip she'd passed along to the cook.

"Gracious, I haven't thought of her for fifty years." Mrs. Goodge sipped her tea and stared off into space. "I liked her. She was intelligent."

"She still is." Ida chuckled. "But she's retired now and lives with a cousin in Fulham. We generally have tea together once or twice a month. When Christopher Gilhaney was murdered, I thought for sure your inspector would get the case, but then he didn't, and I thought no more about him until I met Gracie for tea and she told me the most amazing thing."

Mrs. Goodge wasn't certain she understood. "Gracie knows you pass along a bit of gossip whenever the inspector has a case?"

"Of course not." Ida waved her hand dismissively. "I know that's something you don't want spread about. It was just our regular get-together, but of course the Gilhaney murder came up. Gracie's niece works for one of the Webster family and after the murder there was a big family row. They were very upset because one of the family was a guest at the dinner party on the night Gilhaney was murdered."

"Why would that upset them?"

"Because they didn't want the family name associated with his killing. Turns out that Gilhaney had once worked for Webster's and there had been a scandal. They were terrified the police would find out about the connection to the dead man and the old matter would come up once again."

"What kind of scandal was it?" Mrs. Goodge was fairly certain she could guess, but additional information was always useful.

"Gracie said her niece wasn't sure, but one of the nephews—Leon, I think she called him—was at the center of it."

"Inspector, I've already made a statement. Why don't you just read it and save me from wasting my time. We're very busy here, we've a tender due by noon tomorrow and, frankly, that is more important to me than repeating what I've already told that other policeman." Theodore Bruce crossed his arms and stared at them from behind his massive desk. His hair was dark brown, parted at the side, and slicked back from a broad face. His eyes were small, his nose prominent, and the skin under his chin flaccid.

They were in Bruce's office and, despite the two wing-back chairs available for visitors, the inspector knew they weren't going to be offered a seat.

"We've read your statement, Mr. Bruce. But we'd still like you to answer our questions."

"Oh, for goodness' sake, get on with it, then."

"Was the night of the murder the first time you'd ever met the victim?"

Bruce unfolded his arms and straightened up. "It was."

"Are you certain of that, Mr. Bruce?" Barnes asked softly.

"I am."

"Can you describe for us what happened that night?"

Bruce didn't bother to hide his irritation. "We went to the Chase home for dinner, the purpose of which was to introduce Christopher Gilhaney to myself and other members of the board. It was a most unpleasant encounter and the other guests began to leave as soon as decently possible. We did the same; I put my wife and sister in a hansom cab and then I walked home. You can verify all this with both the Chases and my household servants."

"How long did it take you to get home?" Witherspoon asked.

"Twenty minutes or so. I was in no hurry as I had a head-ache and wanted some fresh air." He reached for a stack of paper. "Now, if that's all, Inspector, I must get back to work. Railway tenders wait for no one."

"We understand that Mr. Gilhaney was very rude that night," Witherspoon said. "Have you any idea why?"

Bruce didn't look up from his work. "None whatsoever. Perhaps he's just a nasty person."

"Did you know your wife was acquainted with Mr. Gilhaney?" Barnes watched him carefully as he spoke.

Again, Bruce didn't look up, but the constable noticed an angry flush creep up his flabby cheeks. "Of course. She was one of the reasons Newton Walker hired the man—she recommended him. Presumably he was some sort of financial genius."

"Would you object to our speaking with your staff?" Witherspoon asked.

Bruce's head jerked up. "I most certainly would. This is a business, Inspector, and I'll not have you pestering my employees when they're supposed to be working."

"Your employees?" a familiar voice said.

Witherspoon and Barnes both turned as Newton Walker stepped through the door. He didn't acknowledge the policemen but kept his gaze on his son-in-law.

Bruce got to his feet and smiled. "You know what I meant, Newton. The railway tender is due by noon tomorrow. I've got the clerks working flat-out and I don't want them distracted. You know how important this contract could be—it's incredibly lucrative."

"Lucrative?" Walker sneered. "You said the same thing about supplying those bridge girders, and that ended up costing us a fortune. I still don't know where all that money went! I don't know why I ever let you convince me and the other directors that expanding into these kinds of commercial enterprises was a good idea. But we'll not air our problems in front of outsiders. I'm going to insist that you allow these policemen to speak to our staff. Answering a few questions will not take much time. Frankly, I want this murder solved as quickly as possible. In case you've forgotten, there are some ugly things being said about us."

"Ugly things," Witherspoon repeated. "What sort of ugly things, Mr. Walker?" He knew from long experience that gossip frequently held the seeds of truth.

"Exactly what you'd expect was being bandied about by our competitors. Gilhaney had just been hired and some people are wondering what was it about our finances that someone in the firm was so desperate to hide that they did the unthinkable."

"No intelligent person believes such nonsense," Bruce argued. "You said it yourself, it's merely our competitors smearing our good name."

"We're a public company now, Ted," Walker snapped. "And I'll not have the scandal of a murder hanging over my good name."

CHAPTER 6

"Mrs. Cwookshank, I'm so pleased to see you."

Luty froze for a split second and then forced herself to smile as she turned to face the brother of the man she'd come to visit. She'd come to the offices of Biddlington and Biddlington, Solicitors, one of the many firms that handled her business affairs, because she needed information for this afternoon's meeting. Ronald Biddlington, who she'd specifically asked to see, could always be counted on to know the latest business gossip.

"I'm right pleased to see you, too, Nelson. Where's your brother? I'd thought I'd be able to meet with him. I know how busy you are. Ronald's always sayin' you're the real brains around here." She extended her hand and they shook. She didn't dislike Nelson Biddlington; she genuinely admired his intelligence and integrity. But Nelson had a problem that kept him in the back office while Ronald, his twin, dealt

with their fee-paying clients: The poor man couldn't pro-
nounce the letter *r*. No matter how often Luty told herself it
wasn't his fault, after just a few minutes of listening to him
she was either trying not to laugh or wanting to scream.

"Wonald isn't well." He took her elbow and led her past
his secretary's small desk and through a door at the end of
a short corridor. "His wheumatism is acting up again so he
stayed home today. But I'll be happy to help you. Please, take
a seat and I'll have Biggs get us tea."

Luty was suddenly ashamed of herself. Nelson was trying
his best to avoid words with an *r* in them and, doggone it,
she was going to keep control of herself and treat him with
the respect he deserved. "Thank you, Nelson, that would be
lovely." She sat down in the chair in front of his desk.

"I'll be wight back." He dashed off and Luty took the time
to have a good look at her surroundings. This was her first
time here; the Biddlingtons generally came to see her when
she needed something done. His office was modest but nicely
furnished, with a brightly colored Persian rug on the floor, a
colorful seaside painting over the unlighted fireplace, and a
huge brass urn filled with a dried flower arrangement that
was quite lovely.

Nelson stepped back into the room. He was a small, thin
man with a shock of curly gray hair, a longish nose, and blue
eyes. "I'm so delighted you've come to visit. Wonald is going
to be sowwy he missed you."

"I hope my bargin' in like this didn't take you away from
something important," she began, but he held up a hand.

"Please, this is a tweat for me. Usually it's Wonald who
gets to see you. Now, what can I do fo . . . uh, to help you?"

"I've got a real delicate problem." Dang, she thought,

Ronald was the one who liked to gossip. She had no idea if Nelson did or not, but she was here, and there was no harm in trying. She had to show up with something this afternoon or the plan she and the other two had cooked up wouldn't work. "I'm not sure how to put it, because it sounds right silly when I say it out loud."

"You awe never silly," he replied. "Just tell me what it is you need and . . ." He broke off as the door opened and a young man carrying a tray loaded with delicate white and green bone china entered. Nelson pointed at the edge of his desk and then waited till the lad left before he spoke.

"How do you take tea?" He stood up, reached for the teapot, and began to pour.

"Cream and one sugar," she replied. She'd used the tiny interlude to come up with what she hoped was a clever way to say her piece. "The truth is, Nelson, I'm thinkin' about investin' in a building company, a big one named Walker and Company." She nodded her thanks as he handed her a cup and saucer.

"Biscuit?"

"No, thanks. Uh, have you ever heard of them?"

"Yes, they're quite well known." He took his tea and a ginger biscuit and slipped back into his chair. "May I ask what made you decide they would be a good investment?"

"Well, I've heard they're makin' a lot of money these days and since they went public last year, this might be a good opportunity. Why? What have you heard?"

Nelson took a sip of his tea and then put the cup and saucer down. "Just the opposite: that the company isn't making money these days and no one knows why. Newton Walker had even gone to the length of hiwing a man from

Manchestew, a consultant of some kind, but he was killed before he could get a good look at the company finances."

"Really?"

"I'm supwised you didn't know that, Mrs. Cwookshank. Wonald tells me you know everything that goes on in London, especially when it comes to mudder."

His words were polite enough, but the smile he gave her was sardonic and didn't quite reach his eyes. Luty suddenly remembered he was a very smart man, but because of a speech problem, she'd fallen into the trap of thinking him less intelligent than he was. Well, Nell's bells, she was the one that was acting dumb. From the way he was watching her, she suspected he knew exactly why she'd come here.

"You're right, I generally do know what's goin' on here in town, especially about murder. Do you know anything about the Gilhaney murder?"

He shook his head. "If I did, I'd tell you. Wonald tells me that there's gossip you help your policeman fwiend solve mudders. I don't approve of mudder. It's wwong to take a human life. I don't believe the state should do it, either—I don't believe in hanging."

Luty knew there'd been some talk about her, but she didn't much care. She'd already made up her mind that if Inspector Witherspoon ever got wind of it, she'd just say it was because of her involvement in one of his recent cases. Her name had been mentioned in the press. "I do; if you murder someone, you should hang. An eye for an eye, that's what it says in the good book."

"That's what it says in the Old Testament," he pointed out. "I believe we should love one another, just like Jesus says in the New Testament." He smiled as he spoke, and this time his smile was genuine. "Why don't you tell me what you need to know and I'll see if I can help. Don't wowwy, I won't tell youh secwet." He giggled. "You could say, my lips are sealed."

"I'm glad everyone is here on time today," Mrs. Jeffries said as everyone took their place around the table.

"It was easy for me." Wiggins shrugged. "It was so cold out, it was hard to find anyone who wanted to chat. I talked to a housemaid from the Bruce home, but you could fill a thimble with the little bit she had to say."

"That's too bad. We'll never get this case solved properly if you can't get people to talk." The cook handed him his cup of tea. "You've had a very bad two days now, haven't you, Wiggins?"

"You said that like it's my fault," he protested. "But it's not. Some days you 'ear a lot, some days not as much. But I've not come empty-handed. I did 'ear something."

"Really?" Mrs. Goodge shoved the plate of seedcake toward Ruth. "That's good, then. Maybe if we all find out a few tiny bits and pieces, we'll catch this killer by Easter."

Mrs. Jeffries' brows drew together, her expression puzzled. It wasn't like Mrs. Goodge to be so sarcastic. The cook was usually the lad's staunchest supporter. "Wiggins, since you've started, tell us what you learned."

The footman shot the cook a quick, hurt look. He knew he hadn't done his best on this case, but he hadn't thought anyone would notice. It wasn't as if the others were doing any better. He took a deep breath and decided he'd stretch what little he'd gotten out of the housemaid as far as he could. "Like I said, I 'ad a word with a housemaid from the Bruce home. She was still up when the family got home that night." He paused and wondered why a lie had popped out of his mouth. But now that he'd started, he couldn't think of a way to stop. Blast a Spaniard, he was really in a mess now. "Usually when the family is out, only one of the housemaids has to stay up, and that night, it was 'er turn and—"

Ruth interrupted. "She was sure it was the night of the murder? She recalls that time specifically?" She stared at him, her expression skeptical.

Wiggins gaped at her. He couldn't believe his ears. She couldn't possibly know he was lying. "She said she did. There's no reason not to believe her." He looked uncertain. "She'd no reason to lie."

"People lie all the time," Luty interjected, "especially young girls wantin' to impress a handsome young feller like you. But go on and tell us what she said."

"She told me that Mrs. Bruce and Miss Bruce got 'ome first." He felt a bit better. This was true, as Mrs. Jeffries had reported hearing it from the inspector. "Mr. Bruce came in later."

"Did she know what time he came home?" Luty asked. "Seems to me that's important."

"I asked, but she said she wasn't lookin' at the clock, so she didn't know." He looked off into the distance to avoid meeting anyone's gaze. "She also said the Bruce home is a right miserable place to work, that Mr. and Mrs. Bruce watch each other like hawks . . ."

"What does that mean?" Mrs. Goodge demanded.

He shrugged. "Just that. She didn't explain it and she was in a bloomin' 'urry so I was practically runnin' to keep up with her. Then she said that if anything was out of place in the 'ouse, the servants were accused of stealing." He spoke more confidently now that he was telling the truth. "Mrs. Bruce accused one of the housemaids of stealing her little perfume bottle, which was silly as it was one of them empty ones and even when Miss Bruce found the bottle in the front garden, they were still watching the maids because Miss Bruce claimed someone had been drinkin' her medicine." He took another deep breath, relieved that he was done. "That's all I found out."

"Thank you, Wiggins. I think you've done very well." Mrs. Jeffries flicked a quick glance at the cook, who met her gaze squarely before folding her arms over her chest.

"I'll go next if no one objects," Phyllis volunteered when the silence started to get awkward. "Actually, I've not much to report. The local merchants either didn't know or wouldn't say a word about Ann Holter."

"Did you go to her house?" Ruth asked.

Phyllis seemed surprised by the question. "No, I just talked to the shop clerks on the high street."

"And no one knew anything?" Ruth gave an exasperated sigh. "Well, this isn't doing us any good at all, is it."

"I tried my best," Phyllis said defensively. "But if people won't talk to you, there isn't much you can do about it." In truth, she'd gone into only one shop and that clerk hadn't been at all helpful. When she'd come out, she'd noticed the omnibus was coming and, on impulse, she'd got on board and gone to the theater district. She'd spent most of the afternoon there and had even treated herself to a light, early tea. But now she felt miserable and she was sure that everyone at the table knew what she'd done.

"Don't feel bad." Betsy gave Phyllis a sympathetic smile. "I didn't find out very much, either. Some days are like that."

"I forget where you said you was goin'." Luty said to Betsy. "Was it to the Longworth neighborhood?"

"It was, but the only thing I managed to find out was that Robert Longworth goes to church every day. He's Roman Catholic."

"Bloomin' Ada, guess they're a strict lot, aren't they," Smythe muttered.

"I don't think Catholics have to go to church every day." Betsy smiled at her husband. "Longworth only started doing it about three months ago."

"So you did find out somethin' useful." Luty nodded in approval. "Could be that Mr. Longworth has a guilty conscience over something."

"Yes, but it couldn't be Gilhaney's murder," Ruth pointed out. "He was only killed six weeks ago."

"That's true, but he could have felt guilty about something connected to Gilhaney from before that." The cook looked at the clock. "We'd better get a move on, it's getting late. I'll go next. Today was a good one for me; one of my sources had plenty to say. To begin with, Leon Webster knew the victim; he didn't just meet him that night at the Chase home. Gilhaney had worked at Webster's Metals before he went to Manchester. It's not that big a firm so Leon must have known him. Secondly, right after Gilhaney's murder was in the newspapers, there was a huge family row at the Webster house. Apparently, they were all afraid that the murder investigation would dig up an old scandal they'd pushed under the rug."

"Did your source know what kind of scandal it was?" Ruth asked.

"No, only that the family was very upset and that Leon

Webster was in the middle of it. When the newspapers began writing that the crime was a robbery gone bad, the Websters were very relieved." The cook helped herself to a slice of cake. "That's all I've got for right now, but I've three more sources coming round tomorrow."

"Gracious, Mrs. Goodge, that's amazing," Ruth gushed. "You found out that one of the suspects knew Gilhaney." She turned her attention to Mrs. Jeffries. "Can you be sure and find out what Leon Webster tells the inspector?"

Mrs. Jeffries nodded. "Of course."

"If we keep diggin', we'll find out everything we need to know," Luty declared. She noted with satisfaction that Mrs. Jeffries looked interested in what was being said. "I'll go next unless someone else has something they're dying to tell us." She broke off and looked at Hatchet. "From that long face of yours, I can see it won't be you." She chuckled.

"No, madam, it won't."

Luty could see his nose was out of joint and that was exactly what they wanted. It turned out that Nelson loved gossip as much as his brother and he'd given her an earful. "I found out a lot today. To begin with, when Newton Walker hired Gilhaney, he was supposed to start working on the Monday, November ninth, after Guy Fawkes Night."

"How is that important, madam?" Hatchet snapped.

"We don't know that yet," she shot back. "Turns out that on the morning of November fifth at the executive meeting, Newton Walker told them that Gilhaney would be starting the next day, Friday morning, November sixth. He was murdered that night. So you see"—she looked at Hatchet—"it might be important after all."

"I don't see how," he muttered.

"That's very interesting," Mrs. Jeffries murmured. Something tugged at the back of her mind, but she ignored it. "But I tend to agree with Hatchet: I don't see how it would impact Gilhaney's murder."

"But it's conceivable it did," Ruth argued. "He was murdered that very evening."

"And don't you always say that it's impossible to know what will or won't be important in an investigation until we have all of the facts?" Mrs. Goodge added.

Mrs. Jeffries hesitated. "Well, yes, I suppose I have said that."

"I wasn't done," Luty said. "I also found out that two years ago, Hazel Bruce wanted to get a divorce from her husband. But her father was against it. He was afraid the scandal would ruin her socially. What's more, he'd given Ted Bruce carte blanche in running the company and it would upset the apple cart to try and get rid of him if the two of them divorced. What's more, it's danged expensive. But this past October, Walker seemed to have changed his mind. He asked a firm of solicitors what steps would need to be taken for her to be free and how much it would cost."

"Is she going to divorce him?" Betsy asked. "They're still living together."

"Yep, but they hate each other," Luty said. "And, like Wiggins' source said, they watch each other like hawks. Accordin' to my source, Newton Walker has bribed someone at the Bruce house to spy on Ted Bruce."

"Which would imply he's definitely relented about helping his daughter get a divorce," Ruth murmured.

"Maybe he doesn't care. Maybe seein' his young'un be

miserable for the rest of her life hurt him too much," Luty suggested.

"But Ted Bruce doesn't own the house," Phyllis pointed out. "He could be forced to leave it. Socially, that would be much easier on Mrs. Bruce than a divorce."

"That's certainly true," Ruth agreed. "Usually, that's how it is done amongst upper-class marriages where the couples can't abide one another. They simply lead separate lives. I wonder what made Walker change his mind about divorce. He's right, you know—as unfair as it is, Hazel Bruce will be the one who is ruined." She shook her head. "If it's all the same to everyone, I'll take my turn. I didn't learn a great deal, but I found out that prior to living with her brother, Florence Bruce took care of their mother in the family home. When she died, Ted Bruce inherited the house and he immediately sold it. Florence was going to go and live with a cousin in the north until Hazel Bruce insisted she come live with them. The two women are very close."

"So it seems," Mrs. Jeffries said. "Anything else?"

"No, I'm finished. I feel badly about having so little information to share. I'll try harder tomorrow."

"Nonsense, Ruth, you've done very well," Mrs. Goodge exclaimed.

"Indeed," Mrs. Jeffries agreed. "Does anyone else have a report?"

There was silence around the table.

"Well, at least some of us had something." Luty frowned heavily.

"We're doing our best, madam," Hatchet said coldly.

"Are ya?" She cocked her head to one side and stared at

him. "Did you contact those rich friends of yours that have helped in the past? You know who I mean, the fellow that's an artist. He and his wife know everyone in town. I'll bet they could help us. So just tell me, Hatchet, what the heck did you do today?"

"Robert Longworth is the last of the guests that were at the Chase home on Bonfire Night," Barnes said as they got out of the hansom cab. "Once we're done with him, we may have time to go back and take a good look through Gilhaney's possessions."

"I'm hoping we'll be able to find out who his solicitor was." Witherspoon stepped onto the pavement. "If not, we'll have to send another telegram to Manchester." Overhead, the sky was threatening rain and the air had gone very cold. He flipped his coat collar up as he studied the Longworth home while Barnes paid the driver.

It was a three-story brown brick house with a small, paved front garden surrounded by a black wrought-iron fence. "This is an expensive area," Witherspoon murmured as the constable joined him.

"It is, sir. The house is well maintained but not particularly opulent. Not as big as some of the others on this street."

"Let's go see what Mr. Longworth has to say," the inspector said as they stepped through the gate and onto the brick walkway.

The front door suddenly opened and a man with thinning blond hair and a mustache watched them approach. His skin was pale and there were dark circles under his eyes. He wore a red cravat around his neck, and both his blue suit and white shirt seemed too big for his thin frame.

He smiled politely. "Good day. You're the police. Abigail Chase told me that you'd probably come and speak with me. Please come inside."

"I'm Inspector Witherspoon and this is Constable Barnes," Witherspoon said as they stepped inside and followed him through a dimly lighted foyer and into the drawing room. The furniture was old-fashioned, with thick claw feet on the cabinets and tables, cream-colored crocheted antimacassars on the backs of the overstuffed brown settee and chairs, and a faded Oriental carpet that was fraying along the borders.

"Please sit down." Longworth motioned toward the chairs while he sat down in the middle of the settee.

"Mrs. Chase told you we were coming?" Witherspoon was surprised to find the chair quite comfortable.

"Indeed, I saw her this morning. We ran into one another at the bank. She's a lovely woman. I was sorry to see her Bonfire Night party ruined."

"Was that dinner party the first time you'd met Christopher Gilhaney?" Witherspoon asked.

"No, I met him a long time ago. He worked for my family's firm. Longworth's Metal Fasteners and Fittings. We had a manufacturing site in Battersea Park."

"How long ago was this?"

"Ten years." Longworth smiled faintly. "He was hired as a clerk in our accounts department. We manufactured metal parts for the building industry: nails, screws, hand tools, that sort of thing."

"You used the past tense, sir," Witherspoon said. "Does that mean your family company is no longer in business?"

"That's correct, Inspector. The business closed nine and a half years ago, six months after Gilhaney was sacked."

"Why was he let go?"

Longworth smiled bitterly. "He was suspected of embezzling funds, so my father let him go. What the old man forgot was that Gilhaney had one of those very rare abilities—he remembered everything he saw."

"Yes, we've heard that about him," Witherspoon said.

"And it is true. He knew to the penny how much it cost to manufacture, transport, and package a hook or nail or a hoe or a pair of brass fittings. He remembered everything. He took that knowledge to our biggest competitor, who then undercut all our prices. Sales dropped precipitously, we lost one contract after another, and within six months, we were closing our doors. Seventy men lost their livelihood. It killed my father."

Witherspoon thought his admissions very odd. He'd just admitted to a motive for Gilhaney's murder. He wondered if he understood they were here to question him and that he might be a suspect. "You blamed Gilhaney for this?"

Longworth blinked. "Blamed? Of course not, it wasn't his fault, my father knew that Gilhaney had a remarkable memory. He shouldn't have sacked him in the first place."

"But if he was embezzling—"

"It wasn't him, Inspector," Longworth interrupted. "I was the one doing it. I'm quite clever with numbers—not on Gilhaney's level, certainly, but I was very good at it, until he had a look at the books. It didn't take him long to see what I was up to so I made certain that he took the blame for the crime." He smiled sadly. "For such a brilliant man, he was quite naive back in those days."

"How have you made a living since then?" Barnes asked bluntly.

"I haven't," Longworth replied. "A few months after my

family died and our assets were sold to pay off our creditors, my mother and I inherited this house from her brother, as well as a modest annual income. We lived quite happily here until she passed away two years ago."

"How did you happen to be appointed as a director at Walker and Company?" Witherspoon thought this one of the strangest statements he'd ever heard.

"My father and Newton were friends. We were one of their suppliers and we've stayed in touch over the years. He's been very kind to me. When he took the company public, he asked me to serve as a director. There's a small stipend attached to the position."

"Did Mr. Walker know of your connection to Christopher Gilhaney?"

"He never told me so directly, but he must have known. He did his best to help my father when the firm was in trouble and I'm sure he cursed Gilhaney's name on many an occasion."

The inspector didn't know what to make of Longworth. "I understand Mr. Gilhaney was quite rude to you the night he was murdered."

"Not really, he made a comment or two that were aimed at me, but then he stopped. Despite his behavior the night of the Chases' dinner, Gilhaney was a decent man. He'd had his fair share of tragedy."

"But he ran your family's firm out of business." Barnes studied Longworth carefully.

"Only after he'd been unfairly sacked. He could have told my father I was the one doing the embezzling, and he could have proved it, but he held his tongue. He didn't need to ruin me in order to get back at the company."

"What do you mean?"

"My father was a dreadful man, you see. He didn't have Gilhaney arrested because the evidence against him wasn't as absolute as it should have been. But if Gilhaney had wanted to, he could have easily proved that I was the criminal. If my father had found out it was me who was the culprit, he'd have prosecuted me to the fullest extent of the law. He was a tyrant at the office and a bully at home. My mother was a good woman, but the happiest day of her life was when he died. Gilhaney did me a great favor by staying silent. If he hadn't, I'd probably still be in a prison cell."

Witherspoon said, "Mr. Longworth, if Mr. Gilhaney hadn't been insulting you that night, why did you leave so early?"

"I wanted to catch the last omnibus, Inspector. Hansom cabs are very expensive. I needed to get home. I'm ill, you see. No"—he smiled—"that's not true. I'm dying."

"I don't know why Mrs. Goodge is makin' it seem like we're not doin' our best on this one," Wiggins said as he followed Phyllis into the drawing room. He put the brass andirons he'd finally finished polishing onto their stand by the fireplace. "It's not fair. We've been doin' the best we can. And it weren't just her, either. Ruth and Luty was actin' like they didn't think we were doin' our share, either. Just because they found out somethin' today, it doesn't mean we've not been tryin'."

Phyllis pulled the heavy curtains away from one of the front windows and ran her feather duster over the sill. "I haven't," she admitted. "And I feel terrible about it." She turned to face him, her eyes welling with unshed tears. "But

I was so upset that we'd have to change our Christmas plans, I didn't want to do my share."

"Come on, Phyllis, I'm sure that's not true," Wiggins cajoled. He didn't want to hear that she'd been deliberately negligent—that hit too close to home.

"But it's true. The only reason I found out anything yesterday was an accident, and today, I spent less than twenty minutes in the Holter neighborhood. I only talked to one shop assistant and barely asked him anything. I went to the theater district and looked at the posters and the playbills, then I treated myself to a nice tea."

Wiggins had no idea what to say or do; he could only stare at her helplessly as the tears started to stream down her cheeks. "Uh, look, there's no reason to get so upset . . ."

She swiped at her face with her free hand. "There's every reason. I'm so ashamed of myself. The inspector is the first employer I've had who has treated me decently. He isn't stingy with food and he heats the house properly. He passes along his magazines and lets me read the books in his library and the one thing I can do to repay him, I failed to do because I wanted a few evenings out. I can't believe I've been so selfish and stupid."

"You're not selfish and you're certainly not stupid." Wiggins hurried over to her and patted her awkwardly on the back. "You've a right to want some time to yourself."

"I have my day out." She moved to the other window and pulled the drapes back. "Mrs. Goodge and the other ladies are right, at least about me. I've been shirking my duty. And I'm not ashamed just because I've failed to help him; that's only part of it. I'm ashamed because I've failed myself. Because of our investigations, I've learned to stand up for myself and to fight for what is right. We stand for the dead who can't stand for themselves and that's important. I never thought I'd do anything important in my life, but because of all of you, I have."

He said nothing for a long moment. "You've not done anything I haven't been doin' as well. The first day we were supposed to be out on the hunt, I spent ten minutes in front of the victim's lodgin' 'ouse before giving up and nipping down to see Craven Cottage. That's where Fulham plays and I was hopin' to see some of the players, but I didn't. And today when I said I'd talked to a housemaid from the Bruce house, I didn't so much talk to her as chase the poor girl, who was tryin' her best to get away from me."

"But she told you things."

"I made part of it up." He smiled sheepishly. "I mean, I know it was true because Mrs. Jeffries and Mrs. Goodge told us that the Bruce ladies went home in a hansom on their own and I just guessed the rest about when Mr. Bruce come in."

"But what about the perfume bottle and the missing medicine and—"

He interrupted. "That was all true, but like I said, the girl was more worried about gettin' the sack than talkin' to the likes of me. But that wasn't the worst. This was early today and I could have stayed out on the hunt. We've a half dozen suspects. I could have gone to their houses, waited about, and found a footman or another housemaid. But you know what I did? I went to Hammersmith because I knew my mate was gettin' off work early. We met up and then went to his pub and talked football for two hours. So you're not the only one that's been shirkin' a bit. I 'ave, too."

She said nothing, but simply looked at him, and then she giggled. "Oh, goodness, we are a pair, aren't we? I wonder how Mrs. Goodge and the other ladies knew we'd been larkin' about?"

"They're smart, that's how." He laughed, delighted that he'd made her smile. "But come tomorrow, I'm goin' back out there and doin' what's right. I love football and I 'ope I get to see the ones I'd planned on seein', but if I don't, that's alright as well. Justice is more important."

"Me, too, no more trips to the theaters. Tomorrow I'm going back on the hunt. Oh dear, it's getting dark. I'd better finish dusting and get down to help Mrs. Goodge with dinner."

Upstairs, Mrs. Jeffries stood at her bedroom window and stared out at the darkening day. Her mood had darkened as well. She wasn't sure what to do. What on earth had gotten into Luty, Ruth, and most especially Mrs. Goodge? She'd never known any of them to be anything other than helpful and encouraging, but today, all three of them had implied that the others were shirking their responsibility, putting their own wants before the cause of justice. Well, she wasn't going to stand for it.

After the inspector came home and dinner was finished, she'd have a word with the cook. But just as she made that decision, another, more unwelcome thought entered her mind. The three women hadn't just implied the others were the only ones shirking their duty; several of their looks and comments had been aimed at her as well.

Shocked by the realization, she stood there until she heard the clip-clop of a hansom come around the corner. She shook herself as it pulled up in front of the house. The inspector was home. She hurried downstairs and was waiting at the front door when he came inside.

"How was your day, sir?" Mrs. Jeffries reached for his bowler and waited for him to unbutton his overcoat.

He paused, his fingers hovering over the row of buttons. "It was strange, Mrs. Jeffries, truly one of the oddest days I've ever had as a policeman. I'll be interested to hear your thoughts about it."

Intrigued, she hurried after him. She had their sherry poured and was sitting across from him within a very short amount of time. "Do tell me, sir, what was so unusual about today."

He took a sip and then stared at the liquid in his glass for a few seconds. "Let me start at the beginning. It helps me to understand the investigation if I go through my day in the order it happened." He told her about his interviews, starting with his visit to Gilhaney's lodging house. "We didn't have time to get back to the station this evening to go through everything. We'll do that tomorrow morning. Hopefully, there will be something amongst his things that will answer some of our questions. After leaving the station, we interviewed Leon Webster."

She listened closely, interrupting him with a question halfway through his narrative. "Brass knuckles, sir? Was there a mention of that in Inspector Nivens' files?"

"Webster claims that he tried to tell Nivens what he'd seen that night, but that Nivens was in such a hurry to leave, he brushed him off. But no brass knuckles were on his person the night he was killed."

"Do you think the killer might have taken them?"

"I do."

"That's interesting, sir. I wonder if Leon Webster had met Gilhaney prior to the dinner party."

"He claimed he hadn't, but I'm not sure I believed everything he said," Witherspoon continued, taking care to tell her not just what Leon Webster had said, but his own impressions of the man. "After we finished there, we went to Walker and Company to have a word with Mr. Bruce. He was annoyed to be interrupted at work, but luckily, Mr. Newton Walker insisted he take the time to speak with us."

"Mr. Walker seems determined to see this matter resolved, doesn't he?" she murmured.

"He does." Witherspoon nodded. "He's quite a decent sort, Mrs. Jeffries. Not at all what you'd expect." He told her about his interview with Bruce. She continued listening, making sure she understood everything he said.

"After that, we went to see Robert Longworth." He took a sip of his drink. "Honestly, Mrs. Jeffries, his statement was very unusual."

"In what way, sir?" She took a sip from her own glass, but tonight she'd not have more than one. She needed a clear head; she needed to have a good long think about this case.

"Thus far, Mr. Longworth is the only person we've found who admitted to having a reason to hate Christopher Gilhaney. Yet, I'm sure he's innocent." He told her about their meeting with Longworth.

When he finished, she said, "So you think he's telling the truth because he is dying?"

"Not just me, Mrs. Jeffries, Constable Barnes shares my opinion."

She wasn't sure what to think, but then she remembered

something David, her late husband, had told her. He said that the police took deathbed confessions seriously, that the dying were the only people to have no reason to lie. "If you're absolutely certain Mr. Longworth is soon to leave this world, sir, then I think I must agree with you and the constable. He'd have no reason to lie and he did himself no honor by telling you the truth about his embezzlement. What will you do tomorrow, sir?"

She knew what she would do and she was now heartily sorry it had taken her so long to realize how foolish she'd been. It had cost them dearly. They'd lost several days, and it was her fault. She was their leader, the one they looked to for guidance, and she'd let them down badly.

"As I said, we'll go through Mr. Gilhaney's personal items and hope we can discover where he put his money and who would have been likely to inherit from him." He grimaced. "Honestly, Mrs. Jeffries, one of the first rules of a homicide investigation is to find out who benefits from the victim's death. But as far as we can tell, Nivens made no attempt to do that whatsoever. According to the Manchester police, he never contacted them. After that, we'll just keep on digging. Gilhaney's old mates from Clapham might have something useful to tell us, and if that fails, I may have to go to Manchester. Gracious, Mrs. Jeffries, I feel like I've made no progress whatsoever on this one. I fear we won't have much of a Christmas this year."

Mrs. Jeffries knew what she needed to do. "Nonsense, sir. Considering all the obstacles you've faced, you've done a splendid job." She jumped right in with both feet. "Inspector Nivens' files were abysmally bad, you've had to conduct interviews and take statements from people who were insulted badly by the dead man, but you've persevered and learned more in a few days than Nivens did in six weeks. What's more, we'll have a splendid Christmas. The tree is coming the twenty-fourth and we're going to decorate it before the guests arrive for the party."

He stared at her over the rim of his glass. "Thank you, Mrs. Jeffries. I appreciate the vote of confidence. I must tell you, I've been very afraid I won't solve this one. I hate to admit it because it seems so vain, but I don't want my record marred by a defeat . . . oh dear, that sounds so conceited. I truly wish to solve this murder because I believe in justice, but—"

"You're human, sir," she interrupted, "and you've a remarkable talent as a detective, so it is perfectly understandable that you'd like to continue on in the same vein. Nonetheless, despite the difficulties you've encountered so far, I've every confidence you'll catch Mr. Gilhaney's murderer. The only difference between this case and the others you've solved is that this crime took place a few weeks ago. It's really no different than if you'd come across a victim who'd been frozen in a winter lake for six weeks." The moment she said the words, she realized they were true and not just for the inspector but for the household as well. They could solve this crime, they would solve this crime, and they'd get it done in time for Christmas.

He looked at her, his expression hopeful. "Do you really think so?"

"Of course, sir!" She laughed merrily. "You'll do what you always do and keep digging until you find the truth."

"Yes, indeed I will." He sat up a bit straighter. "I think I'll go back to Walker and Company tomorrow as well."

"Why there, sir?" She was curious.

"Because I've a feeling the reason for the murder has something to do with Gilhaney coming back to London."

Mrs. Jeffries already had a pot of tea made when Mrs. Goodge, with a meowing Samson at her heels, shuffled into the kitchen. The cook stopped in her tracks. She hoped the housekeeper wasn't still annoyed with her—they'd barely said two words to one another after yesterday's meeting. She eyed the housekeeper warily. "You're up bright and early."

"That's because we've much to do today." She grinned.

"You're not angry?"

"Of course not. The three of you were rather rough on us, but you were right to do so. Come have a cup of tea before the others get up. We've a lot to discuss."

Mrs. Jeffries got the meeting started as soon as the front door had closed behind the inspector and Constable Barnes. The constable had stopped in the kitchen and added a few details to the information Mrs. Jeffries had learned from Witherspoon. In turn, they shared what had been garnered by the household.

"First of all, I want everyone to know that we've got much territory to cover in the next few days if we're going to help our inspector have this case sorted by Christmas," Mrs. Jeffries began. "The inspector learned quite a bit yesterday, so everyone listen carefully."

It took less than ten minutes to repeat everything. As she spoke, she noticed Luty, Ruth, and Mrs. Goodge exchanging knowing glances. She gazed at the faces around the table and noted that Phyllis and Wiggins were nodding eagerly as she spoke, but the others still looked mutinous. "Now, I know this case has many drawbacks, but we can do this, so let's not be so down in the mouth about it."

"What do you want us to do?" Betsy grumbled. "We can't make people talk to us."

"You most certainly can," Ruth insisted. "You do on all the other cases. You're very good at it, Betsy. All of you are."

Betsy opened her mouth to argue, then clamped it shut again.

"This is a hard one." Smythe patted his wife's hand. "And we're all het up because we had some nice plans."

"I imagine Christopher Gilhaney had some nice plans, too, but he's dead now, ain't he," Luty charged.

"You're not being fair, madam," Hatchet snapped. "It's not as if the man was murdered recently. He was killed six weeks ago, so no matter how hard we try, we'll probably not find out anything useful."

"So we only try to do the right thing when it's easy," she shot back. "All of ya brag about how important justice is to ya, how workin' hard to do what's right has made yer lives have a meaning beyond how the world sees ya. But here ya are, wantin' to shove it aside when it interferes with your plans."

"That's hardly the case, madam." Hatchet's eyes narrowed angrily. "What we're all upset about is working our fool heads off for an investigation that's impossible to solve. The killer will have gone free yet everyone's Christmas plans will still be in shambles."

"Who says it's impossible to solve," Ruth interjected. "It's not. Have more faith in yourselves! If you keep telling yourself it's impossible you'll be bound to fail. But I know each and every one of you and all of you are intelligent, resourceful, and, usually, determined. Sometimes, when it looks as if women will never get the vote, or even basic, decent equality, I think of the murderers *all* of you have helped to bring to justice. I think of the innocent lives that were saved because the wrong person wasn't arrested and I'm inspired to keep on going, to keep on fighting for what is right regardless of the cost. So stop selling yourself short and just get on with it."

CHAPTER 7

"Let's hope Gilhaney's strongbox has something useful in it." Barnes closed the lid of the suitcase and flipped the clasps shut. "All we've found so far are the two rings and a key. Other than those, the only things in this were his clothes. Mind you, he dressed well—the labels on his suits and shirts were from Henny's in Bond Street. They must have cost a pretty penny." Barnes lifted the suitcase off the desk and put it on the floor alongside the one the inspector had just finished searching.

They were in the duty inspector's office at the Ladbroke Road Police Station and had just spent the last thirty minutes examining both cases.

"Perhaps that's why he may not have had an estate," Witherspoon said. "He spent all his money on clothes. But be of good cheer, Constable. I'm sure the box will tell us something useful."

Barnes picked up the heavy wooden box and placed it on the duty desk. "It's not a proper strongbox." He examined it carefully. "It isn't metal. But it's got a good heft to it. I've never seen one like this. It's been sanded and stained and the fittings are perfect."

The box was made of a dark hardwood and stood eighteen inches high with a brass handle on the top. Brass fittings had been screwed into the corners and there was a sturdy brass lock on the front. Witherspoon inserted the key and twisted. The mechanism resisted for a second and then turned, unlocking with a tiny click.

"Our luck is holding." He opened the lid and stared in dismay at the jumble of books and papers. "Gracious, going through all this is going to take some time. But we've no choice in the matter, not if we want to learn more about the victim. Let's start with the books." He pulled out the first one, looked at the title, and then handed it to Barnes. "It appears Mr. Gilhaney was interested in drawing."

"'*List of Colours and Materials for Drawing and Water-Colour Painting*,'" Barnes read aloud. "'Manufactured by Winsor and Newton, thirty-eight Rathbone Place, London.' Perhaps he liked to draw, sir." He flipped the cover open. "No, wait, there's an inscription here."

"What does it say?"

"'For Polly, with hope for our new beginning.'" He looked at the inspector. "I wonder who Polly was."

Witherspoon pulled out another volume. "More of the same—this one is *The Art of the Portrait, Techniques and Materials*." He opened the cover. "There's no inscription here. Just a name, Polly Wakeman, and a date, March fifth,

1878." He yanked out the third and last book. "This is just about accounting. Let's keep on with the rest of it."

They searched through stacks of receipts, old invoices for Gilhaney's clothes and personal items, and a half dozen letters from the Manchester Institute of Accountants, of which Gilhaney was apparently a member in good standing. Beneath the stack of letters was a green file box lying flat on the bottom.

"Hopefully, this is where Gilhaney kept his important documents," Witherspoon muttered as he lifted it out. Laying it next to the strongbox, he undid the tiny metal latch and released the cover. He rifled through it. "It's mainly correspondence. Let's start with the top one." He read it and handed it to Barnes. "It's a letter from Harold Whitley, a trustee of the Fulham Workhouse. He's agreed to recommend Gilhaney to apprentice as an accounts clerk, but the interesting part is the next paragraph."

Barnes scanned it quickly and then read it aloud. "'Christopher, at nineteen you are far older than most candidates for this position, but I explained to Mr. Adderman that you've recently had a bereavement and that you wish to change your current circumstances. Additionally, I told him about your remarkable abilities with both mathematics and memory. He has agreed to bring you into the company but, unfortunately, cannot compensate you anywhere close to what you earned as a journeyman carpenter. He has asked that you report to his firm on Monday morning, July twelfth.'"

"Interesting, isn't it." Witherspoon picked up another paper and unfolded it, and a yellowed newspaper clipping fell onto the desktop. "No one has mentioned that Gilhaney was a carpenter."

"Perhaps they didn't know, sir," Barnes suggested. "Frankly, I think there is a lot we don't know about the victim."

Witherspoon had picked up the clipping and was reading through it. "You're right, Constable . . . Take a look at this." He handed it to him.

Barnes squinted to read the tiny, fading print. "Now we know who Polly Wakeman is," he said when he'd finished. "According to this article, she was killed when the roof of an unfinished office building collapsed. Ye gods, the poor thing was only eighteen years old. What was she doing there?"

"I'm not sure," Witherspoon said. "But it happened a month before Gilhaney changed professions. I've no idea if it has anything to do with his murder, but my 'inner voice,' as Mrs. Jeffries likes to call it, is telling me that Gilhaney's unusual past may have some bearing on it."

"It's worth looking into, sir, and perhaps after we've finished the interviews at Walker and Company, we should go to Clapham and have a chat with one of Gilhaney's old mates."

Wiggins was determined to make up for his negligence. He pulled his jacket tighter against the cold wind as he walked past the Chase home. He'd decided to start here because this was where Gilhaney set out on the journey that ended his life.

He reached the corner and started to cross the road when he saw two young women come out of the walkway on the side of the Chase home. One was wearing a heavy coat and muffled in a red scarf while the other was buttoning a short green jacket over her housemaid's dress.

Wiggins crossed the road and knelt down. He pretended to tie his shoe as he watched them. The maids turned the corner and he gave them a few moments to get ahead of him before going after them. Moving as quietly as possible, he darted back to their side of the street and got as close as he dared.

They chatted as they walked, but he couldn't hear everything they said, just the occasional word. But he heard enough to know that one of them was going to the shops while the other one had her day out. They turned the corner onto the high street and Wiggins rushed to catch up, moving past them as they came to the omnibus stop. He kept on walking till he reached a haberdasher's shop. He stopped and pretended to examine the goods displayed in the window while watching them from the corner of his eye.

They stood there for a few moments until the omnibus arrived and he saw one of the housemaids get on. He hesitated for a split second, wondering if he ought to jump aboard the vehicle before it pulled away. He might have more luck getting the maid on her day out to chat, especially if she had a long journey. But girls were leery of men on public conveyances and there was always the chance she was taking the omnibus to the train station. If he kept following her, he might end up somewhere in Kent. So he made a quick decision and stayed put, staring in the window while the other maid went past.

He watched her amble up the busy street, obviously in no hurry to get back to her duties, until she reached the greengrocer's stall. Wiggins stayed where he was until she went inside and then he made his move, hurrying so that he could be in the right spot when she came out. He leaned against the corner of the bank next door to the stall and waited. He was taking a big risk, but it was a trick that had worked before. The trouble was, if he timed it wrong he might do some real damage and there was always the chance she might get angry, no matter how much he apologized. But he was desperate to find out something to bring to the meeting.

The maid reappeared, holding a bundle of vegetables wrapped in newspapers. Looking down as if searching for something he'd dropped, Wiggins shot forward and directly into the lass.

She yelped as the bundle went flying into the air before landing with a thud on the pavement. Potatoes, carrots, and a turnip spilled out and rolled in different directions. "Oh no," she cried as she dived for the potatoes.

"I'm so sorry, miss, it was all my fault." Wiggins scrambled to grab the runaway vegetables, scooping up the turnip and the carrots. "I didn't mean to run into you like that. I was looking for a sovereign I dropped and not payin' attention."

She captured the rolling potatoes and then reached over and yanked up the newspaper before turning to him. But he didn't give her a chance to speak. "I'm ever so sorry, miss. I'll be happy to replace anything that's ruined. If you'd like, I'll take your veg inside and have them wrapped again." He cradled the remainder of her vegetables against his middle. "I feel awful about this, miss. I hope I didn't hurt you?"

"I'm fine," she muttered. She stared at him for a moment. "And the vegetables seem fine as well. Let me just wrap them up."

"No, please, let me." He tugged the paper out of her hand,

squatted down, and spread it out. He put the turnip and the carrots in the center and then took the potatoes she handed him. Wrapping it all up, he stood up. "I'm so sorry, miss."

She'd recovered a bit and now looked at him with interest. "It's alright. If I'd dropped that much money, I'd look for it, too." Her hair was blonde and curly, her face as round as one of Mrs. Goodge's mince tarts, and her eyes blue.

"I'd just found it when I run into you." He smiled and she blushed. Wiggins wasn't conceited, but he knew he was nice looking. "Please, miss, let me make it up to you. There's a café up the street, it's a decent place, and I'd be pleased to buy you a cup of tea if you've the time."

"Well, I should get back, but the cook usually pops upstairs for a lie-down about this time and the mistress isn't home. Alright, I'd love one."

Five minutes later, Wiggins put their tea down next to the plate of buns he'd bought and sat down opposite her.

"Thank you," she said. "You never said your name."

"It's Albert, Albert Jones," he lied. He always used a false name when he was on the hunt. If she happened to speak to the inspector again, the only thing she could possibly say was that a fellow named Jones had asked her a few questions. "What's yours?"

"Margaret Newley, but everyone calls me Peggy." She smiled shyly.

"Do you work around here, Peggy?"

"I'm a housemaid nearby."

"I work for a newspaper." He was making it up as he went along and he thought he might have come up with a way to get down to business quickly. "I'm just a copyboy now, but I'm hoping to get promoted soon."

She helped herself to a bun. "To what?"

"A reporter. But the only way for that to happen is if I can bring my guv something interestin'—you know, something about a bank robbery or a murder, or something like that. But it's hard." He reached for his cup and took a sip. He'd sensed she was pleased with the attention he gave her and he expected she'd want to impress him a bit. He was counting on her knowing the police had been to the Chase home to talk to the master and mistress and hoped the word "murder" might get her chatting.

"I know something about a murder." She glanced around the café.

He pretended to be shocked. "Are you teasin' me?"

She giggled. "Of course not, I'm serious. You know that man that was killed on Guy Fawkes Night, the one all the papers said was a robbery?"

"Of course I do. I'm in the business, remember. What about it?"

"Before I say anything, you've got to promise you'll not tell anyone that I was the one you heard it from. I mean, it's not all that interesting, but you might be able to use it to get your promotion."

"I'll make sure your name never leaves my lips. Go on, then, tell me what you know."

"The Chases have been decent to me and I'll not say a word against them, so don't you go sayin' they did something wrong just to sell newspapers."

"Peggy, I just gave you my promise and I never go back on my word." He gave her what he hoped was a reassuring and trustworthy smile.

"I'm sure you don't." She returned his smile with a shy one

of her own. "Well, the police have been around to see the Chases again. It turns out the fellow wasn't just robbed. I overheard the mistress say the police now believe it was straight-out murder and the killer only took a few of his things to make it look like a robbery."

"Really?" Wiggins reached for a sticky bun. "A straight-out murder? Now that could be useful to me. What do you remember about that evening?"

"It was a dinner party for Bonfire Night and Mrs. Chase had been looking forward to it because she was anxious to meet Mr. Gilhaney. Mr. Chase had spoken about him several times. I serve at dinner and I'd overheard him." She took a quick bite of her bun. "I was serving at dinner that night. Mrs. Chase had called in Mr. Wicket to serve as well—he's from a domestic agency and costs the earth, so she only brings him in when it's a very fancy do. Anyway, it was obvious, even to us downstairs, that the dinner wasn't goin' very well and then, of course, when the guests started leaving it went from bad to worse. All of a sudden, everyone was dashing to and fro; poor Mr. Wicket sent one of the street lads to get Mr. Walker's carriage and even us girls were sent out that night." She broke off and frowned. "I don't know what else to tell you. It wasn't a very successful do and poor Mrs. Chase was at her wits' end."

"Did you happen to see anyone suspicious hanging about the neighborhood?" Wiggins was beginning to think he should have followed the other girl. Peggy wasn't telling him anything he didn't already know. "I mean, when you went out to find a cab."

"I only went out the one time." She made a face. "I was out there for ages and ages waitin' for a hansom, but I didn't see anyone. Mind you, it was Bonfire Night and there were lots of people about the streets."

"I guess that's why it took you so long to get a cab," he muttered. Blast a Spaniard, by the time he got out of this situation, it might be too late to learn anything today.

She snorted. "There were two cabs at the stand, but one was a growler and the other a four-wheeler. Mr. Bruce told me to make sure I got a hansom, so I had to stand about in the cold until one pulled up."

"Why would he have wanted a hansom?"

She shrugged. "I don't know, but Mr. Bruce was adamant that I was to send a hansom and nothing else."

Gordon Chase led the inspector into the office. "This was going to be Gilhaney's, but the poor man never even got to see it. Please, sit down." He motioned toward a leather chair as he took a seat behind the ornate carved desk.

Witherspoon took a seat and studied the room. The firm had gone to some trouble to make the place appealing. There were green-and-coral-striped drapes on the window, an etching of the Old Bailey courthouse over the unlighted marble fireplace, and a shiny brass bucket filled with coal on the polished hearth. The walls were painted a deep forest green and there was a colorful Oriental rug on the floor.

"Newton has told me you're to have a free hand in interviewing the staff," Chase said. "I've put your constable in the staff room and he won't be disturbed while he's conducting interviews. Will this space do for you?"

"Yes, this will do nicely," Witherspoon replied. "But before you go, there's a few questions I'd like to ask you."

"Of course, though I'm not sure what I can tell you, I

only met Mr. Gilhaney twice. What little I know of the man is only what I've heard from others." He gave a rueful smile. "But do go ahead with your questions."

"Mr. Gilhaney had been in London since the middle of October. When was he due to start his employment here?"

"He was originally supposed to start on Monday, November ninth. But at our executive committee meeting, which was November fifth, Newton suddenly told us that he'd be starting Friday morning, not Monday."

"Did Mr. Walker give a reason for the change of plans?"

"No, and Theodore Bruce was quite put out about it." He steepled his fingers together. "I was quite surprised as well . . ." He broke off as there was a sharp knock on the door. A moment later, a young clerk with rolled-up newspapers under his arm and carrying a bundle of wood stepped inside.

"Mr. Walker sent me to build a fire, sir," he explained. Chase nodded and the lad hurried to the fireplace.

"You were saying, Mr. Chase?" Witherspoon pressed.

Chase hesitated, with a glance at the kneeling clerk, who'd just put the newspapers under the grate and struck a match. "As a matter of fact, we were all surprised."

The lad put a bundle of kindling on the grate and then fanned the flames on the paper.

"Why was that?" Witherspoon coughed softly as a shaft of smoke wafted in his direction.

"Because Mr. Walker generally isn't one to make changes at the last minute—" He broke off, frowning, as a billow of gray smoke burst out of the grate. "Be careful, Hodges."

"The wood is a bit damp, sir." Hodges leaned across the bucket, picked out several hunks of coal, and placed them on the smoking grate.

"You were saying?" Witherspoon's eyes began to water as even more smoke poured out of the fireplace.

"Mr. Walker likes order, Inspector, and considering there had already been a row about the mistake in Mr. Gilhaney's desk and that was only being sorted out that afternoon, it was simply surprising that he insisted on changing anything else. But he did, and despite Mr. Bruce's objections, he told him to have all the company books on Gilhaney's desk—" He broke off again, choking, as the room filled with smoke. "Ye gods, Hodges, what have you done? You're going to suffocate us. Open the window." He got up, as did the inspector, and both men headed for the door as the hapless Hodges raced to the window. He tugged at the bottom frame but had no success in raising it. "It's stuck, sir," Hodges called.

Down the hall, Barnes looked up from his notebook. "Do you smell smoke?"

Lloyd Ridgeway, Newton Walker's secretary and the chief accounts clerk, sniffed the air and then pursed his lips. "Don't worry, Constable, it's not a fire. It's that silly Hodges being too lazy to go downstairs and get the dry kindling from the porter. He's used the leftover damp wood from yesterday. The office gets terribly damp at night—we've complained about it, but it does no good. You'd think a huge building firm like ours could have premises that kept the wet out, but apparently, that's impossible."

Barnes was relieved he didn't have to run for his life, but he did want to get this interview over. "Tell me what happened here on November fifth. I just need a general statement as to what went on here that day."

Ridgeway stroked his short, rather sparse beard. "It

started out like any other. I typed the agendas for the executive meeting and gave them to Mr. Chase. He asked if the correct desk for Mr. Gilhaney's office had been delivered yet and I told him they were going to exchange the desks that afternoon. He was annoyed and asked why it had taken so long. He said Mr. Walker was quite upset about the mix-up and it needed to be sorted out before Mr. Gilhaney started on Monday. I told him it wasn't our fault—I even showed him a copy of the original order that we sent to the shop and it specified the carved mahogany desk. But the clerk at the shop had the audacity to claim that someone from here had used that infernal contraption to contact them and change the order. Gracious, Mr. Walker had a fit when he saw they'd sent an oak desk instead of the mahogany one. I overheard him and Mr. Chase have a rather heated discussion about the matter. Mr. Chase claimed he'd not been the one to ring the shop and tell them to bring the cheaper desk. Of course, he'd not admit it if he had, would he. But just between you and me there's only the three managers in the office that are allowed to touch that infernal contraption—"

Barnes interrupted. "By 'infernal contraption,' do you mean the telephone?"

"That's right." Ridgeway shuddered. "Every time the wretched thing rings I just about have a heart attack. But as I was saying, Mr. Bruce, who generally isn't near as concerned with keeping expenses under control as Mr. Chase is, was very indignant when he found out how much that mahogany desk cost."

Barnes knew he shouldn't have asked such a broad question. Good Lord, the man was going to tell him every little detail about that day. "Yes, that's all very well. What happened next?"

"Then Mr. Chase came out and told me to get the complaint file ready so that he and Mr. Bruce could go over it after the meeting. After that, the managers went into their monthly meeting and we got on with our work. When the meeting was over, I grabbed the complaint file and rushed it in to Mr. Chase's office and then Mr. Bruce left rather quickly as he had a meeting with Manfred Stowe, which was odd as well, because I'm in charge of the appointment calendar and there was nothing listed for Mr. Bruce, but then again, he and Mr. Chase and even Mr. Walker often got called away when there was a problem at one of the building sites." He leaned across the table. "Let me tell you, sir, taking care of the appointment calendar for all the management is a very difficult task, very difficult indeed."

"I'm sure it is," Barnes remarked. "Go on, please."

"There's really not much more to tell. Uh, let me see, Mr. Walker left rather abruptly, but of course he didn't tell us where he was going." He shrugged. "The only other incident of the day was the desk for Mr. Gilhaney's office. They delivered it and then there was a bit of a row between Mr. Chase and the deliveryman. The fellow kept insisting that we'd only paid for the oak desk, not the mahogany—"

Barnes interrupted. "Did anything else happen?"

Ridgeway drew back. "No, nothing untoward happened for the remainder of the day. You asked for an accounting, sir, and that was what I was giving you." He sniffed. "There's just no pleasing some people."

"She's a right mean old cow." The boy used his grubby sleeve to wipe his nose. "But at least she pays a bob or two more than most."

Phyllis nodded in understanding. "Would you like another bun?"

She and the lad were standing at the counter of a workmen's café by the river. She'd spent the morning on the high street, questioning the shopkeepers and clerks about Ann Holter. She'd been using the old "lost address" trick, but despite her best efforts, she'd found out nothing. She'd almost given up hope when this young lad had followed her out of the butcher's. "I know that lady," he'd said as he tugged on her elbow. "If you give me a tuppence, I'll show you where she lives."

She already knew where Ann Holter lived, but of course she had to keep up the pretense, so she reached into her pocket for a coin. But as she'd handed it to the boy, she'd taken a moment to really look at him. His arms were as thin as matchsticks, his clothes frayed and dirty, and the ill-fitting jacket he wore so threadbare it could do nothing against the cold December winds.

Suddenly she had a moment of awareness that was so strong she felt tears come into her eyes. She was different now. Working for justice had changed her; it had made her see not just that the innocent shouldn't hang, but that all manner of injustice walked this world. This child wasn't responsible for being born poor, just as it hadn't been her fault she'd been born into a family that could neither afford her nor feed her. She blinked to hold back a sob as a weight of guilt lifted off her shoulders. She'd always felt that somehow she'd deserved going hungry and being cold and worrying about keeping a roof over her head, but that was foolish. Being born into poverty wasn't her fault, nor was it this young boy's. She had grinned at the lad. "No, I won't pay you yet."

His face had crumpled. But before he could cry, she said, "I'll buy you a cup of hot tea and some buns first. Is that okay?"

His jaw had dropped. "You're not havin' me on, are ya?"

In answer, she'd taken his hand, led him to the café, and ordered hot tea and buns.

"Ta, miss." He grabbed the pastry, stuffed it into his mouth, and chewed like a madman.

"Don't eat so fast. You'll choke. I'll buy you another one."

"That'd be good, but can I take it home with me?"

"Don't worry about saving it for your supper. I'll give you enough to buy a meal."

"That's not it." He looked down at the scratched linoleum floor. "I've got a little sister and a bun would be a real treat for 'er."

"Then we'll order two of them for her," Phyllis said softly. "Now, tell me what you know about Ann Holter. I mean, other than the fact that she's a right mean old cow."

He grinned. "She drinks a lot. So I hang about her house and as soon as the old lady leaves for the station, Miss Holter comes out the back door and sends me to Maywood's. She says the same thing every time: 'Be careful, now, Jamie, make sure you don't break them.'" He sneered. "I'm not a baby, you know. I know how to carry so it don't break."

"What do you bring her, Jamie?" She felt guilty for not having asked him his name. He had a name and she should have done him the courtesy of decent introductions.

"Two bottles of red wine."

"Two bottles of red wine each time you go, or two bottles altogether for the week?" Phyllis wanted to make sure she understood what he was saying.

"Two on Saturday and two on Tuesday." He grinned. "She likes that sour stuff, can you believe it? I tasted it once when my uncle Jonas come to visit and it was ruddy awful."

"When you speak of the 'old lady,' who is that?"

"Her mother. Old Mrs. Holter. She goes to visit her sister in Rye on Saturdays and Tuesdays. That's when Miss Holter drinks herself silly—leastways, that's what my mum says. Miss Holter don't want anyone to know how much she drinks so she waits until her mother's gone."

"Don't they have servants?" Phyllis had seen the Holter house and it was four stories tall, in a good neighborhood, and only slightly run-down. It was the sort of place that had to have servants.

He shrugged. "There's a housekeeper, but she only comes twice a week, and there's a maid, but Mrs. Holter is half-blind so the maid has to take her to the station and fetch her in the evenings."

Phyllis was fairly certain she could guess the rest. The maid knew what was what and once she took the mother to the station, she took her time coming back. Phyllis didn't blame her. She'd have done the same if she'd ever been lucky enough to find herself in such a situation. "But surely when her mother came home, she'd see her daughter had been drinking."

"I told ya, she's half-blind, and my mum says when you get old, your sniffer don't work worth a tinker's damn, so she'd not even smell the liquor."

"You're right, I'd not thought of it like that." He was

obviously a smart lad. Why was he working the streets? "Why aren't you in school?"

"I'm eleven," he declared. "I'm just small for my age. My mum needs me to bring in some coin and they don't pay you for goin' to school."

"Did you like school?" Phyllis had gone to a church school until she was twelve and had loved learning.

"It was alright, but I 'ave to bring in coins, otherwise we'll not have enough to eat. It takes all my mum's wages to keep a roof over our heads. Are you goin' to get me that bun?" Tommy asked, his expression anxious.

She nodded and bought three more buns. "Can you wrap them in paper, please," she asked the serving girl.

Jamie's eyes widened with delight when she handed him the bundle. "Here, this is for you and your family. Why did you call Miss Holter a mean old cow?"

"'Cause she is." He tucked the bundle under his arm. "She never smiles when she pays and she's got a nasty tongue. I move as fast as I can when she sends me off to Maywood's, but no matter how quick I get back, she complains about how long it took me. Once, she even forgot to pay me what she owed. She just left me standin' at her back door. I thought she'd gone to get me money, so I waited and waited, but she never come back, so I went inside. I was scared, too, but I needed that money to buy a half loaf for our supper." He took another quick sip of his tea and Phyllis wished she'd bought him another cup. It took her a moment to realize he wasn't just thirsty; he'd picked up his cup to hide his face. He looked as if he was trying not to cry.

"Did she pay what she owed?"

"No, and she was actin' right funny—she scared me so bad that I left and I almost didn't go back the next time." He put the cup down. "But I needed the coins, so I made myself knock on her back door the followin' Tuesday as soon as I saw old Mrs. Holter and the maid gettin' into a hansom. She acted like nothing was wrong." He looked at her, his expression disbelieving. "She just handed me the money for Maywood's and told me to be quick about it. I don't think she even remembered what she'd done."

"What happened that day, Jamie? How did she scare you? I know it's hard to remember some things, but this is important."

Jamie angled his chin and stared at her. "You're not wantin' to take a note to her, are you? That was just a way to find out about her, wasn't it?"

She couldn't lie to him. "That's true. I know this isn't easy for you to understand, but I work for someone who is trying to catch a killer."

"You mean like the police or one of them detectives."

"That's right, so please, tell me what happened that day."

"Miss Holter didn't kill anyone," he replied. "Mind you, I think she could." He took a deep breath. "Anyways, like I said, I thought she'd just gone to get my money, but when she didn't come back I went into the house. I called her name, but she never answered. I wanted my coins, but goin' into someone's house is scary, so I decided to leave. But then I heard thumping, like footsteps comin' from one of the front rooms. So I went down the hall and when I got to the big parlor, there she was . . ." He broke off and shuddered.

"What was she doing?"

"She was dancin' around the room, holding this fancy dress up. I didn't know what to do, but I wanted my money . . . and then all of a sudden she saw me and she stopped. I tried to tell her I'd just come to get my coins. She stared at me for a second and then went to a cabinet by the window. I breathed a bit easier 'cause I thought she was goin' to pay me. But when she turned back, I could see her pointin' somethin' at me. The room was so dark, I couldn't see what it was. So I asked her to pay what she'd promised, but she just kept comin' toward me, and then I saw what she had in her hand." He swiped at his eyes as they filled with tears.

She knew the memory was causing him pain, but her instincts told her it was important. "What was it, Jamie? What did she have in her hand?"

"I kept tellin' her I'd just come for me coins, that I meant no 'arm. I was backin' away as fast as I could, but she kept comin' toward me. I've never been that afraid in my life, so I just kept tellin' her that I was sorry, that I'd never trouble 'er again, but she kept pointin' that thing at me. I knew what it was and I knew it could hurt me bad. My aunt Helen, the one that no one in the family will speak to because my mum says she's taken to the streets, she had one and she showed it to me last Christmas when I saw her outside Brackman's Pub. She said she carried it in case that Ripper feller come back."

"What was it?" Phyllis repeated, but she suspected she knew exactly what it was.

"It was a gun. It was a little one, like I said, just like Aunt Helen's, but I knew from the way Miss Holter was lookin' at me, that if I didn't get out of there, she was goin' to use it on me."

* * *

"One doesn't like to repeat gossip, Lady Cannonberry, and normally, I'd not say a word about such a delicate situation, but honestly, she was quite rude to me at Lydia Benson's tea last week."

"I'm so sorry, that must have been dreadful for you." Ruth smiled sympathetically at her fellow women's group member, Marion Tavistock, and silently prayed they'd not be interrupted. Marion was a portly woman with curly light brown hair, heavy eyebrows, and a prominent overbite. She had only recently joined their cause and Ruth didn't know her well. But this morning, she'd gone to visit her friend Octavia Wells, the treasurer of their group. Octavia knew all the gossip about the moneyed classes of London and she used that knowledge for the fight for equality and women's rights. Unfortunately, her friend was suffering from a bad case of laryngitis and for the first time in all the years Ruth had known her, she couldn't talk. When Ruth explained why she'd come, Octavia wrote her a note that read, *Talk to Marion Tavistock at today's meeting. She loathes Hazel Bruce.* Ruth had sought Marion out and Octavia had been right, it hadn't taken more than a mention of Hazel Bruce's name to get the woman talking.

"It most certainly was. But I'm trying very hard to be a bigger person and, as our Lord says, to turn the other cheek." She gave Ruth a brief stiff smile. "You being a vicar's daughter can certainly understand that."

"I try to understand it, but the truth is, turning the other cheek has always been very hard for me. I've prayed about it many times, but I'm afraid it's still a character flaw the Almighty has not seen fit to correct in my nature," Ruth replied. It wasn't true, at least she hoped it wasn't true, but she wanted to establish a sense of shared trust with Marion. She had seen the surprise on the woman's face when she'd sat down with her and started chatting. "You must be a very special person, Marion, and I envy your character."

Marion's homely face transformed as she smiled in delight. Ruth felt momentarily guilty and silently vowed she'd make a special effort to get to know her better. She refused to be the type of person who was only being nice to get information out of a person.

"That's very kind of you to say," Marion said.

Ruth patted her hand. "I'm not being kind, I'm being truthful. I've never met Mrs. Bruce, but I've heard she has quite a sharp tongue."

Marion's pleased smile disappeared. "You've heard correctly. The woman has no manners. I couldn't believe the way she spoke to me." She put the elegant rose-patterned teacup down so hard it rattled loud enough that the ladies at the next table turned to look at them.

Marion caught herself. "Just because her family has money, she thinks she can say what she likes without any social consequences. Well, she has another think coming. I'm going to make sure she doesn't get invited to the Shipleys' ball next month. Leona Shipley is a dear friend and one word from me and Mrs. Bruce will be taken off the guest list." She snorted delicately. "She thinks too highly of herself because of her family's wealth. But there's more to society than just money. Breeding and ancestry are far more important than a bit of silver in the bank. I'm from an ancient and honorable family with a lineage that goes back to the Conqueror."

Ruth refrained from pointing out that most people's lineages, whether peasant or king, went back just as far. But she wanted information so she held her tongue.

"We've connections to court, you know. But that didn't stop her from publicly saying, in front of everyone at the luncheon, 'Isn't it sad that some bloodlines traded on ancient lineages rather than modern-day success?'"

"I take it she aimed that comment at you specifically? Why? Does she resent you for some reason?"

"Of course." Marion smiled bitterly. "Her family's company built our conservatory last year, the large one we added onto the main house. But they made a mess of it: bad workmanship, inferior materials . . . the place leaked terribly and the paint began to chip less than a week after it was applied. The conservatory was so badly constructed we couldn't use it and we had to hire another firm to come fix their mess. Naturally, my husband refused to pay them what they claimed was owed and they've threatened us with a lawsuit. Well, I say let them sue us, then everyone will see what shoddy work that firm does." She stopped her tirade and smiled self-consciously. "I'm sorry, I shouldn't get so upset about it. I suppose it was my bad luck to run into the woman at the tea and, of course, she was rude."

"That was unfortunate," Ruth murmured.

"She sat there with her nose in the air as if she was better than the rest of us. I did my best to ignore her comments, but everyone in the room knew we were in the midst of legal actions. What's more, from what I know, she's no right to hold herself in such high regard. She's no better than a Whitechapel street tart."

Ruth's eyes widened. "Really!"

"No, that's not correct. She's worse than a tart. Hazel Bruce has been unfaithful to her marriage vows."

Mrs. Jeffries put the linens into the cupboard, closed the door, and then leaned against the wood. She stared out the small third-floor window over the landing and saw nothing except the skeletal branches from the top of a tree. But she wasn't interested in the view; she was trying to assemble all the facts they'd learned thus far into an idea or a theory she could work with.

To begin with, the first picture they had of the victim was wrong. He'd been incredibly rude on the night of the murder, yet other people claimed he was a kind and decent man. Which was it? Something Witherspoon had said tugged at the back of her mind, but it was gone too quickly for her to make sense of it. She bit her lip, trying to force it back, but the only thing she could recall was that it was a tidbit she'd heard the first time they'd discussed the case.

She closed her eyes and tried again. What did they know? But because she'd not been listening properly and, more importantly, hadn't been thinking about what was being said, the few details she could recall didn't make any sense. Leon Webster hadn't gone straight home that night, Florence Bruce took laudanum, Newton Walker owned the Bruce home and apparently paid someone to spy on his son-in-law, Abigail Chase was furious her dinner party had been ruined, and Robert Longworth was dying.

But none of these facts pointed her in any direction whatsoever.

She sighed. She was in a mess of her own making and they were all going to suffer for it unless they got this case solved. At least Phyllis and Wiggins seemed to have come to their senses and even Hatchet had come along a bit. But Betsy and Smythe were both still angry at the situation and, though she could understand why, she knew they'd hate themselves if they didn't do what was right.

"Hepzibah," Mrs. Goodge shouted up from the bottom of the back stairs. "We've company. It's Dr. Bosworth."

Mrs. Jeffries shook herself and raced down the staircase. When she came into the kitchen, the cook had the kettle on the boil and was at her worktable slicing a malt loaf.

"Dr. Bosworth, how nice to see you." She smiled in genuine pleasure. If Bosworth was here, he had something important to tell her.

"Forgive me for barging in, but I had a bit of luck with the late Mr. Gilhaney's postmortem and I wanted to tell you what I'd found out."

"Don't say anything until I've the tea made," Mrs. Goodge ordered. She put a slice of cake in front of him. "It'll just be a minute."

He looked at his plate and then at the two women. "Aren't you two having any?"

Mrs. Goodge poured the boiling water into the waiting kettle. "We'll have ours with the rest of the household. They'll be here shortly."

"Would you like to stay?" Mrs. Jeffries asked. The others knew he could be trusted, as he'd worked with them many times before.

"I'd love to, but I've an appointment soon." He forked up a bite of cake.

They spoke of pleasantries until the tea had brewed and all of them had a cup in front of them.

"Now, what have you found out?" Mrs. Jeffries asked.

"As I said, we had some luck on this one." Bosworth grinned. "Dr. Sullivan—he's that friend I told you was interested in pathology—did indeed watch the procedure. He not only got a good look at the bullet wounds before Dr. Spicer arrived to do the postmortem, but he took specific measurements."

Mrs. Jeffries smiled in delight. "Gracious, Dr. Bosworth, you ought to be so proud. Obviously, your ideas and methods are having an impact on the whole profession."

"I like to think so." Bosworth grinned in pleasure. "I shouldn't admit it, but I am rather pleased about it. A number of the younger doctors seem to be following my lead. But I digress. From the measurements of the bullet holes, Sullivan was certain the shots were fired from a small weapon. He is of the opinion they were fired from a revolver."

CHAPTER 8

"The two of 'em hate each other," Flora Benning exclaimed. "All of us are tryin' our best to find other positions, but it's hard, you know."

"It is difficult, isn't it? Good positions aren't easy to find." Betsy nodded in sympathy. She had gone to the Bruce home determined to have something to report at their afternoon meeting. What's more, she knew that Smythe was back on the hunt as well and she didn't want him to best her.

She and Smythe had been fuming after yesterday's meeting but by this morning's meeting, their anger had turned to guilt. So after they left the Witherspoon house, they'd gone home, had a long talk, and discovered that both of them were willing to give up the Paris trip, but they'd been convinced the other would be crushed if it was canceled. After a good laugh, Betsy had asked Elinor to look after Amanda

while her husband went off to see his main source, a source
that Betsy knew would probably have plenty to say.

"Especially without a reference, and Mrs. Bruce might
not give me one if I was to leave." Flora yanked a handkerchief out of her coat pocket and blew her nose. "It's nice of
you to walk with me. I get lonely on my afternoon out. My
family lives on the south coast and that's too far to go for
just an afternoon, add to that the cost of the train fare."

She was a small slip of a woman with red hair twisted into
an unattractive knot at the nape of her thin neck, a porcelain
complexion, and a high forehead. The navy blue jacket she
wore was so big the sleeves reached to her knuckles and the
gold scarf wound round her neck was frayed in spots and
missing half its fringe. At first, Betsy had thought her a young
girl, but up close the lines etched around her mouth and eyes
revealed she was closer to thirty than twenty.

"I understand," Betsy replied. "I used to get lonely on my
afternoons out as well." They were walking along the Chelsea Embankment and there was a cold, stiff breeze off the
river. Betsy had waited till after the luncheon hour before
going to the Bruce home. She knew the neighborhood and
guessed that the Bruce home was big enough to need a substantial number of servants; that meant the maids couldn't
go for their afternoon out together, but had to go one at a
time to make certain their masters weren't inconvenienced
in any way. She'd been right and just after one o'clock, Flora
Benning had come out the servants' entrance.

It cost her a sovereign to make Flora's acquaintance, because she'd immediately claimed the coin when Betsy pretended to pick it up from the pavement and asked her if she'd
dropped it, but Betsy didn't mind. She could afford it and

poor Flora looked as if she needed it. "Why won't she give you a reference if you get a better position?" she asked.

"Because they have trouble keeping help." Flora made a face. "And Molly Dunning told me that they wouldn't give the last girl who left them a reference. Mr. Bruce said he was tired of the way Mrs. Bruce managed the house and if she couldn't keep the servants she had, he'd not let her have any more. Of course, she laughed in his face when he said it. She told him straight-out that it was her father's money that paid for their household and she'd have as many maids as she liked. Mind you, I don't think she knows that Mr. Newton Walker—he's her father—is payin' Molly to tell him everything that goes on."

"Oh, my goodness, really? Why would he do such a thing? Doesn't he trust his own flesh and blood?" Betsy slowed her steps. She didn't want to reach the end of the embankment too quickly.

"He trusts Mrs. Bruce; it's Mr. Bruce Molly is to keep an eye on. Molly doesn't know that I know what she's up to, but I saw Mr. Walker payin' her last month. I wasn't spyin' or anything nasty like that. I just happened to be under the back stairwell adjustin' my stockin's when Mr. Walker paid her. She gave him an earful, too. Told him all about how Mr. Bruce would slip out the servants' door when he thought Mrs. Bruce had gone to bed—not that they shared a room, but that didn't stop Mrs. Bruce from watchin' him like she was afraid he was sellin' off the family silver."

Betsy saw that they were almost at the end. "Let's cross the road." She took Flora's arm and stifled a twinge of guilt. The woman was so desperate for company she was talking her head off. Betsy remembered how that felt and she knew how crushing it could be. "Flora, I hope you won't think me overly bold, but there's a nice pub around the corner, it's a decent place with a female owner, and I'd like to treat you to a glass of wine or a nice whiskey. I've enjoyed your company so much and you've saved me from an afternoon on my own."

Flora smiled broadly. "That would be lovely. I'm usually too afraid to go in on my own, but there's two of us."

Clearly irritated at the interruption, Theodore Bruce looked up from his ledger. He frowned when he saw Inspector Witherspoon standing in his doorway. "What is it now?"

Witherspoon stepped into the room. "I've some questions for you, sir. It won't take long."

"Yes, yes, just get on with it. What do you want to know?"

"I understand that Mr. Gilhaney was due to start work here on Monday, November ninth, but at the morning meeting on November fifth, Mr. Walker announced he'd be starting work the next day, Friday, November sixth. Is that correct?"

"It is. What of it?"

"Did Mr. Walker give a reason for this change?"

"Walker never explains himself." Bruce tossed his pencil onto the open ledger. "He merely said that Gilhaney was going to be here on Friday morning instead of Monday."

"I understand you were a bit upset by the change?"

"Who told you that?" Bruce leaned forward.

"Mr. Bruce, that doesn't matter. But I would appreciate your answering the question," Witherspoon said. He wished the man would offer him the empty chair in front of his desk. His knee was beginning to twinge.

"Humph, it was probably Gordon, the man doesn't know how to hold his tongue. Not that it matters, but yes, I was annoyed. We were up to our ears in work and bringing anyone new into the office is always disruptive."

"Even someone with Mr. Gilhaney's background, someone who has been described to me as a genius who can recall everything he sees."

Bruce gave a short, harsh laugh. "Newton might believe that nonsense, but I certainly didn't. No doubt Gilhaney was good at his work, but I hardly think he was a genius."

Witherspoon nodded. "Who recommended Mr. Gilhaney to Mr. Walker?"

"I'm not certain. I think Newton said some business acquaintances in Manchester put forward his name."

"Your wife told us she was the one who recommended him to her father." The inspector watched him carefully, but Bruce's expression didn't alter.

"Perhaps she did, Inspector. But what does it matter? My wife has friends in Manchester that she visits often. It could well be that those friends and Newton's business acquaintances are one and the same." He reached for the pencil. "Now, if that is all you wanted to know . . ."

"That's not all, sir. After you learned that Mr. Gilhaney was to start the following day, what did you do?"

Bruce looked puzzled. "Do? I'm not sure what you mean—I worked."

"Here in the office?"

"For part of the day, yes," he replied. "I went out for a few hours to meet someone and then I realized I'd left some papers at home so I dashed home and then came back."

"Thank you, Mr. Bruce. I'll try not to trouble you again."

*   *   *

"I knew you'd come," Blimpey Groggins announced as Smythe walked into the Dirty Duck Pub and sat down opposite him. Blimpey looked at the man polishing a tray of glasses behind the bar. "Ya owe me a quid, Eldon. I told ya he'd come."

Eldon groaned and then gave Smythe a good frown. "What ya doin' 'ere now? One more day and I'da been the one winnin' the quid."

Groggins was a buyer and seller of information with a network of informants all over the south of England. He had people at the newspapers, the courts, the shipping lines, hospitals, the Houses of Parliament, and, there were even some rumors, at Buckingham Palace. He knew everything that went on in London and that knowledge was one of the reasons he owned the Dirty Duck as well as a half dozen other properties. He was a portly man with a broad smile, red cheeks, and wispy ginger hair.

"I wasn't sure I wanted to spend my money on this one," Smythe admitted.

"But you've 'ad a change of heart?" Blimpey laughed. "I hear you and your little family were goin' to Paris right after Christmas."

"We were, and we are if we get this ruddy case solved. That's why I'm 'ere." Smythe wasn't surprised that Blimpey knew of his plans, nor that he knew why he'd showed up today. He didn't beat about the bush. "What can you tell me about Christopher Gilhaney? More importantly, can you tell me anything about who'd be wantin' to kill 'im?"

"I've not put my people on it," Blimpey admitted. "I kept waitin' for ya, but ya never came until today. Do ya want me to start now?"

"How fast can you get me some information?"

"By tomorrow, but it'll cost ya extra."

Smythe thought for a moment. It wasn't the money that worried him, it was that it was already too late. But he wanted to make up for the way he'd acted. He'd been sure Betsy would be crushed if their trip was canceled, but he'd been wrong. She'd only been sulking in front of the others because she thought he'd be crushed. Truth was, they could go to France anytime they wanted. "Do it. Gilhaney was killed in Chelsea, in Kilbane Mews after leaving a dinner party. He was due to go to work for Walker and Company; they're a building firm. What else do you need to know?"

"The guests at the dinner party, are they suspects?"

"Yes, most of them were either employees, shareholders, or board members of Walker's. I can tell you who they are . . ." He rattled off the names quickly, knowing that Blimpey could easily remember them. He stood up. "Do your best, Blimpey. Gilhaney was murdered in cold blood—shot three times—and then the case was handed off to someone who made a right mess of it."

"Nigel Nivens. He's not known for his brains, but he's got excellent connections. So he made a cock-up of it, did 'e. Sit back down, Smythe, I do 'ave a few bits to share with ya."

"Why didn't ya say so," Smythe complained. "Blast a Spaniard, we're already behind on this one. Tell me what ya know."

Hatchet shifted his weight and then realized he'd do better by sitting still. The chairs in the tearoom were harder than planks and attempting to find a comfortable position was pointless. But despite the posterior-numbing seats, the Oak

Tree Tearoom was filled with patrons. Elegantly dressed matrons, giggling young women, and at least three courting couples occupied the small round tables.

He nodded his thanks as a waiter brought them a pot of tea and a three-tiered plate filled with madeleines, petit fours, ginger cakes, almond slices, and mince tartlets. "I hope this is to your liking, Mr. Wicket. Please, help yourself."

Horatio Wicket's watery hazel eyes widened at the sight of the food. "I didn't expect all this, Mr. Willow, but I'll gladly partake. Now, what was it you needed to speak with me about?"

Hatchet, or Mr. Willow, as he called himself for the purposes of this meeting, had decided to go as close to the truth as he dared. "It's a delicate matter which requires the utmost discretion. I have it on good authority that you were at the home of Gordon and Abigail Chase on November fifth."

"That's right." He reached for a ginger cake. "They were having a dinner party and needed a butler. They always ask for me; I've served there many times." He took a bite.

"Yes, I know." Hatchet had visited every domestic agency in Chelsea and Knightsbridge before he'd found the one that supplied extra help to the Chases. Luty's words had stung him to the core and he'd vowed to have something to say at this afternoon's meeting. After finding out that his friends, generally one of his most reliable sources when it came to hearing the latest London gossip, wouldn't be back in town until tomorrow, he'd embarked upon this course of action, and to his surprise it was turning out to be quite successful. "But what I'm trying to ascertain is if anything unusual happened that night?"

"Mr. Willow, I'm not stupid." Wicket took another bite,

chewed, and then swallowed. "So don't treat me as if I am. Of course something happened that night—the dinner party was ruined by an obnoxious guest who was then subsequently murdered."

"Yes, that's precisely what I wanted to know. Did anything else happen that night, anything odd or unusual?"

"Not that I can recall. The party was a shambles, the guests left early, the mistress was furious with her husband, and the minute she went up to bed, he took off like a shot."

Hatchet hadn't heard this before. As a matter of fact, he'd definitely been under the impression that neither of the Chases had left the house. "Gordon Chase went out after the others had gone?"

Wicket reached for a madeleine. "That's right. He was gone for a long time. I remember looking at the clock in the kitchen just before Mr. Chase came in the back entrance. It was almost eleven."

Hundreds of miles north, Inspector Nigel Nivens started down the wide staircase of Lord Ballinger's Scottish estate. He was in no hurry to join the others in the drawing room and fervently wished he'd stayed in London for Christmas instead of nagging his mother into getting him invited to this wretched place. He'd foolishly assumed that the other guests would be interesting, witty, and able to help him climb the ladder at Scotland Yard. Instead he'd found himself in the company of social-climbing mothers trying to foist their daughters onto Ballinger's only son and drunken aristocrats with empty titles and no influence whatsoever.

He stopped halfway down the stairs as a roar of laughter bellowed out of the great hall; it was Lady Ballinger. She sounded like a horse being slaughtered. Closing his eyes, he leaned against the staircase. Good Lord, what was he to do? He didn't think he could stand this much longer. Lord Ballinger's ancestral home was nothing more than a pile of old stones that should have been torn down five hundred years ago. The rooms were damp and drafty, the furnishings ancient and smelling of mold, and most of the servants so old they could barely move. It took ages just to get a ruddy cup of tea and when you finally did, it was likely to be cold.

What was worse, Ballinger was so cheap he wouldn't pay to have the London papers delivered, so Nivens had no idea if Witherspoon had solved Gilhaney's murder.

Another screech filled the air and he bolted straight up, grabbing the pitted wood of the banister for support. Ye gods, he had to get out of here. He was hungry, cold, and worried to death that Witherspoon had solved that wretched case. He'd look a right fool if the great man had managed to catch the killer in just a few days.

"There you are, Nigel." Lady Ballinger, all fifteen stone of her, waddled out of the great room and propped herself against the archway. "We've been waiting for you. Come along and have a drink. Timmy's brought a lovely whiskey."

Timmy, or *Sir* Timothy McClelland, as he reminded everyone in earshot, would drink rotgut gin if that was all he could get his hands on. "It's a bit early for me." Nigel started down again. "Actually, I was thinking I'd go into the village . . ." He broke off as the butler, moving slower than he thought humanly possible, appeared from the back corridor. "Mr. Nivens, sir," he yelled as he held up a silver tray. "There's a telegram for you, sir."

Nivens rushed down to the bottom, praying it was Barrows

canceling his leave and ordering him back to London. He grabbed the envelope, opened it, and read the message. *Witherspoon not up to snuff. Stop. Case dead as doornail. Stop. Barrows furious. Stop.*

"I do hope it isn't bad news." Lady Ballinger hiccuped.

Nivens broke into a broad smile as he read the message a second time. He'd paid one of his flunkies, a constable that was ambitious and willing to do anything a superior asked of him without question. "Just the opposite, Lady Ballinger. Actually, I do believe a drink sounds splendid."

Mallings and Brockworth, Woodworkers and Cabinetmakers, was located on North Street in Clapham. Witherspoon glanced at Barnes as he paid the driver of the hansom cab and hoped he wasn't pushing the constable too hard. After leaving Walker and Company, he'd noticed the lines of fatigue around Barnes' eyes and he'd wanted him to go back to the station and then go home. But the constable had insisted on accompanying him here to interview one of Gilhaney's old friends.

"Let's go see if Paul Woodford is on the premises," Witherspoon said.

Barnes stepped in front of him and pushed open the door. They entered a cavernous space filled with the scent of sawdust and the sounds of men hammering, sawing, and scraping as they labored behind their individual workbenches. Stools, armoires, and half-finished cabinets were placed along the side of the room. Hand tools were hung along the walls and wood shavings littered the floor. At the back, a large double door stood open to the elements.

A tall, muscular man with black hair and a full beard

standing behind the closest workbench put his saw down and walked toward them. "Can I help you?"

"We'd like to speak with Paul Woodford. I'm Inspector Witherspoon and this is Constable Barnes."

"I'm Woodford." His brown eyes narrowed slightly. "You're a bit late, don't you think. That fellow you sent here six weeks ago was about as useless as a headless hammer. So unless you've come to tell me you've found his killer, I don't think I've much to say to you."

Witherspoon wasn't going to pretend he didn't know what the man was saying. "You're understandably upset, Mr. Woodford. Your friend's murder was not investigated properly and I'm heartily sorry about that."

"You lot couldn't be bothered to listen to me properly before, so why are you here now?"

"Because despite what you may think about the previous investigation into Christopher Gilhaney's murder, it is different now. We'll listen to anything you have to tell us. Constable Barnes and I will do our very best to ensure Mr. Gilhaney's murderer is caught and brought to justice."

Woodford crossed his arms over his chest and tried to scowl, but he ruined the effect by the tears pooling in his eyes. "He was my best friend in the world and when you come up the 'ard way, like we did, friends are important. They take the place of family. Chris didn't deserve what happened to him."

"Nobody deserves it, sir, and I promise you, we'll do our best to catch whoever took his life."

"I want his killer to hang." He took a deep, ragged breath. "Right, then, let's go to the back. I've a lot to say. There's an office there and we'll not be disturbed."

* * *

Betsy, with Amanda in tow, was the first to arrive for their afternoon meeting. Mrs. Goodge eyed her warily as she set a plate of scones next to the teapot. Betsy and Smythe had both seemed a bit annoyed at the way she, Luty, and Ruth had ganged up on them the previous day, and this morning they'd both been quiet. Smythe had waved good-bye when he left, but Betsy had stomped off in a sulk. The cook hoped the lass had forgiven her; she'd hate there to be bad feelings between them.

But Betsy gave her a sunny smile as she wheeled Amanda's pram into the kitchen. "Hurry up and sit down, Mrs. Goodge. Amanda wants a cuddle and if you're not careful, Luty will get here and snatch her up. I'll finish getting the tea ready."

The cook was so relieved she almost cried. "Thank you, Betsy." She plopped into her chair and held out her arms. Amanda laughed in delight as Betsy pulled her out of the contraption and put her on her godmother's lap.

Within a few minutes, the others arrived and took their places. Mrs. Goodge glanced at Hatchet. He was harder to read, but this afternoon, he looked happy enough. It was Luty who was glaring at her. "You ain't goin' to keep hoggin' the little one, are ya?"

"Of course not." The cook laughed and patty-caked Amanda's hands together. "You just sit down and wait your turn."

"She's had her nap so she ought to be in a good mood." Betsy pulled out her chair and sat down next to Smythe. "She'll want hugs and playtime with both her godmothers," she assured the elderly American.

"We've a lot to cover today so let's get to it," Mrs. Jeffries said. "If no one objects, I'll go first." She paused for a brief second and then plunged straight ahead. "Dr. Bosworth stopped by today and had some very interesting information about this case."

"We haven't seen him in a long time," Betsy murmured. "Fancy him stopping in just when we've a case."

"He came because I asked for his help," Mrs. Jeffries explained. "I went to see him after my disastrous attempt to find out something about Robert Longworth."

"Don't be so 'ard on yourself," Wiggins protested. "Sometimes we just don't get people to chat."

"It happens to all of us," Phyllis added.

Mrs. Jeffries held up her hand. "You're being kind, but let's be honest here, none of us are proficient at everything. We all have our specific talents, but one of mine isn't getting information out of shopkeepers. Now, as I was saying, I asked Dr. Bosworth for help. The doctor that did the original autopsy was so incompetent his report couldn't even speculate as to the kind of firearm used to murder Gilhaney. Luckily for us, one of Dr. Bosworth's colleagues, a young man who is interested in Bosworth's theories, happened to be at the hospital morgue when the body was brought in. He measured the wounds and thinks the bullets were fired from a revolver or some other small handgun."

Phyllis gasped and everyone turned to look at her. "Sorry, didn't mean to interrupt you, Mrs. Jeffries, it's just that I found out that one of the Bonfire Night dinner guests owns a gun. From the way it was described to me, I thought it was a derringer, but it could just as easily be a revolver. But I'll wait my turn to tell you the rest."

"No, go ahead, I'm finished."

"Well, as I said, I found out that one of the dinner guests owns what is possibly a revolver, but that wasn't the most important bit I heard today." Phyllis told them about her encounter with Jamie, the street lad. She left nothing out and took care to repeat his words accurately. "Poor little mite was terrified." She reached for her tea. "He was certain she was going to kill him."

"Now, that's a woman with lots of troubles." Luty shook her head. "Dancin' around with a fancy dress and threatenin' to shoot a little boy."

"Did Jamie say what color the dress was?" Betsy asked.

"What difference does the color make?" Wiggins stared at her incredulously.

The women ignored him. "I asked him and he thinks it might have been white, but the light was so dim, it could easily have been a pale pink or blue."

"Then it was probably a wedding dress," Mrs. Goodge guessed.

"Well, what difference does that make?" the footman complained. "I mean, oh, what am I not seein' 'ere that you women do?"

"If it was a wedding dress, but she's not married, it means that something may have happened to her fiancé," Phyllis explained. "And that might explain her animosity to Gilhaney. Perhaps he did something and she blamed him."

Mrs. Jeffries started to tell them that they mustn't let their imaginations run wild, that speculation at this point was dangerous, but she caught herself. Perhaps in this specific instance, it wasn't as risky as in their previous investigations. Perhaps a bit of imagination was exactly what they needed to get this case solved. "If she was once engaged, it's worth finding out who was the fiancé and what happened to their wedding plans."

"Let me handle that," Hatchet volunteered.

Ruth looked at him. "Are you sure? I've some resources that I can tap . . ."

"I'm sure you do"—he interrupted with a broad grin—"but I've friends that I've not seen and as Madam pointed out yesterday, they have far-reaching resources as well."

Luty poked him in the ribs. "They've helped us before and they know how to hold their tongues."

"They do. What's more, I think I've hurt their feelings by not consulting them on the last few cases."

"Then I'll leave it to you," Ruth said. "But do let me know if you need my assistance."

"I will," he promised. "If it's all the same to everyone, I'd like to go next. I've not much to report, but I did find out that Gordon Chase left his house on the night Gilhaney was killed."

"How'd you find that out?" Luty demanded.

"It was easy, madam. With skill and intelligence, one can find out simple things such as where the suspects might have been on the night in question." Hatchet would die before he'd admit he'd gotten his information by bribing Mr. Wicket. "But how I learned the information isn't relevant. What's important is that Gordon Chase left his home as soon as his wife went up to bed. The butler was helping to clear up, so he was still there when Chase returned. He said it was close to eleven o'clock when Chase returned and that he was very disheveled."

"Now, that's very interesting," Mrs. Jeffries commented.

"The inspector and Constable Barnes both implied neither of the Chases had left the house that night."

"But do we know if they asked 'em?" Smythe said. "'Cause to me it sounds like they either didn't ask or they haven't taken statements from the household servants."

"Good point." Mrs. Goodge glanced at Luty. "I suppose you want your turn."

Amanda, who saw that she was now the center of attention, pumped her little arms and giggled in delight.

"Sure do." She grinned as Hatchet got to his feet, scooped the toddler into his arms, and deposited her safely in Luty's lap. When he sat back down, he angled his body so he could catch her if she squirmed out of her godmother's grasp.

"This evening, I'll make it a point to bring up the Chase servants," Mrs. Jeffries said. "For all we know, Gordon Chase and Gilhaney might have known each other."

"But he didn't insult either of the Chases," Betsy pointed out.

"That doesn't mean that one of them didn't have a reason to murder him," Ruth said. "We need to know who doesn't have an alibi. If Mr. Chase was out and the servants were cleaning the kitchen and dining room, even Abigail Chase could have gone out without anyone being the wiser."

"I'll drop a hint or two about them when I speak with the inspector tonight." Mrs. Jeffries looked at the clock. "Oh dear, it's getting late."

"I've more to report," Ruth said. She told them about her meeting with Marion Tavistock. "She loathes Hazel Bruce," she finished, "so I'm not sure if we can believe her when she claims Mrs. Bruce has been unfaithful to her marriage vows."

"Who was the man? Did she say?" Mrs. Jeffries asked.

"No, we were interrupted. But I'm going to do my best to find out. I've some sources I can see tomorrow."

"What I think is interestin' is the fact that she's accused Walker's company of doin' shoddy work." Luty cuddled Amanda and rocked from side to side. "That goes along with what I heard from Nelson Biddlington. Like I said yesterday, the gossip he heard about Walker's was that they was losin' money and no one knows why. But maybe it is part and parcel of them doin' shoddy work. I'll look into that. If it's all the same to everyone, I'll go next. I had morning coffee with Henrietta Parry today."

"So that's where you slunk off to right after breakfast," Hatchet charged. "You took Nicholas with you, didn't you?" Nicholas was just a lad, but he was street smart and resourceful and he adored Luty. He could be trusted to keep an eye on the elderly American and summon help if she got into difficulties.

"Don't be ridiculous, it was broad daylight and I was in the carriage. Henrietta's a gossip, but I don't think she'll shoot me. Now, as I was sayin', Henrietta has her nose in everyone's business—it's one of the reasons she's about as welcome in most homes as a case of shingles. But I like the woman, she's just lonely and likes to talk . . ."

"Yes, yes, madam, do get on with it," Hatchet said impatiently.

"Anyway, when I mentioned Leon Webster and Webster's Metals, I pretended I was thinkin' about investin' in 'em, and Henrietta just about split her corset to tell me the dirt on them. Turns out the reason they were so nervous when Gilhaney got killed was because years ago Gilhaney was the one who found out Leon Webster was embezzling money from his family's business. Leon likes to gamble."

"How long ago was this?" Mrs. Jeffries asked.

"About eight years or so. The family swept it under the rug and put Leon in a position where he didn't have access to the company money. Gilhaney left London and went to Manchester to work, but he knew the truth about what had happened. That's all I found out."

"I'll go next," Wiggins offered. "Mine won't take long. I followed two housemaids from the Chase house today and I picked the one that didn't know much of anything." He told them everything he'd found out from Peggy Newley. "It's not much, but it was the best I could do today. I'm hoping for better luck tomorrow."

"I wonder why Theodore Bruce insisted on a hansom cab." Phyllis reached for a scone. "It sounds as if the poor girl was out in the cold for ages."

Wiggins shrugged. "He probably didn't want to be near his wife; it sounds like they don't like each other."

"They hate one another," Betsy confirmed. "That's what my source said." She repeated what she'd learned from Flora Benning, taking her time and making sure she didn't leave out any details.

"Blast a Spaniard," Smythe complained. "You've stolen my thunder, woman. That was what I found out. Well, that's not all, but it was a big part of it." He repeated the only information Blimpey had given him, taking his time and stretching it out so it sounded better than it was. "The only other bit I 'eard was that Gilhaney surprised all his friends in Manchester when he accepted Newton Walker's offer. He told a colleague that he was going to flat-out turn it down, that he'd had two other offers that paid more and that he didn't like Walker. Then all of a sudden, something made him change his mind and the next thing everyone in Manchester knew, Gilhaney had up and come to London."

Witherspoon was exhausted when he came home. Mrs. Jeffries hung up his coat and bowler and then ushered him into his study. "Do sit down, sir. You look as if you're dead on your feet."

"It has been a tiring day, Mrs. Jeffries, but we're making progress." He smiled gratefully as she handed him a sherry.

"Now, do tell me, sir. You know how I love hearing all the details of your day. Start at the very beginning, sir, there's no hurry for dinner. Mrs. Goodge has made you a lovely pork roast, but she's only just taken it out of the oven and she likes it to sit for a good while before she carves."

"With roasted vegetables?" he asked eagerly.

"Of course, sir. Mrs. Goodge always makes your favorites when you're working on a difficult case."

"I'm a lucky man, Mrs. Jeffries, my people take excellent care of me." He took a sip. "As you requested, I'll start from the beginning. Before we went to Walker and Company, we had a good look through Gilhaney's things. We found two rings in one of the cases, the ones his landlady had told us about. One was very ornate, while the other was a delicate, pale green stone. I sent one of the constables to the jeweler's down the road from the station to find out exactly what kind of stones they might be, but as we didn't get back to the station this afternoon, I won't know until tomorrow. But we did find some very interesting things in his strongbox." He told her about the books, the newspaper clipping, and the correspondence.

She listened carefully, making certain that nothing escaped her. "Do you think there is a connection between the newspaper clipping and Gilhaney's changing professions?"

"Indeed there is." He smiled approvingly. "But I'll hold that tidbit back until I get to the end of my day. Oh, and we did find the name of a solicitor in Gilhaney's correspondence with the Manchester Institute of Chartered Accountants."

"Do you think he might be Gilhaney's solicitor? Someone who would know if he had a will?"

"We're hoping so. We sent off a telegram to the firm and we should hear back tomorrow. Unfortunately, there wasn't time to read through all the correspondence as carefully as I'd like. I wanted to get to Walker and Company and have another go at questioning them."

Again, she listened closely, hoping that she could recall what he said long enough tonight to write some of it down. When he mentioned Gordon Chase, she interrupted. "I'm so glad you mentioned him, sir. I'd quite forgotten about him." She was taking a risk here, but she felt she had no choice. There was so much information to pass along to Constable Barnes tomorrow, she had to try to get some of what they'd learned to the inspector on her own. Barnes did his best and usually could be counted upon to come up with "an informant" or "a recollection" when he was sharing the bits and pieces they'd found out with Witherspoon. But it wasn't fair to expect him to do it all on his own.

"What about him?"

"Mrs. Holcroft thought she saw him on Bonfire Night"— she smiled self-consciously—"I happened to run into her right as she was on her way to the station. She was taking the train to the continent to join her son; he lives in Italy somewhere. But I digress. She was sure she saw Gordon Chase walking along the Chelsea Embankment on Bonfire Night. She used to work a few doors down from the Chase home so she knew him by sight."

"How did his name come up?"

She was ready for that one. "Oh, Inspector, you know how proud we all are of you—I'm afraid I was being a bit of a braggart and as we were chatting I said you'd been given this difficult case because no one else could solve it, and apparently, I mentioned Mr. Chase's name. I'm sorry, I know it was indiscreet of me, but I said nothing more than what had been reported in the press." This was a bold-faced lie— she'd no idea what the original press reports had said or whose name had been printed.

He beamed. "Don't worry, Mrs. Jeffries, I'm sure you said nothing untoward. Mrs. Holcroft was certain it was Gordon Chase she saw?"

"She was, sir. I should have taken down her address in Italy, in case you needed confirmation."

"That's alright, we'll have a word with the Chase servants. I should have done so already."

"I didn't mean to interrupt your narrative, sir. Please, go on."

He held up his empty glass. "Do we have time for another?"

"Of course, sir." She got up and refilled their glasses.

"After we left Walker's, we went to Clapham."

"That's right"—she handed him his drink and took her

seat—"one of the housemaids at his lodgings knew where one of his friends lived."

"Paul Woodford. We went to his home and his mother told us where he worked," he said. "We had a word with him and, I must say, what he told us was quite amazing."

"Really, sir?"

"It might explain the reason Gilhaney was so rude to everyone at the Chase dinner party. More importantly, I'm sure it has a direct bearing on his murder."

"My goodness, sir. Do tell. I'm all ears."

"Christopher Gilhaney was raised in the Fulham Workhouse. As a child, his extraordinary abilities were noted and he could have been or done anything he liked. Several of the trustees offered to take him as a ward and educate him, but he refused."

"Why wouldn't he want such an opportunity?"

"Because he'd become attached to a young girl there. Her name was Polly Wakeman and if it is possible for children to fall in love, those two did. He gave up any and every opportunity that came his way so he could stay close to her. When they came of age, they left the workhouse. She went into service and he became a carpenter's apprentice. They were going to marry. Unfortunately, the family she worked for discovered she had a fiancé and sacked her. She had no family and no place to go. Gilhaney was living in a workmen's dormitory, but he was desperate to keep a roof over her head until he could make other arrangements."

"Gracious, how could anyone do that to a defenseless young woman?" Mrs. Jeffries stifled a surge of anger at the injustice of it. "Her only crime was being engaged!"

"That's right. Polly Wakeman had kept it a secret, but her fiancé had given her an engagement ring and she made the mistake of showing it to the daughter of the house. Someone she thought she could trust. This was eighteen years ago and there were still some households that followed the old-fashioned customs and their rule was, no men under any circumstance." He shook his head in disbelief. "They made her leave that very day."

"I take it the daughter wasn't trustworthy?"

"Correct. Paul Woodford thinks she was jealous of the maid. Apparently, she wasn't the sort to attract young men herself and resented the fact that her housemaid could. But that's just a guess on Woodford's part."

"A good guess, I'll wager," Mrs. Jeffries commented. "What happened then?"

"Gilhaney couldn't take her to his dormitory. No one would rent them a hotel room and, according to Woodford, neither of them had any money. Gilhaney had used what he had to buy the engagement ring, and the quarter had just started so Polly wasn't due any wages."

"Where did he take her?"

"To a half-built office building. Gilhaney wasn't working on the site, but he'd been there and knew how to get in and out of the place. The company he apprenticed with was due to start the carpentry work as soon as the snow let up. It wasn't ideal, but it would at least keep her out of the cold and wet. He took her there, got her inside, and made her as comfortable as possible. He told her he'd be back early the next morning to get her. But when he returned at sunrise, the roof had collapsed and Polly Wakeman was dead. What he didn't know was it wasn't just the snow that had halted work on the building, there were some dreadful structural flaws."

"How terrible for that poor girl. I hope she was sound asleep when it happened. But how does this connect to Gilhaney's behavior the night he was murdered?"

"Because most of the people at the dinner had some part in Polly Wakeman's death, at least that's what Gilhaney thought. She worked at the Holter home."

"And it was Ann Holter who betrayed her confidence?"

He nodded. "That's correct. Mrs. Holter sacked the girl. But that's not all of it. The actual roof collapse happened for two reasons: The metal fastenings that had been supplied and used in the beams were the wrong size and poorly made. The fastenings had been supplied by Webster's Metals. During the investigation that followed, Webster's claimed they'd notified the builder not to use the defective parts but that the manager of the project was in a hurry and he ignored their instructions. He claimed he never received any such notice."

"That explains Leon Webster."

"It also explains Theodore Bruce," Witherspoon added. "He was manager on that project. He was courting Hazel Walker at the time and her father didn't approve of him. He didn't want to do anything that would make him look incompetent in Walker's eyes. Finally, we get to the builder and I'm sure by this point you can guess who it was."

"Walker and Company," Mrs. Jeffries murmured.

"That's right." Witherspoon drained his glass. "Gilhaney did everything he could to force both companies to take responsibility for her death, but because he'd broken into the place, the inquest ruled that Polly Wakeman's death was an accident. Gilhaney was so furious, he burst into Newton

Walker's office and swore he'd make him pay, before he was tossed out; and when he tried to confront the Websters, they were on the lookout for him and had him dragged away before he could get past the clerks.

"How dreadful. But surely Walker should have recognized him?"

"It was eighteen years ago, Mrs. Jeffries, and the first time we interviewed Walker, he told us that Gilhaney looked familiar but he was terrible with faces. He simply didn't recognize the man."

"Didn't he recall the scandal? Recognize Gilhaney's name?"

"That's just it, there was no scandal; her death was barely mentioned in the press. Walker's is a huge firm and Newton Walker wasn't in charge of that project. Once the inquest was over and Gilhaney was dragged out of his office, he forgot all about the fellow. But her death affected Gilhaney deeply. He started drinking heavily, and fighting, and finally he lost his apprenticeship. Then he decided to change his life. He asked one of the trustees from the Fulham Workhouse to help him get an accounting apprenticeship. Woodford says he thinks it was always Gilhaney's plan to exact vengeance on the ones he considered responsible for her death. He just decided to use intellect instead of anger so he could do it properly."

"But if he blamed them, why did he subsequently agree to work for Newton Walker?"

"According to Woodford, it was because of a specific set of circumstances," Witherspoon explained. "Gilhaney was going to refuse Walker's offer and tell him the reason, that he considered Walker partially responsible for the death of his fiancée, but suddenly, he changed his mind and took the position. When Paul Woodford pressed him on it, all he'd say was that, for once, providence had smiled on him and all his enemies would be in the same place at the same time."

CHAPTER 9

Mrs. Jeffries locked the back door and went back to the kitchen. The house was quiet except for the ticking of the carriage clock and the jangle of a horse's harness as a hansom went past outside. Sleep was impossible now—she had too much to think about and, if she was brutally honest, she was too excited.

She opened the bottom cupboard of the pine sideboard and pulled out the brandy she kept for emergencies. Putting it on the table, she grabbed a glass and uncorked the liquor. This wasn't precisely an emergency; it was actually more of a celebration. Her chat with the inspector had changed everything. She was certain she knew why Christopher Gilhaney had been killed and now that she knew the "why," the "who" would soon follow.

She pulled out her chair, sat, and poured herself a generous quantity of brandy. She gazed across the room, letting her eyes unfocus as she thought about the victim. Why had he been murdered and why at that particular time?

The answer was simple. Someone at that dinner party realized Gilhaney had come back to London for vengeance.

In the years he'd been in Manchester, he'd not married nor, it seemed, formed any lasting romantic connections. He was still obsessed with his dead love. More importantly, he was now respected enough and probably wealthy enough to go after those he thought responsible for the death of his beloved. Gilhaney could do real damage now and that made someone very afraid. Fear, she knew, often led to murder.

She took a sip just as an unwelcome idea sprang into her mind. He was murdered with a gun, something most guests didn't bring to a dinner party. Putting the glass down, she considered the problem. He was killed with a gun, probably a revolver. Which meant that unless the killer carried the weapon with him or her all the time, he or she would have had to know beforehand that Gilhaney was going to be there that night.

But it wasn't a secret. According to what Gordon Chase had told the inspector, they knew he was coming. They'd ordered furniture and supplies for his office. What's more, Newton Walker had insisted the Chases invite the man to their home, so it was entirely possible that not only did the people at the office and the Chase home know, but the other guests could have easily found out as well. Which meant that whoever wanted him dead had armed him- or herself accordingly and Gilhaney had foolishly walked right into a trap.

She sipped her brandy as she thought about every detail they knew, but no matter how she looked at the crime, the only motive she could see for Gilhaney's murder was fear, plain old fear.

Occasionally, an idea that didn't quite fit popped into her head, but she brushed it aside. Not everything they learned was connected with the murder. Some of it was just extra bits and pieces they picked up along the way.

She yawned as she realized she was now sleepy. She put the brandy away, washed her glass, and picked up the small lamp she'd brought downstairs. She understood exactly what to tell the others they must do to put this one to bed. They would have their Christmas and none of them would have to cancel their plans, she was sure of it.

Despite the brandy, Mrs. Jeffries didn't sleep well. She awakened early and went downstairs, making enough noise as she put the kettle on to boil to wake the cook. She had the tea ready when Mrs. Goodge and a very cranky Samson came shuffling out of her quarters. Over tea, she told the cook everything.

"So that's the reason Gilhaney was killed." Mrs. Goodge tapped the rim of her teacup. "Someone was afraid of him?"

"That's right. Now our task is to find out who it was," Mrs. Jeffries said.

Mrs. Goodge wasn't as certain. It sounded to her like a flimsy excuse for a murder, but this early in the morning, she wasn't at her best and couldn't think of how to say what she felt. "Right, then. I'll get dressed and we'll see what we can get out of Constable Barnes."

"We've much to share with him," Mrs. Jeffries said cheerfully. "So let's hope he comes early."

But he didn't. If anything, he was later than usual, so they rushed through their report and kept hurrying him as he filled in some of the details of the previous day's activities.

Mrs. Jeffries was still in a positive frame of mind when the others arrived for their morning meeting. "We've a lot of information to share, so we'll need to get started immediately." She told them everything they'd learned from Witherspoon and Barnes.

Wiggins was the first to react. "Cor blimey, so that's why someone killed him."

"It's such a sad story," Phyllis murmured. "Poor Polly. She must have been so terrified."

"No wonder Gilhaney wanted vengeance." Smythe grabbed Betsy's hand under the table. "He lost the only thing that meant anything to him."

Mrs. Goodge helped herself to another cup of tea and glanced at Mrs. Jeffries. "If Gilhaney was murdered because someone at the dinner party was scared of him, how are we going to find out which one of them it was? Except for the Chases and Robert Longworth, all of them had a hand in what happened to Polly Wakeman."

"But it was so long ago." Ruth's brow furrowed. "And are we sure that Gilhaney had enough power to hurt any of them?"

"I considered that question," Mrs. Jeffries admitted. "I finally decided it didn't matter whether in fact he could do them any real damage, what mattered was that one of them believed he was capable of it. Look at it from the killer's point of view. After eighteen years, they meet Gilhaney at a dinner party, and what does he do? He immediately goes on the attack, not just to one of them, but to everyone at the party who had some involvement in Polly Wakeman's death."

"What about Robert Longworth? He didn't have a hand in her death," Luty pointed out, "but Gilhaney made some nasty comments to him."

"Only because of his past association. Longworth did let Gilhaney take the blame for his crime," Mrs. Jeffries replied. "And Longworth himself said that Gilhaney stopped almost immediately. He told the inspector he thought Gilhaney realized he was ill."

"It's like 'e was sendin' all of 'em a message," Wiggins said.

"Right, or as Mrs. Chase commented to the inspector, 'It was almost as if he'd prepared a script for the evening.' But Mrs. Goodge is right, it will be difficult to find out which of them felt threatened enough by his presence here in London to take such drastic action," Mrs. Jeffries said.

"Do you have any idea how we should go about finding this person?" Ruth asked.

"Unfortunately, the only thing we can do is keep on as we've been doing, uncovering as much information as possible about all of them."

"We do know that one of them has a gun, Ann Holter. But did she take it with her to the dinner party?" Betsy said.

"I can try and find out," Phyllis volunteered. "Today's Tuesday and the housemaid always takes Mrs. Holter to the train station. I know she doesn't go back to the Holter home—she waits somewhere near the station for Mrs. Holter to come back on the afternoon train. I'll try to find her and see if she'll tell me anything useful."

"Do that," Mrs. Jeffries said. "We know that Leon Webster didn't go straight home and Gordon Chase went back out after Mrs. Chase went upstairs, but what about the rest of them? I think we should find out if Ann Holter, the Bruces, and Newton Walker all went straight home that night."

"That should be easy enough," Hatchet said. "But does that mean we shouldn't continue to find out other specific information? I was going to see my friends and try to discover who Ann Holter's fiancé might have been."

"And you should definitely do that," Mrs. Jeffries said quickly. "We really should do both tasks; they're equally important."

"Good." Ruth grinned. "I was quite looking forward to seeing if I can uncover who Hazel Bruce's alleged lover might be."

Leon Webster frowned as Witherspoon and Barnes were led into the outer office of Webster's Metals. Shoving his chair back, he jumped up from his desk and stalked toward the policemen. "What are you doing here? I've already told you everything I know. This won't do, Inspector, it simply won't do. I'll not be subjected to this kind of harassment."

Barnes edged himself between the angry man and Witherspoon. "We're not harassing you, sir. But we do have more questions. You can either answer them here or you can accompany us to the station. It's your choice, sir."

Webster's mouth flattened into a grim line and his hands clenched into fists. "Follow me," he muttered. He stormed down the hall, shoving the door open to the file room and stomping inside.

They trailed after him. When they stepped inside, Webster sat at the head of the table. He gave them a sour look and waved them toward the rickety chairs. "Go on, then, ask your damned questions."

Barnes closed the door before he took a seat. He pulled out his pencil and notebook.

Witherspoon waited till the constable was settled before he spoke. "Mr. Webster, you said you went to the White Hart Pub when you left the Chase home, is that correct?"

"That's correct. What of it?"

"You also said that no one would remember you because this happened so long ago, correct?"

"Again, yes. What of it?"

"You were wrong, Mr. Webster. We sent a constable there to confirm your statement and lo and behold, someone did recall your being there on Bonfire Night. I'm surprised it slipped your mind."

"What do you mean? What are you saying?"

"You ran into someone you knew that night, a former worker here at Webster's Metals, and you bought him and his uncle a drink. Why didn't you tell us about that encounter?"

He shrugged, but the bluster had disappeared. "I forgot. It happens, you know. One can't be expected to remember every little thing one does. It was weeks ago, Inspector."

"I'm not sure I believe you, Mr. Webster. I think you neglected to mention it because if you had, we'd have tracked these witnesses down and they would have told us that you didn't arrive at the White Hart when you told us you had. You didn't get there until ten minutes before last call, so it was very nearly half past ten."

"You left the Chase home at eight thirty or thereabouts,"

Barnes said. "The White Hart is less than half a mile from there. Where were you all that time?"

Webster swallowed and pulled a handkerchief out of his pocket. He dabbed at his forehead. "I went for a walk, a very long walk. I was most upset. Christopher Gilhaney had been very rude."

Barnes said, "Were you scared of him? He once accused you of supplying inferior products to a building site where a roof collapsed and a young woman died as the result of your actions. She was his fiancée and her name was Polly Wakeman."

He gasped. "How did you know that? It was years ago and our company did nothing wrong. It was an accident, an accident, I tell you."

"Nonetheless, he considered you partially responsible. You were in charge of Webster's during that time, weren't you?" Witherspoon guessed.

He looked like he was going to cry. "Her death was an accident, a terrible, terrible accident. I wasn't responsible."

"But Gilhaney didn't see it that way," Barnes pointed out. "If I were you, Mr. Webster, I'd tell us where you went when you left the Chase house that night. This is a murder investigation."

"I went to a house down by the river—there's always a card game there." His voice had dropped to a mere whisper. "But you can't tell my family. If they find out I'm gambling again, they'll cut me off completely."

"It's about time you came to see us." Myra Manley handed Hatchet a cup of tea. "We were beginning to think you'd forgotten us."

"Never." Hatchet laughed. He adored Myra and her husband, Reginald. The three of them were having tea in front of a roaring fire in Myra's lovely day room. The walls were papered with cheerful blue and red flowers on a cream background, the furniture was overstuffed, elegant, and comfortable, and an amazing portrait of Myra hung over the white marble mantelpiece.

Reginald, an artist, had captured his wife's true beauty. Most people would have regarded her as homely; her once-dark hair was laced with gray, her face was narrow, and her teeth protruded ever so slightly. He had captured her perfectly. The painting portrayed a woman of great compassion, humor, and character. It was one of the most beautiful portraits Hatchet had ever seen.

"Now, don't look so skeptical," he chided as he saw their expressions. "I have been by several times in the last few months and each time, you two are off somewhere having an adventure."

"I'll admit, we've been doing a lot of traveling, but I've been working, I'll have you know." Reginald nodded toward the portrait. "What do you think of that one?"

"Reginald," Myra chided. "What do you expect the poor man to say, I'm sitting right here."

"I'll be brutally honest, then." Hatchet studied the painting again. "It's almost as beautiful as the subject." He looked at his friend. "I hadn't realized you were such an excellent portrait artist, Reginald."

"We all have our talents." Reginald Manley was a man of late middle age, with gray streaks in his black hair, blue eyes, and the kind of bone structure that seemed to defy the passing years. Before marrying Myra, he'd been a not very successful artist.

Myra was from one of the richest families in England. The two had met at the onset of middle age, fallen in love, and been told by everyone that it was impossible. But they'd been married for a number of years now and were as devoted to one another as the day they fell in love. Hatchet came to them for information because they believed in justice, had a wide circle of friends from both the aristocratic and artistic worlds, and knew how to hold their tongues.

"That's very kind of you, Hatchet." Myra blushed prettily. "But it is Reginald's talent that makes the work so compelling."

"Nonsense, darling." Reginald patted his wife's hand. "It was your beauty that inspired me."

"Why haven't you always done portraits?" Hatchet took a sip of his tea.

"I've done quite a few. The problem is, if I paint the person as I see them, sometimes they get upset."

Myra chuckled. "His portrait of Lady Vernay wasn't well received. She claimed he made her look quite unattractive."

"That's because she has an ugly character," Reginald said. "As I just told you, I paint what I see. What's more, that awful woman tried to get out of paying me. I had to threaten to put the painting on Nelson's Column to get what she owed."

They laughed and then Hatchet put his teacup on the side table. "I need your help."

"We thought you might," Myra said. "Your inspector friend is now investigating the Gilhaney murder, right?"

"Yes, how did you find out?"

"We have our sources, Hatchet." Reginald chuckled. "Since we've been helping you, we've become very interested in murder. You should have seen Myra questioning poor old Ridley at dinner the other night."

"The Home Secretary?"

"Oh yes, I peppered him with questions." Myra's eyes twinkled. "That's how I knew about the reassignment of Gilhaney's murder to Inspector Witherspoon. Someone at the Home Office wants the killer caught. I tried my best, but I couldn't pry that name out of him."

"It's a very difficult case," Hatchet said. "The original investigation wasn't done properly and now six weeks have passed. But despite the difficulties, we're doing our best. Do either of you know a family called Holter? They live in Chelsea."

"I know them," Myra replied. "They had a country estate in Suffolk near my cousin's home, but it was sold years ago. There was a scandal about their daughter, Ann."

"When was that?" Hatchet asked.

"I'm not sure of the exact year. I think it was eleven or perhaps twelve years ago. Why? If it's important, I can find out for you."

"That won't be necessary, at least not yet," Hatchet murmured. The time frame was right; Gilhaney was still in London at that point. But that didn't necessarily mean the Holter scandal was connected to him. "Do you remember any of the details?"

"Are the Holters suspects?"

"Ann Holter might be," he said. "She was one of the last

people to see Gilhaney alive. They were at the same Bonfire Night dinner party. Gilhaney made some very rude comments to her. It was shocking, really. He said things no gentleman would say to a lady, especially a lady who later told the police she'd never met Christopher Gilhaney before the night he was murdered. We know she was lying."

"How do you know that?" Reginald eyed him curiously.

Hatchet told them about the connection between Ann Holter, Polly Wakeman, and Gilhaney. When he finished, he could see from their expressions they were shocked and disgusted.

"I'd heard that the Holters were old-fashioned," Myra said, "but to toss a servant girl into the street in the dead of winter, that's monstrous."

"It was indeed," Reginald agreed. "And her only 'crime' was falling in love and getting engaged. God, I hope the old boy is rotting in hell."

"It was Ann Holter who betrayed her," Myra reminded him. "And she knew exactly what she was doing. My cousin always said she was a mean-spirited, spiteful girl. Now I don't feel so badly for her."

"You mean about the scandal," Hatchet prompted.

"I don't know all the details, but I know enough. Apparently, she was going to get married. She'd already been labeled a spinster and I suspect she felt this was her last chance at happiness. But the wedding never took place. The banns had been read and the announcement had run in the *Times*, but something happened at the very last moment. The family tried to hush it up, but when a wedding is canceled only minutes before the ceremony, it's impossible. The gossip was that someone had interfered and managed to talk the groom out of going through with it." She frowned in concentration. "I wish I could recall more. But I do know the church was filled with people, the reception was ready, and then her father had to stand up and tell the guests to go home."

"Were you there?" Hatchet asked hopefully.

"No, I'd been invited, but I didn't go." She smiled ruefully. "I can't remember why, something must have come up."

"How could someone interfere merely an hour before the nuptials?" Hatchet didn't understand that part of it.

"I know about that part of the whole fiasco—my cousin gossiped about it incessantly that whole summer," Myra explained. "Apparently, her fiancé had proposed because he thought the family still had money. Ann didn't disabuse him of that notion—as a matter of fact there were some that said she got what she deserved because she'd lied about the family money to get a ring on her finger. The Holters were once very wealthy, but for years now all they've had is the family house here in London and a small investment income. Someone made it his business to tell her fiancé the real state of the family's financial affairs. He then declined to go through with the wedding."

"Do you have any idea who it was?" But Hatchet thought he could guess.

"I can't remember anyone ever saying, but it had to be someone who was privy to the Holter family finances."

"I'll bet it was Gilhaney." Reginald sipped at his tea. "As Hatchet said, after Polly Wakeman was killed, he made it his business to find out as much as possible about the ones he considered responsible for her death."

"But how would he know how much money they did or didn't have?" she argued.

"You know something about their finances," he pointed out.

"Only because they had an estate next to my cousin and Sophie is one of the nosiest people in the world. But in general I'm not privy to such things."

"You never needed to be." Reginald took his wife's hand and kissed it. "Darling, for such a brilliant woman, you're wonderfully naive."

Myra looked at her husband curiously. "Why do you say that?"

"Because before I met you, I could tell you to a penny how much a London socialite was worth and I wasn't even an accountant."

"Don't be absurd—you make yourself sound as if you were a gigolo, and that's not true." She snatched her hand away. "You had patrons, people who could see how talented you were."

"Gilhaney was a talented man as well." Reginald grabbed her hand again and wouldn't let go when she tried to pull away. "Don't be angry at me, darling. I'm trying to make a point."

She opened her mouth to argue and then laughed. "You can make all the points you want, but I'll not have you demean yourself. You weren't a gigolo, you were an artist, and the women who helped you knew that."

"What is your point, Reginald?" Hatchet shifted uncomfortably. This conversation was getting awkwardly personal. Reginald hadn't been a gold digger or anything of the sort; however, before marrying Myra, he'd had a series of liaisons with a string of wealthy women who'd supported him while he painted. To his credit, he'd always been faithful to his ladies.

"I'm sure you already know." He grinned. "If I could find out how much someone was worth, so could Christopher Gilhaney. It would have been child's play for him to discover that Ann Holter was lying about how much money her family had, and once he did, he used that knowledge to publicly humiliate her and ruin her life, just like she'd ruined his."

"Do you think we should have put a constable on Webster?" Barnes asked as he and Witherspoon climbed into a hansom for the trip to Walker and Company. "He's scared and scared men often make a run for it."

"I considered it, but I'm not sure he had anything to do with Gilhaney's murder." The inspector braced himself as the cab lurched forward. "If he was telling the truth, he's an alibi for the time that Gilhaney was killed. We should have the answer to that question when we go back to the station."

They'd sent a message through the fixed-point constable to get some of the local lads to the house where Webster claimed he'd been playing cards. He'd even supplied them with the names of two witnesses who could vouch for him.

"I'm not sure I think much of his 'witnesses,'" Barnes muttered. "They're a hard lot down by the river and most of them would just as soon spit on a policeman's shoe as tell him the truth."

"That's true, but this is a murder, Constable, so let's hope for the best." Witherspoon grabbed the handhold as the cab hit a pothole.

They discussed the case as the hansom drove through the

crowded London streets. Barnes was grateful that Mrs. Jeffries had been the one to tell the inspector about Gordon Chase leaving his home on the night of the murder. At least he was saved from coming up with a story about that one. He'd spent much of today passing along the rest of the information he'd picked up from the housekeeper and the cook, but it was blooming difficult. He sank back against the seat, going over in his mind everything they'd told him and hoping he'd dropped enough hints and vague references so that Witherspoon knew as much as he did. By the time they reached their destination, Barnes was fairly confident he'd not left anything out.

"You're back again," Lloyd Ridgeway said as they stepped into the office. "If you're here to see Mr. Walker, he's already left for the day. He works short hours and Mr. Bruce is gone as well. He didn't say if he was coming back."

"We're here to see Mr. Chase," Barnes said.

"That's alright, then. If you'll wait here, I'll announce you." He disappeared down the hall. Witherspoon glanced at the clerks. There were four of them in two rows of two each. He noticed Hodges, the one who'd filled Gilhaney's office with smoke, sitting at the closest desk. The lad looked up from the stack of invoices he'd been sorting and saw Witherspoon. He got up. "Uh, I'm sorry about the other day, sir."

"That's alright, no harm done. It was just a bit of smoke."

"Is that why you're back, sir, to finish speaking with Mr. Chase?" He brushed a strand of dark blond hair off his forehead. He was a thin lad with long, coltish legs and oversized feet.

Witherspoon realized Hodges had a point; he'd not completed that interview and just before they'd fled the room, Gordon Chase had been about to tell him something. "That's right."

"Is it hard to get into the police?"

Two of the other clerks snickered, but a glance from Barnes shut them up.

"I'm not sure it's hard, as you say, but there are standards," Witherspoon explained. "But we're always hoping to attract fine young men of good character. If you're interested, we're currently taking applications."

"I am, sir." Hodges sat back down as Ridgeway returned. He gave the old clerk a measured look. "Very interested."

"This way, please," Ridgeway said.

Chase looked up from his work as they entered his office. "Mr. Ridgeway, could you please bring another chair."

"Yes, sir." He dashed off and returned a few moments later with a straight-backed chair exactly like the one already in front of Chase's desk.

"Thank you, Ridgeway. Please, Inspector, Constable, do sit down." He said nothing until they were settled. "How can I help you?"

"We didn't finish our interview when I was last here," Witherspoon said.

Chase laughed. "That's right, Hodges choked us with smoke. As I recall, you'd just asked me about how the managers had reacted to Newton's announcement that Gilhaney was coming on Friday morning, November sixth, rather than the following Monday, and I'd said something to the effect that we were surprised, because Newton wasn't one to make changes at a moment's notice and that Mr. Bruce was a bit annoyed."

"You have a good memory. Was that all Mr. Walker said at your meeting?"

He acknowledged the compliment with a quick smile. "That was it, except that Newton wanted all the financial records on Gilhaney's desk before he came in the next day. Frankly, I don't blame Mr. Bruce for being a bit put out over the matter."

"Why is that, sir?" Witherspoon moved his hips in a vain attempt to find a comfortable position.

"Because half of those records are stored in the box room upstairs. Bringing down the ledgers from the past ten years was going to take the clerks half the afternoon and we were already behind schedule on the monthly invoices and receivables."

"The past ten years?" Witherspoon wondered if that was a standard procedure, but before he could ask, Barnes said, "Mr. Chase, did you leave your home after the dinner party was over?"

Chase drew back, his expression surprised. "Yes, I did. Abigail was so furious with me, I went down to the river to watch the bonfires. It was quite a sight—there were half a dozen of them still blazing."

"Why didn't you tell us this before?" Witherspoon asked.

"You didn't ask me." He looked confused and then his expression cleared. "Oh, I see, you think I might have slunk out and murdered Gilhaney. Gracious, I had no idea I was a suspect."

"Everyone who was there that night is being asked to account for his or her whereabouts at the time of the murder," the inspector assured him. "It was remiss of us not to have asked you about this previously."

"How long were you at the river, sir?" the constable asked.

"Quite a long time," Chase replied. "I wanted Abigail to be sound asleep when I got home. I don't know the exact time I arrived home, but the servants were still in the kitchen, so one of them might have noticed. I came in the servants' entrance. My best guess is it was probably close to eleven o'clock."

"Did you see anyone you know while you were there?"

"Three of my neighbors." Chase chuckled. "Mickey Harlow—he lives across the road from us at number eleven—and Mr. and Mrs. Blodgett—they live around the corner on Marshall Place, number fourteen."

"Did any of these people happen to notice the time you arrived at the river?" the inspector asked. There was no apparent reason for Chase to have followed Gilhaney and murdered him, but Witherspoon wanted to be thorough.

"Indeed they did!" Chase laughed. "The first thing Mrs. Blodgett asked me was, why was I at the river at nine o'clock? She knew we were having guests, you see. Unfortunately, once I told her it was over, it wasn't difficult for her to guess the dinner party hadn't been a success. But to her credit, she was sympathetic and insisted that her husband share his flask of fine Irish whiskey with me."

"She sounds like a very nice lady." Witherspoon chuckled. "Did your friends stay with you the whole time you were there?"

"The Blodgetts went first; the wind had come up and it was very cold so they left about ten minutes before Harlow and I. We walked together and said good night in front of my house." Chase cocked his head to one side. "But I assure you, Inspector, I had nothing to do with poor Mr. Gilhaney's death. I was looking forward to him coming into the firm. We desperately needed someone with his skills and talent. As a matter of fact, I'm hoping to have a word with Newton about finding a replacement for him."

"I see," Witherspoon murmured. "We've been told several different reasons for Mr. Walker's decision to bring Gilhaney into the company. He said that he was thinking of selling the firm and needed Gilhaney's expert advice on the real worth of the company, but Mr. Bruce implied it was because business had increased substantially and they simply needed more management talent. Would you mind telling us what you were told?"

Surprised, Chase stared at him. "I don't understand, Inspector. There's no reason for Newton to have brought Gilhaney in to give him that sort of advice—the fellow wasn't an expert at assessing assets or receivables or even determining the real worth of current contracts."

"Then why was he brought in?" Barnes asked.

"He was hired to find out where all the money had gone," Chase replied. "That's why Newton wanted him to examine the ledgers from the past ten years."

"She carries the gun everywhere she goes." Joy Kemp, the Holter housemaid, took a quick sip of her tea and then stared curiously at Phyllis. "How'd you know she had one?"

She was a pretty young woman with brown eyes, a wide mouth that smiled easily, porcelain skin, and light brown hair worn in a loose coil at the back of her neck.

Phyllis had trailed the housemaid and the elderly Mrs. Holter from their home to the train station. She'd waited until the maid had put her charge on the train and then followed her. It hadn't taken much effort to fall into conversation with the girl and from there into a café. "I have my sources. I told you, I work for a private detective and Miss Holter's name has come up as a possible witness in a very serious crime."

"You're not answerin' my question." Joy grinned. "Come on, then, I've played along nicely. What kind of crime is it, then?"

"Murder." Phyllis decided there wouldn't be any harm in sticking as close to the truth as possible. "Miss Holter isn't as clever as she thinks she is—she's been seen waving her gun about."

"I don't doubt that, she's quite a stupid woman." Joy sighed. "Who did she kill?"

"I didn't say she'd killed anyone." Phyllis reached for her teacup. "Why? Do you think she'd capable of such a thing?"

"Of course she is—that woman doesn't have a heart. She's a nasty, mean-spirited, vindictive cow. She looks down on the rest of us like we were bugs. I should have left that house a long time ago. Maybe if she's killed someone and arrested, I can go."

"Why do you have to wait till she's arrested?" Phyllis couldn't believe the turn this conversation had taken.

"Because then old Mrs. Holter will have to go live with her sister." She laughed. "The only reason she keeps the house here is because her sister and Miss Holter can't stand each other. Once Mrs. Holter is safe there, I can scarper. The only reason I stay is because I'm scared of what would happen to her if I go. The old woman's been good to me and I'll not leave her with that horrid excuse for a daughter. Do you know, I once saw her slap Mrs. Holter—smacked her right across the face—and then told me if I mentioned it to the neighbors, she'd sack me. I kept my mouth shut because even if I'd said something, no one can do anything about it, not if Mrs. Holter refuses to leave."

Shocked, Phyllis stared at the housemaid. But before she could say anything, the girl kept on talking. "Look, you think I'm hangin' about the streets here for the fun of it, but I'm here because Ann Holter drinks herself silly on the two days of the week her mum's gone and she's a mean drunk with a gun. Oh, why am I tellin' you all this? I guess it's because you've a nice face and I get so lonesome and bored hangin' about waiting to get Mrs. Holter off the ruddy train when she comes home."

"But isn't she mean when you and Mrs. Holter get home?" Phyllis blurted out. In truth, she was so stunned she could barely think of anything to ask.

Joy shook her head. "She's passed out. By then she's had a whole bottle of wine and she's dead drunk and snoring in her bed."

"There's a gentleman to see you, sir," Constable Griffiths, who was on duty behind the counter, said when Witherspoon and Barnes stepped into the station. "I've put him in the duty inspector's office."

"Who is he?"

"He's from Manchester, sir, and he says he's a solicitor."

They hurried past him and into the corridor that led to the offices and the cells. Witherspoon got there first, flung open the door, and stepped inside. A short, burly man with a handlebar mustache and wearing a dark blue suit stood up as they entered.

"Good afternoon," he said. "Are you Inspector Gerald Witherspoon?"

"I am"—he nodded toward the constable—"and this is Constable Barnes. Who might you be, sir?" He went around the man to the duty desk and sat down. Barnes closed the door and leaned against it.

"I'm Barnabas Smalling; I'm from Manchester. I'm a partner at Smalling and Truelove. I came as soon as the Manchester police contacted me. I'm here about Christopher Gilhaney."

"Were you his solicitor?" Witherspoon asked.

"I was, and until his estate is settled, I still am." He sank back into the chair, his expression confused. "I don't understand any of this, Inspector. Why wasn't I notified of his death?"

"We only just found your name in the late Mr. Gilhaney's personal property." Witherspoon glanced at Barnes, who was tight-lipped with anger. The inspector felt just as furious but was determined not to let his fury show. Once this case was over, he was going to speak to Chief Superintendent Barrows. Inspector Nivens hadn't just made a mess of the case—his failure to go through the deceased's effects to find out who should have been notified of the death was dereliction of duty, plain and simple.

"That's hardly an excuse, Inspector. From what I understand, my client was murdered six weeks ago. Is that correct?"

"That's right. I'm surprised it wasn't in the Manchester newspapers. He was a well-known local businessman."

"It probably was, Inspector." He sighed and rubbed his

hand over his face. "But it was six weeks ago and I only recently returned from the continent. However, had the firm been notified, I'd have come back immediately. But that is neither here nor there. Where is Mr. Gilhaney buried?"

Witherspoon gaped at him. "Where is he buried?"

"That's right." Smalling leaned down and picked up a briefcase. He propped it between his knee and the edge of the duty desk. Opening it, he yanked out a set of bound papers and waved them at the inspector. "According to Mr. Gilhaney's will, upon his death, he was to be buried at the Fulham Palace Road Cemetery. He wished to be buried beside a young lady named Polly Wakeman. When he had Miss Wakeman's body moved from a pauper's grave to the cemetery, he made arrangements to spend eternity alongside her."

"I'm not sure where he's buried," Witherspoon admitted. "I'll make inquiries. You do realize if he's already in the ground—"

Smalling interrupted. "He'll have to be exhumed and reburied. Don't concern yourself, Inspector. I'm aware of what needs to be done. I've done it before. As I said, Miss Wakeman's remains were not only exhumed and moved, but rehoused, as it were, in a very nice casket. So if you'll just find out where Mr. Gilhaney is currently resting, I'll start the necessary steps to get him moved."

Barnes shoved away from the door. "I take it Mr. Gilhaney had a will?"

"Of course." Smalling smiled slightly as he looked at the constable. He flattened the bundle of papers on his lap and began to leaf through the pages. "He was a very wealthy man."

"Was he married?" The constable didn't think it likely,

but if there was a wife who didn't even know he was dead, that would be very bad indeed.

"No, he was not."

"Did he have any other relatives?" Witherspoon asked.

"He had some distant cousins, but they aren't his heirs. He didn't know them and left them nothing. Mr. Gilhaney did not believe blood was thicker than water." Smalling had reached the last few pages and was skim-reading them.

"Who exactly are his heirs?" the inspector asked. "You understand, the man was murdered and knowing who benefited from his death could have a bearing on our investigation."

"I understand, Inspector, and as he's dead, I've no objection to telling you—ah, here we are," he said. "His estate is worth approximately sixty thousand pounds."

"That's a lot of money for an accountant," Barnes muttered.

"He was a smart man, Constable, and he lived simply and invested wisely. He's left ten thousand pounds to be divided amongst three of his old friends from the Fulham Workhouse. The other fifty thousand has been split as follows: Twenty-five thousand pounds to be placed into a scholarship fund in the name of Polly Wakeman; according to Mr. Gilhaney, she was a very talented artist herself. The scholarship is to be administered by the trustees of the Fulham Workhouse and given to young persons residing in the workhouse and showing talent in painting or sculpture." He ran his finger farther down the page. "Ah, here it is, the final twenty-five thousand pounds is left to Mrs. Theodore Bruce, nee Walker, currently residing in the Royal Borough of Kensington and Chelsea, London."

"Mrs. Theodore Bruce," Barnes repeated. He looked at the inspector. "Now, that's going to put the cat amongst the pigeons. Why on earth would Christopher Gilhaney leave Hazel Bruce twenty-five thousand quid?"

CHAPTER 10

"I'm here, Mrs. Jeffries," Wiggins called as he raced down the corridor to the kitchen. Fred, who was getting a bit deaf, raised his head from his spot by the cooker and started to get up as the footman sped into the room. He stopped and knelt by the dog. "Stay still, old boy. I'll take you out later." Fred thumped his tail and curled back onto his rug. "Sorry to be late, but I was havin' a bit of luck." He leapt up, shedding his jacket as he raced to the coat tree, and then took his seat.

"We've only just started, lad." Mrs. Goodge cut a huge hunk of Victoria sponge cake, plopped it onto a plate, and put it next to the tea she'd just poured for him.

"Ta, Mrs. Goodge. Did I interrupt?"

"Nope, I'd only said a couple of words," Luty said. "But like I was sayin', I went back to one of my sources and got an earful. I shoulda spent more time listening the other day when

I saw him." She'd gone to see Nelson Biddlington again, and this time, she'd not been in a hurry to leave. "Seems that Newton Walker came out of retirement a year or so ago because he was worried about what was happenin' to all the money. The company is very successful, they're building things left and right, have been for years, but somehow, there never seems to be as much profit as there should be. There's no sign someone was embezzling or stealing—there just doesn't seem to be as much money as there should be."

"Then someone must be doin' one of those things," Smythe pointed out. "Either that, or Walker overestimates how much money should be coming into his coffers."

"That's what I think, and apparently, it's worse now that the company has gone public. That's why Newton hired Gilhaney—he wanted someone who was really good to have a look at the books. But I think we'd all pretty much guessed that already. That's all I heard."

"Everything is useful information, Luty." Mrs. Jeffries glanced at Phyllis, who was staring down at her tea with a puzzled expression on her face. "Is everything alright, Phyllis?"

She looked up and saw everyone staring at her. "I'm fine, it's just I'm trying to understand what I heard today. It's somewhat shocking and I'm not sure what to believe." She told them about her encounter with Joy Kemp. When she finished, she shook her head in disbelief. "The question is, the maid claims she's staying on at the Holter house because she's afraid of what Ann Holter might do to her own mother. Which means she's sure the woman is capable of violence."

"But is she tellin' the truth?" Smythe asked. "Or is she bein' a bit dramatic. Wasn't it old Mrs. Holter that tossed Polly Wakeman in the street?"

"That's quite common, Smythe," Mrs. Goodge said. "But it doesn't mean that it was Mrs. Holter that made the decision. It was an old-fashioned household so it was probably Mr. Holter that made his wife sack the poor girl."

"Joy said that Mrs. Holter complains to her that her daughter is just like her father," Phyllis added. "Oh, I forgot to mention the most important thing—she carries her gun when she goes out, especially at night. So she had it with her the night Gilhaney was murdered. That's all I have."

Hatchet grinned at Phyllis. "My day was almost as interesting as yours. I had a nice chat with my friends and I found out why Miss Holter has a wedding dress but no husband." He repeated what he'd learned from the Manleys and then sat back with a satisfied smile on his face.

"Your friends didn't know for certain that it was Gilhaney who convinced the fiancé not to go through with the wedding?" Mrs. Jeffries poured herself another cup of tea.

"They did not, but one of them made a very compelling argument that it must have been him and I'm inclined to agree with that assessment. That's the extent of my information."

"I'll have a go next," Betsy offered. "I didn't find out much, but it wasn't for lack of trying. I tried to find someone from the Webster house to chat with, but there was no one about, so when it got close to one o'clock, I went back to the Bruce home."

"Findin' another housemaid." Smythe poked her in the arm.

"Yes, and I'm glad I did," Betsy retorted. "This one was Molly, the girl that Newton Walker is paying to spy on Ted Bruce. She didn't have much to tell, but she did say that Hazel Bruce has a revolver—"

Wiggins interrupted. "Cor blimey, does every woman in London carry one of them things? What's this world comin' to?"

"It's no worse than it's ever been," Ruth said. "But remember, those Ripper murders frightened everyone, most especially women."

"But guns are dangerous."

"I know how to handle mine," Luty declared.

"And many upper-class women know how to handle them as well. Hunting is done by both sexes and shooting parties are a part and parcel of their world." Ruth shot Betsy a quick, apologetic smile. "Sorry, do go on."

"There's not much more to tell."

"How did the maid know Hazel Bruce owned one?" Luty demanded. "I've got my Peacemaker, but I don't go showin' it to every Tom, Dick, and Harry." She waved her hand around the table. "All of you know about it because of what we do, and some of my help knows about it, but most of 'em don't."

"She claims she saw it." Betsy was reluctant to admit she simply wasn't sure Molly hadn't been lying her head off. The truth was, she'd had to bribe the girl to get anything out of her and it might have been the sight of the sovereign rather than real facts that had loosened her tongue. On the other hand, this was a murder and if she had doubts about the truth of what she'd been told, she had to pass her misgivings along. "But I'm not sure I believed her."

"Why not?" Mrs. Jeffries asked.

"I'm not certain, but I had a feeling about her. There was something sly in her manner," Betsy admitted. "And supposedly, she'd seen the gun weeks ago when Mr. Bruce put it back in his wife's vanity after cleaning it. The only other thing she said was that Mr. Bruce has a 'hidey-hole' in his office that no one knows about. He had it put into the floor under his desk chair when his wife was on one of her trips to Manchester and he did it when all the servants were out of the house."

"Then how did Molly find out?" Phyllis asked.

"When Bruce gave everyone the day off, she suspected he was up to something." Betsy laughed. "She crept back into the house and saw the workman tearing up the floorboards. That's it for me." She smiled at her husband. "What about you? Find out anything?"

Smythe narrowed his eyes. "Not as yet, but I'm seein' my source tomorrow mornin'." Blimpey should have something useful by then, he told himself.

"I've not much." Wiggins shot the cook a quick, intense glance. "But it wasn't because I was larkin' about. I tried my best, but sometimes ya just can't find anyone who'll give you the time of day."

She patted his arm. "I know. Go on, then, tell us what you did find out."

"I finally got an accounts clerk from Walker's to talk to me." Wiggins didn't add he'd had to bribe the lad by buying him a pint and paying for his lunch. "The only thing he had to say was that he caught a tongue-lashing when Newton Walker came into the office the morning after Gilhaney's death. Mind you, none of them knew he was dead at that point, but he said Walker came stompin' out of Gilhaney's office, demandin' to know why the ledgers and financial documents weren't on Gilhaney's desk."

"And why weren't they?" Mrs. Jeffries asked.

"Because Mr. Chase hadn't told anyone to have them at the ready," Wiggins explained. "About that time, Mr. Chase and Mr. Bruce arrived and there was a nasty row about who was supposed to have told the clerks to get them ready."

"So who was supposed to have told them?" Mrs. Jeffries really didn't care; it seemed like a silly argument. People made excuses when something hadn't been done and no one wanted to shoulder the blame.

"Mr. Chase, but he insisted Ted Bruce had said he'd do it." He scooped the last bite of sponge onto his fork. "That's all I've got."

"I've something." Ruth had deliberately waited till the others were finished. She didn't like being the center of attention, but she wanted to make certain all of them listened to what she had to say. She knew it was important. "Hazel Bruce told the inspector that she'd met Christopher Gilhaney socially while visiting friends in Manchester. But that's not true. At least, that's not what my source told me."

Ruth had spent the entire day racing around London in her carriage and calling upon everyone that loved to gossip. She'd even gone back to the Wells mansion and asked Octavia, who still had laryngitis, to tell her what she knew. Luckily, Octavia was a very fast scribbler and the two of them had communicated by note. Little by little, Ruth pieced together what she learned and realized there was only one conclusion. "Hazel Bruce and Gilhaney were lovers. They'd carried on an affair for several years."

"Is that why she kept goin' back to Manchester?" Wiggins asked.

"I expect so," Ruth replied. "Apparently, they were very serious about one another and one of my sources told me

Gilhaney was the reason Hazel Bruce wanted a divorce. But her father refused to help her and so she broke it off with him."

"Why? Was her husband gettin' wise to her?" Luty suggested.

Ruth shook her head. "No, my source says that Gilhaney wasn't Hazel's first liaison and that Ted Bruce has looked the other way for years while his wife does what she wants."

"Maybe she didn't want her father findin' out," Mrs. Goodge muttered.

"But why would Gilhaney be with her?" Wiggins' forehead wrinkled in thought. "He thought Mrs. Bruce's father and husband had a hand in Polly Wakeman's death. So why would he have anything to do with the woman?"

"'E might not have known who she was when he approached her," Smythe said. "If they met socially and he didn't know of her connection to Newton Walker or Theodore Bruce, he might 'ave fallen for 'er before he understood how she was related to that lot."

"Or maybe he didn't hold her responsible," Phyllis suggested. "She wasn't married when the roof collapsed, and as Walker's daughter, she had nothing to do with his business."

"We can talk about this till the cows come home," Luty interjected. "But it seems to me the one with the real motive here is Florence Bruce. If Mrs. Bruce got a divorce, Florence would be the one with the most to lose. We already know her brother sold the Bruce family home out from under her. He'd do alright if Hazel tossed him out on his ear, but Florence wouldn't have a roof over her head."

Witherspoon smiled as he handed Mrs. Jeffries his bowler. "I think we're making real progress today, Mrs. Jeffries.

Let's have our drink and I'll tell you all about it." He started down the hall and then stopped at the open door to the drawing room. "Oh, my goodness, this is lovely."

Mrs. Jeffries joined him by the door. "Thank you, sir. Mr. Cutler brought the evergreens this afternoon. He's bringing the tree on the twenty-fourth." She pointed to a bare spot by the fireplace. "I've taken that big chair out so we can put the tree there."

"It looks so festive." He grinned. "It's perfect, Mrs. Jeffries. You've done a fine job."

Pine boughs decorated with bright red velvet ribbons lay along the top of the fireplace mantel and at each end stood an elaborate silver candelabra holding rose-scented white candles. In the middle of the mantelpiece was a brilliant china crèche with the holy family, manger, shepherds, angels, and a surprisingly large number of sheep. Mrs. Jeffries had found it in the attic, cleaned it, and brought it down for their enjoyment. Woven wreaths were hanging in the windows and holly branches with their crimson seeds were arranged in tall vases and placed strategically around the big room. The usual cotton table runners had been replaced with festive green satin ones and gold satin streamers had been hung along the curtain rails.

"Thank you, sir. Regardless of what happens with the case, we're going to enjoy our Christmas together."

"Don't despair, Mrs. Jeffries. I've a feeling we'll do more than just have our Christmas together. Come along and let me tell you about my day."

They went to his study and she poured their sherry while he relaxed into his chair.

"Thank you, Mrs. Jeffries." He took his drink. "It's been

the most extraordinary day. To begin with we had another chat with Leon Webster. I must say he didn't look pleased to see us when we arrived." He told her about their interview. "Fortunately for Webster, the local constables were aware of the gambling house so we were able to confirm his whereabouts quickly. The, ah, proprietor verified that Webster arrived on Bonfire Night around eight forty-five, which is only ten minutes or so after he left the Chase home."

"And you said that Mr. Chase claimed Gilhaney and Newton Walker left his house at eight forty-seven, so that means Webster couldn't have been in Kilbane Mews committing the murder." She took a sip of sherry. "Is this gambling person reliable? If Webster's a regular customer, he might lie to give the man an alibi."

"We thought of that," Witherspoon replied. "But the local constable assured us that despite running a gambling den, the owner isn't one to lie to the police. After we left Webster's Metals, we went to Walker and Company." He repeated the interview he'd had with Gordon Chase.

When he'd finished, a question popped into her mind and she blurted it out without thinking. "Mr. Chase didn't happen to mention which of them was supposed to have instructed the clerks to bring the records down, did he?"

Witherspoon looked surprised by the question. "No, actually, he didn't."

"It's not important, sir, it's just something that passed through my mind and landed on my tongue." She wracked her brain, trying to think of ways to hint about the information the household had learned over the day. "I was just surprised that something Mr. Walker had been so adamant about hadn't been done." Again, she had no clue where that comment had come from and it certainly wasn't moving the inspector along the path she wished him to take. She tried to think of a comment that would get him looking at Ann Holter again. If Phyllis' source was to be trusted, Ann Holter was both vindictive and capable of murder. What's more, from what Hatchet had told them, she blamed the dead man for ruining her life. "I take it you've sent constables to speak with Mr. Harlow and the Blodgetts."

"Yes, and they were able to get back to us before we left the station today. Mr. Harlow confirmed that he and Gordon Chase had walked back to their homes together and Mrs. Blodgett verified the time Chase arrived at the river."

"So he's no longer a suspect?"

"Not really. Besides, he had no known past connected with Gilhaney."

"That means he had no motive that you could find. But what about the discrepancy between what Newton Walker told you and what you've heard from other, reliable sources about the company?"

He frowned over the rim of his glass. "I'm not sure I know what you mean."

She had to tread carefully here because she didn't want to divulge anything that the household knew but which Barnes hadn't been able to pass along to the inspector. So she chose her words carefully, but before she answered him, he said, "Oh, I see what you mean. Walker said he'd hired Gilhaney for advice about selling the company, but, of course, that was only part of the reason he'd brought the man on board, so to speak. Gilhaney was also going to sort out the finances." He tapped his chin. "I can't recall who said it, but I know someone said the company wasn't making the sort of profits it should be making. What's more, apparently, that's been happening for quite a long time. But I expect that is true of most companies, isn't it?"

She had no idea. But before she could make another comment, he continued. "I've not told you the most interesting thing that happened today. When we got to the station, Gilhaney's solicitor was there."

"Good gracious, sir, was it the one from Manchester, the firm you telegraphed?"

She stopped fretting over what to say next and just listened.

"He was and he was quite annoyed that he hadn't been notified of Gilhaney's death." Witherspoon grimaced. "I'm not one to complain about a fellow officer, but when this case is finished, I'm afraid I'm going to have to speak to Chief Superintendent Barrows."

She stared at him hopefully. "About Inspector Nivens?"

"Yes." He put his glass on the table next to him, taking care not to touch the prickly holly leaf. "If Nivens had gone through Gilhaney's personal effects in a timely manner, he'd have found his solicitor. As I said, Mr. Smalling was very upset when we saw him." He told her about their encounter with the solicitor.

She interrupted at one point. "He's going to have Gilhaney reburied? Gracious, sir, can you do that?"

"One can; it's difficult, but as Gilhaney's wishes weren't carried out in the first place and he has no family to object, Mr. Smalling should be able to do it. Apparently, he knows all about the process, as he had Polly Wakeman's body moved from a pauper's grave to the Fulham Palace Road Cemetery some years ago. Gilhaney is going to be buried next to her. But the most astounding information we learned was about Gilhaney's heirs."

"He had a substantial estate?"

"He was very rich. The estate is worth sixty thousand pounds." Witherspoon picked his glass up and drained it. He told her the terms of the will, taking care to mention both the legacies for Gilhaney's old friends and the scholarship fund to be set up in Polly Wakeman's name. "He left the remaining twenty-five thousand pounds to one of our suspects and, for the life of me, I can't think why."

"Who was it, sir?" But she had a feeling she already knew the answer.

"Hazel Bruce," Witherspoon announced. "What's more, Smalling said that Mrs. Bruce was fully aware she was one of Gilhaney's principal heirs."

"Did Gilhaney tell her he was leaving her a fortune?" Mrs. Jeffries asked.

"No, Smalling let it slip when he'd had too much to drink. It happened in Manchester. She's actually the reason Gilhaney hired him to handle his legal affairs. She recommended him." He ran his finger around the rim of his glass. "Last October, they were at a dinner party at her friend's home and she made some . . ." His voice trailed off for a moment. "Smalling didn't tell us exactly what she said, but she made some very disparaging remarks about Gilhaney. He took offense on his client's behalf and blurted out that she ought to watch her tongue, that he was leaving her twenty-five thousand pounds."

Once again, Mrs. Jeffries found herself in the kitchen late at night. The house was locked up and she was at the kitchen table. But tonight she wasn't celebrating with a glass of brandy; she was thinking. The inspector had made a clear and compelling argument for Hazel Bruce as the chief suspect and for the most part she agreed with him.

As a matter of fact, she had even more evidence that pointed to Mrs. Bruce as the killer. The inspector didn't know what they had found out about the woman; he didn't know that she loathed her husband and had a history of taking lovers; he didn't know that Gilhaney had been one of her lovers nor that she had a gun. The question now became, how to make certain the inspector learned all of this as quickly as possible so that their Christmas plans weren't ruined?

She stared off into space, trying to come up with solutions to this problem. Some of it could be fed to him through Constable Barnes. He could say that an informant had come forward and told him about the weapon. Yes, that could easily work—she nodded as the idea took form in her mind. And guns weren't sold on every street corner, A revolver was expensive and only bought by those with plenty of money.

But what about the fact that she and Gilhaney had been lovers—how could Barnes have learned about it? She thought for a long time, going over each and every detail that she could recall in an attempt to find that little something that would explain the constable stumbling across that tidbit of information.

She sat for another half hour, going over everything she could remember, before she gave up and went up to bed.

Pulling back the bedclothes, she got under the covers, closed her eyes, and fell asleep. But she slept fitfully, waking a half dozen times as one thought after another took residence in her mind and refused to leave.

By the time she got up the next morning, she doubted

that Hazel Bruce had killed anyone. If she was going to commit murder, the most likely victim would have been her husband, but he was still alive and well. Mrs. Jeffries hurried into the kitchen and put the kettle on to boil.

"You're up early." Mrs. Goodge yawned and then looked down as Samson butted her with his big, wide head. "Hold on, lovey, I've got to get your scraps out of the wet larder."

"I'll make the tea," Mrs. Jeffries offered as the cook and the cat shuffled down the hall.

Five minutes later, Samson was hunched over his food bowl and the two women were at the table with their hands wrapped around their mugs of tea. "You've figured it out, haven't you, Hepzibah."

"I'm not sure," she admitted. She looked at the carriage clock. "And we're running out of time. Wiggins will be up in a few minutes to light the fires and heat the house and I don't want to be interrupted." She repeated what the inspector had told her. "At first, I agreed with him, but I was awakened a dozen times last night and every time, another idea or another fact came to mind and now it seems to me that the evidence is pointing to someone else."

"What are we to do, then?" Mrs. Goodge looked worried. "Let me speak plainly, Hepzibah. I'm more likely to trust your judgment than I am the inspector's, though I mean him no disrespect. But if he has evidence of her guilt, he's going to want to make an arrest soon, possibly even today."

"He mustn't. I'm sure she's innocent." Mrs. Jeffries rapped her fingertips against the table as she tried to think of what could be done. "Perhaps Constable Barnes—"

Mrs. Goodge cut her off. "No, don't even think it; the constable is a good policeman, but unless you have enough evidence to convince him you're right and our inspector is wrong, he'll not try and stop an arrest. Do you have enough evidence?"

She closed her eyes for a brief moment and thought of all the bits and pieces that had played havoc with her rest. She knew she was right and now she had to come up with a way to prove it. "Not yet, but I'm going to try and find it."

When Barnes arrived, the two women passed along their information and listened as he provided a few more details the inspector had missed.

"Do you think you're getting to the end of this one, Constable?" Mrs. Goodge asked innocently as he finished his tea.

He put the cup down, shoved his chair back, and rose to his feet. "Indeed I do. I've a feeling we'll all be able to have our Christmas plans after all."

"Are you that close to making an arrest?" Mrs. Jeffries got up as well.

"I am now." He grinned. "Now that your lot has discovered Mrs. Bruce owns a gun, we've an excellent reason to interview her and her servants again."

"Are you going there this morning?" Mrs. Jeffries needed to know how much time, if any, she had.

"We'll be going to the station first to read the reports. The inspector sent several constables out yesterday evening to look for witnesses. If Mrs. Bruce left her home after she claimed to be retiring, someone might have seen her. Then we'll be going to Scotland Yard—there's a meeting the inspector must attend—and after that, we'll pay a call at the Bruce home."

"But how could she have gone out once she got home? Everyone reported the woman was so sleepy she could barely stay awake at the dinner party," Mrs. Goodge argued.

"She was faking." Barnes started for the back stairs. "If the inspector's theory is correct, that was the excuse she used to get away from the Chase house early. Once there, she could have slipped out a door or even a downstairs window and gone after Gilhaney." He waved and disappeared up the stairs.

Betsy and Smythe were the first to arrive for the morning meeting. Betsy put Amanda down and the toddler immediately rushed to Mrs. Goodge and tugged on her skirt.

"Just a minute, lovey, let me put this dough to rise and then we'll have a nice cuddle."

"Luty and Hatchet were pullin' up at the back gate," Smythe said as he kept a watchful eye on his daughter.

"Let's hope everyone gets here quickly." Mrs. Jeffries took her seat. "We've much to do today and everyone might have to get out and about."

"You've figured it out." Betsy pivoted from her chair to the worktable and pulled Amanda into her arms so the cook could finish her task. "Oh, thank goodness, I really wanted to go to Paris. Let's start as soon as everyone gets here."

Mrs. Goodge covered the dough with a clean cloth and put the bowl by the cooker. She took her seat and held out her arms. "Give me my darling," she demanded, "and be quick about it. The back door is opening and it might be Luty."

It was Ruth, but Luty and Hatchet were right behind her. Mrs. Jeffries started before they even had their tea poured.

She told them everything she'd learned from the inspector, including the fact that he was sure Hazel Bruce was the killer. "But I think he might be wrong," she finished.

"Why?" Betsy stared at her, curious. "It sounds like she's the only one with a real motive for wanting Gilhaney dead. She's going to inherit a huge amount of money."

"She already has money," Mrs. Goodge pointed out. "And what's more, I think she loved him and he loved her."

"I thought his true love was Polly Wakeman." Phyllis looked disappointed in the dead man.

"You can love more than one person in a lifetime," Ruth said. "I loved my husband very much, but I also care deeply for Gerald." She turned her attention to Mrs. Jeffries. "Do you think Gerald is going to arrest her today?"

"I think it's possible, but I'm not sure. What I'm more concerned about is that once the inspector questions her again, the real killer will get away."

"You know who did it?" Ruth pressed.

"I think so, but it's going to be difficult to prove."

"What do you want us to do?" Phyllis asked.

Mrs. Jeffries took a deep breath and thought for a moment. In her mind, it was very clear, but collecting the sort of evidence needed to make an arrest was another kettle of fish altogether. "I want you to go back to the Chase home and speak to one of the servants who was serving on the night of the murder. I need to know if anyone was in the dining room alone while the dinner was being served. At one point in the evening, Gordon Chase made everyone go outside to see the fireworks. We need to know who, if anyone, stayed inside for more than a moment or two after the others had gone out."

"I can go and have a word with Peggy," Wiggins offered. "She was servin' that night."

"I've another task for you," Mrs. Jeffries replied.

Phyllis looked doubtful. "I'll do my best, Mrs. Jeffries, but that's going to be difficult. It was weeks ago and it's not the sort of thing you'd remember unless you had a reason to remember it."

"What about me?" Betsy asked.

"Go and see Molly. Find out what else she knows about Ted Bruce's 'hidey-hole.' From what you've said, she sounds a very greedy person, so if you need to, cross her palm with a bit of silver."

Betsy nodded. That method had worked before. "Molly does know more than she told me; people like her always hold something back."

"What do ya mean?" Wiggins looked confused. "How do ya know?"

"Because she's already discovered that snoopin' is a good way to earn money," Phyllis told him. "And people like that are always on the lookout to get as much as they can. I'll wager she watches both the Bruces and holds a bit back so she has something to tell old Mr. Walker."

"The biggest problem will be getting to her. She's just had her afternoon out and won't get another till next week. I'll have to get into the Bruce house."

"Be careful," Smythe warned. "I don't fancy my wife gettin' arrested for trespassin'."

"Not to worry, I'll come up with something." Betsy patted his hand. "Can Amanda stay here or should I take her home? I'm sure Elinor can watch her for me."

"Leave her here," Mrs. Goodge said. "Between the two of us, she'll do just fine."

"What can I do, Mrs. Jeffries?" Hatchet asked.

"Ann Holter took a hansom home the night Gilhaney was killed." Mrs. Jeffries hesitated. "I need to know if the cab took her straight home or if it stopped anywhere. Also, we need to find out if she left her home once she got there."

Hatchet raised an eyebrow. "I can easily get cabdrivers to talk; my problem is the same as Miss Phyllis', getting them to remember her. It can't be helped, I suppose. Let's just hope Miss Holter was memorably obnoxious that night."

"I'd like to do something as well," Ruth offered.

"Can you find out how much laudanum it would take to make someone sleepy but not unconscious and how long it would take before the person felt the effects of the drug?"

Ruth considered it. "I'm not sure—would a doctor know this?"

"A doctor would claim to know this, but unless he dosed himself with it on a daily basis, he'd tell you what he read in a medical book and we need to know what happens in reality. I'd rather you find out from someone who takes laudanum," Mrs. Jeffries explained. "Do you know of any such person and would they tell you?"

"I do and they would." Ruth grinned. "I don't have to tell you who I speak to, do I? I shouldn't like to violate their privacy and, well, they're quite well known in some social circles."

"No, we don't need to know their identity."

"Is there somethin' in particular ya need me to do?" Smythe looked at the clock. "Because I'm pretty certain my source will 'ave somethin' useful to tell me this mornin'." He wanted to get to Blimpey before the Dirty Duck opened for business and he had to queue up to speak to him.

"I suspect your source is important." Mrs. Jeffries knew whom he meant. "But do try to get back as quickly as possible."

Smythe squeezed Betsy's hand, pushed back his chair, and stood up. He stopped long enough to drop a quick kiss on Amanda's curls before disappearing down the hall.

"What do ya want me to do?" Wiggins asked.

"Go and talk to your source at Walker's." She told him what she needed him to find out. She gave him his instructions.

"That doesn't sound 'ard. Hodges likes to chat. But I probably can't get to 'im before lunch. So I'll be gone till then—is that okay or is there something else you need me to do?"

"No, lunchtime will do, but do get back as early as possible."

"Why?" Luty studied her. "You think somethin' is goin' to happen today?"

Mrs. Jeffries wasn't one to believe in silly nonsense like messages from the spirit world, but she did believe in intuition, though if she were taxed with having to explain the difference between the two of them, she'd be hard-pressed to do so. "I think it's possible. But it could just be my imagination running away with me."

"Then let's get out on the 'unt," Wiggins said.

Betsy eyed the two godmothers as she headed for the coat tree. "Don't you spoil her, now. She's not to have too many sweet biscuits, and make her take a nap."

"Stop fretting, I'll not let her have too many biscuits," Mrs. Goodge promised.

"She'll have a nap after we have our playtime together."

Luty had her fingers crossed behind her back. "So don't you worry about her, she'll be just fine with us."

Blimpey was drinking a tea and reading the newspaper when Smythe arrived.

"You want a cuppa?" Blimpey waved his mug in the air.

"Just 'ad one." He sat down across from him. "What 'ave you got for me?"

Blimpey chuckled and folded the newspaper and laid it on the table. "I've 'eard quite a bit—some of it you lot probably already know. But as I don't know what you know, I'll tell ya everything. To begin with, Newton Walker doesn't trust his son-in-law, Ted Bruce. Mind you, this is after givin' Bruce a free hand in running his business for more than fifteen years."

"We did know about that bit."

"Did ya know that Walker actually retired three years ago, but after Bruce took the company public, he went back to work a year ago and brought in Gordon Chase as well?"

Smythe thought for a moment. "We knew Walker had retired. Why? What have you found out?"

"Why?" Blimpey laughed. "Because goin' public was supposed to increase the profits, but instead, things got worse."

"We heard that, too. It looks like someone is embezzlin' and that's the real reason Walker hired Gilhaney."

"Probably, and my guess is that Walker thinks the guilty party is Ted Bruce. But that's not the important thing. One of my sources at Thomas Cook's said that this same Mr. Bruce has booked a one-way passage on the *Tartar Prince*. She's sailing from Southampton at midnight tonight."

"Where's she bound?" Smythe got to his feet.

"South America—he bought a ticket to Buenos Aires. He also bought a first-class ticket on the London and Southwestern Railway for the five o'clock from Waterloo. That should get him to Southampton in plenty of time."

"Amanda's just had her lunch. I've put her in my room for a nap," Mrs. Goodge explained to Smythe as she came out of her quarters by the back stairs. "Betsy isn't back, nor is Wiggins. But the others are."

"We can't wait for them." He hurried into the kitchen. "We've got to 'ave our meeting now. Something's going to happen today; one of our suspects is makin' a run for it."

Luty and Hatchet, who'd just come in from getting some fresh air in the communal garden, hurried to the table. Phyllis dropped the last of the dirty silverware into the soapy water in the sink and raced toward her seat. Ruth, who'd just taken off her cloak, shoved it onto the coat tree.

Mrs. Jeffries shoved the stack of household bills into the sideboard as everyone took their spot. "What's happened?"

"I don't know who you think our killer is, but Theodore Bruce is leavin' the country. He's takin' the five o'clock train from Waterloo to Southampton and sailing for South America. He booked a single, one-way passage, so he's not takin' the missus."

"Oh dear, I was afraid something like this would happen," Mrs. Jeffries said. "But he's not leaving until five o'clock? Good, that buys us a bit of time."

"I suppose our information has now been rendered irrelevant," Hatchet said. "Pity, really. I was successful."

"It's not irrelevant," Mrs. Jeffries replied. "I need as many facts as possible to come up with a way to get the inspector to see that it isn't Mrs. Bruce who is the killer, it's Ted Bruce. You found out Ann Holter's movements?"

"Indeed, she was obnoxious, but that isn't why the hansom driver remembered her," Hatchet said. "She got into the cab in front of the Chase home and then insisted the driver stop at a wine merchant's, a shop named Maywood's. She paid him extra to go inside and buy her a bottle of a cheap brand of pinot noir, which she then opened herself with a corkscrew she had on her person. Then she had him drive her around Hyde Park several times while she drank it. He helped her into her house at half past ten."

"No wonder he remembered her," Phyllis muttered.

"By then she'd have been too drunk to kill Gilhaney," Mrs. Jeffries said. "I was fairly sure she hadn't done it, but we have to be certain. Other than Ted Bruce she was the only one I couldn't eliminate until now." She looked at Phyllis. "Any luck?"

Phyllis gave a negative shake of her head. "No, I'm sorry. I did manage to speak to Peggy, but she was in the kitchen when Mr. Chase took the guests outside to watch the fireworks. She had no idea if anyone lingered in the dining room."

"Don't be sorry, I didn't have much hope in finding out that tidbit." Mrs. Jeffries smiled reassuringly and then glanced at Ruth. "Did you speak with your friend?"

"She was quite surprised by the question, but willing to answer. According to her, a person who hadn't taken laudanum previously could be made sleepy with a very small amount, no more than a half ounce. More than that and they'd drop off very, very quickly. I'm assuming from the task you gave Phyllis that you think the laudanum was administered to someone at the dinner party?"

"Ted Bruce slipped it into his wife's wine." Mrs. Jeffries was sure of it now. "He didn't want her knowing when he came home that night."

"But they had separate rooms," Luty pointed out.

"But they watched each other all the time, remember. That night was the one time he wanted her sound asleep. He didn't want her snooping around watching what he was doing, especially if he was putting Gilhaney's jewels and brass knuckles into his 'hidey-hole.'"

They heard the back door open and everyone turned as Wiggins came into the room. "Sorry to be so late, but it took ages to get back."

"Did you speak to the clerk?"

"I 'ad to buy the little sod two gins," Wiggins said. "But that loosened 'is tongue. He said that it was Bruce who was supposed to tell 'em about bringin' down the ledgers and such from storage and give them the key as well. But 'e never said a word about it and the clerks couldn't go up on their own, not without the key."

"And when the row between Chase and Bruce was going on, the one where each accused the other of having not done it, he was too intimidated to speak up, right?" Mrs. Jeffries said.

"That's right. He said Bruce is a nasty sort and he didn't want to say anything. He heard Mr. Bruce tellin' Mr. Chase that he'd let the clerks know, that he'd stop on his way out as he was meetin' someone."

Again, they heard the door open and, this time, footsteps running up the corridor. Smythe leapt to his feet as his wife raced into the kitchen. "I'm fine." She stopped and caught her breath. "Sorry to be so long, but I got an earful." She grinned at Mrs. Jeffries. "You were right, Molly talked a blue streak once I'd given her a bob or two. Mrs. Bruce had a visitor this morning and Molly, being the sort she is, made sure she caught his name. It was that Mr. Smalling, Gilhaney's solicitor."

"No doubt he told her more about her legacy," Mrs. Jeffries said.

"But that's not the most important bit," Betsy continued. "Mrs. Bruce knows about her husband's secret compartment under his desk. As soon as the solicitor left, Mrs. Bruce marched into his office and helped herself to whatever he had in there. He keeps it in a big, battered brown briefcase. Molly watched her take it upstairs. She put it in her bedroom and then locked the door."

CHAPTER 11

Betsy's excitement faded as she saw the serious expressions on the faces around the table. "What's wrong, what's happened?"

"Ted Bruce 'as bought a one-way ticket to South America. His ship leaves late tonight," Smythe explained quickly.

"Cor blimey, you think that solicitor tellin' Mrs. Bruce she's inherited a lot of money means that she's tossin' him out?"

"It could." Mrs. Jeffries needed to have a good long think about this development, but knew that wasn't possible now. Events were moving too quickly.

Ruth looked at the housekeeper. "This doesn't sound good."

"No, it doesn't." Mrs. Jeffries rested her elbows on the table and entwined her fingers together. "It's possible she knows what her husband is planning and if she confronts him, it could be very dangerous." She looked at Betsy. "Did Molly have any idea how long Mrs. Bruce has known about the hiding spot?"

"She didn't say and I didn't think to ask," Betsy replied. "What should we do?"

"The inspector and Constable Barnes were going to interview Mrs. Bruce today," Mrs. Jeffries said slowly. "They were going to the station first to read the constables' reports and then to the Yard for a meeting. So perhaps things will work out properly . . . oh, that's ridiculous. They've no idea what Bruce is planning."

"How do we tell them?" Mrs. Goodge got up. "I'm going to make tea, it'll help us think."

"Was Ted Bruce still at the office when you spoke with Hodges?" Mrs. Jeffries glanced at the clock and did some quick calculations.

Wiggins' face creased in thought. "I don't know . . . Wait a minute, he did say something. When he demanded a second gin, I said wasn't he worried about bein' late back and he laughed. He said Mr. Chase wouldn't care and Mr. Bruce was takin' the afternoon off."

"He probably has shopping to do," Hatchet said.

Luty poked him in the arm. "Don't be flippant, this is serious."

"I am serious, madam. Buenos Aires is in the Southern Hemisphere; right now it's summer there. Bruce probably went to buy some clothes."

"We have summer here, you know. Why wouldn't he take his own clothes?"

"He can't risk packing a bag, madam." Hatchet folded his arms over his chest. "Remember, the Bruces watch each other closely. He'd not want his wife to catch him tossing his seersucker suits into a case. Besides, South American summer is warmer than our English ones. Trust me on this, I've been to both Argentina and Chile in January."

"You're right, that's probably why he took the afternoon off," Mrs. Jeffries said. "A quick trip to Oxford Street and then home to grab whatever he has in his hiding spot."

"What do you think it is?" Ruth asked.

"I know what it is," she said. "Money. He's been embezzling from Walker's for years. Small amounts some years, larger ones other years. That's why he murdered Gilhaney." She took a deep breath. "We may have a bit of time. But we've got to get a message to Constable Barnes."

"Well, at least you managed to discover where Mr. Gilhaney was buried," Smalling said. "Now I can get the legal process started and the poor man moved and laid to rest next to Miss Wakeman. When can I take my late client's possessions?"

"Not until after we make an arrest," Witherspoon said. "Some of the items in his strongbox might be used in evidence."

"But that's absurd!" Smalling sprayed spittle as he spoke. "Absurd, I tell you. You've had six weeks to search them properly. They belong to the estate and I want to do a proper appraisal so his property can be sold and disbursed as he wished. I liked Christopher—he wasn't just a client, he was a friend . . ." He broke off as his eyes filled with tears. "And I mourn his loss deeply. I hate the idea of his clothes and his papers being in a stranger's care."

Witherspoon's irritation faded. He knew grief when he saw it. "I'm sorry for your loss, Mr. Smalling. Losing a friend is very hard."

"Thank you." Smalling brought himself under control.

"Right, then. I've much to do. Luckily, I got one task off my plate. I saw Mrs. Bruce and got the documents signed so her legacy could be properly disbursed. It's amazing how much paperwork there is even in a straightforward inheritance."

Barnes looked at the inspector. "That was quick," Witherspoon finally said.

"True, but there shouldn't be any issues with the probate—he had no family and his instructions are quite simple." He frowned. "Oh dear, I've just remembered, there was a bank certificate I neglected to have her sign. I suppose I'd better take care of that as soon as possible. I've an appointment tomorrow to meet with the Fulham Workhouse trustees and that might take all day."

There was a rapid knock on the door, then it opened and a constable stepped into the doorway and handed Barnes a folded sheet of paper. "Message for you, sir. It was brought in by a street lad; he claimed it was from one of your informants."

Barnes' heart beat faster as he reached for the paper, but he kept his composure. "They always say that." He forced a chuckle and then stepped as far away from Witherspoon's chair as he dared. The message was short and to the point.

Ted Bruce taking five o'clock train to Southampton, boarding ship to Argentina.

Mrs. Bruce not the killer. Evidence she's going to confront husband today.

She's in danger. Get to Bruce house.

"Is it important?" the inspector asked.

For a moment, Barnes wasn't sure what to say, but then he realized the truth would be best. "I think we'd better get to the Bruce home, sir. My informant claims Mr. Bruce is getting ready to take a ship to South America."

"Mr. Bruce?" Witherspoon was confused, but nonetheless got up. "You'll have to excuse us, Mr. Smalling, we must go."

As Barnes moved quickly toward the door, he crumpled the paper into a tight ball and shoved it into his pocket. He held the door as Smalling and the inspector hurried out into the hall.

"Shall I fetch a couple of constables to take with us, sir?" Barnes asked as soon as the solicitor had disappeared.

Witherspoon's brows came together. "Well, it couldn't hurt. This is most odd, isn't it? I've no idea what is actually going on, do you?"

"Not really, sir, but if the information is true, I think we'd better have a word with Mr. Bruce before he gets on a ship." He sprinted down the corridor and was back a few moments later with Constables Griffiths and Evans in tow. "Ready, sir?"

"As ready as I'll ever be," Witherspoon replied.

He thought about the situation as he stood on the pavement while one of the constables flagged down a four-wheeler. It was possible this was all a bit of a hoax, he thought as he buttoned his overcoat against the cold wind. On the other hand, Barnes had a remarkable network of informants and this information was very specific. The carriage pulled up at the curb and he climbed inside, took the corner seat, and began to go over each fact he knew about Ted Bruce and Walker's.

Smythe, Wiggins, and Hatchet watched from the windows of Luty's carriage across the street from the station. When the policemen's four-wheeler disappeared around the corner,

Hatchet thumped the ceiling and they pulled away. He'd already instructed Luty's driver to stay far enough back to avoid being seen. "Well, let's see if anything happens." He shrugged. "At the very least, the arrival of the police might keep Bruce from leaving London."

"What time is it?" Wiggins asked.

Hatchet pulled his pocket watch out, flipped open the cover, and said, "Half past three."

"If we're lucky, the police arrivin' will at least keep the bastard from catchin' the five o'clock train," Smythe muttered. "I'm not sure this is goin' to do any good. The bloke can always catch another one."

"The note did say that Mrs. Bruce was in danger," Hatchet reminded him as the carriage careened around the corner, causing all three of them to grab for a handhold. "That implies that Ted Bruce is the killer. That should get the inspector thinking. I'm sure he'll ask some discerning questions."

"Only if 'e had enough time to think about it properly." Wiggins looked unsure.

"Don't worry, lad, Inspector Witherspoon is no fool. He's got twenty minutes or so to consider the evidence and he'll come to the same conclusion as Mrs. Jeffries. I'm sure of it," Hatchet declared.

"You sure about this one, Hepzibah?" Luty asked as Mrs. Jeffries paced back and forth between the back stairs and the cooker.

She stopped and looked at the three women sitting at the table. For a moment, she was tempted to stretch the truth, to tell them that of course she was certain she was right, but as she contemplated their expressions, she realized they would only settle for the truth. "Not completely. But I think it's the most likely solution."

"That's honest." Mrs. Goodge grinned. "But I think you're being hard on yourself. You've always been right in the past."

"Stop doubting yourself, Hepzibah," Luty ordered. "Come sit down and have another cup of tea. You're wearing a hole in the floor."

"Or perhaps you'd like something stronger." Ruth looked at her half-full cup. "I've had more than enough tea. I need something to settle my nerves. Why don't I go across the garden and get a nice bottle of sherry or brandy." She started to get up.

"We've got one here." Mrs. Jeffries waved her back to her seat. "But we'd best hurry, Betsy will be back soon."

Betsy had taken Amanda home to be looked after by her neighbor. She'd wanted the little one out of the way and safely tucked in her own bed.

"And when she gets here, we'll give her a glass as well," Mrs. Goodge added. She got up and went to the sideboard. "You go sit down. I know where the brandy's kept and we can all use a nip or two."

Witherspoon climbed out first and stood on the pavement as he waited for the others.

"Let's hope Mr. Bruce is here to answer our questions." Barnes came to stand next to the inspector. The constables spread out behind him. "I'll have the lads wait out here, sir."

"That's best. I don't want the Bruce household to feel we're an invasion force."

Barnes had just started up the walkway when all of a sudden the front door burst open and a housemaid stumbled out, screaming at the top of her lungs, "Help! Help! They've all gone crazy!"

All four of the policemen raced to the house. Barnes reached the foyer first, with Witherspoon and the constables hot on his heels. He skidded to a halt and the inspector narrowly avoided crashing into his back.

Smalling was sprawled against the wall, his legs splayed apart, a briefcase and papers scattered on the floor around him, and blood oozing out of his forehead. "I just wanted her to sign some papers." He pointed down the hall. "They've gone insane, both of them, utterly insane."

The sound of a gunshot came from down the corridor. There were more screams and footsteps pounding toward them. A second later, two maids, their caps askew, raced into the foyer and out the front door. "Run for your lives!" one of them screamed as she leapt over Smalling's feet and out the door.

"Get him outside," Witherspoon ordered Evans. "Send one of the maids for the fixed-point constable." Then he and the remaining two policemen ran down the hall.

The door of the drawing room was open and Constable Griffiths reached it first, followed by Witherspoon and Barnes. The inspector peeked inside.

All the chairs were turned over, the tables were upturned, and the cushions from the sofas and settees were scattered everywhere.

Another shot rang out and Witherspoon jerked back into the corridor.

"You looking for this?" It was a woman's voice. Her tone was taunting.

Barnes dropped to his knees and looked. Inside, Hazel Bruce was behind an overturned love seat. She was waving a battered brown briefcase over the top of the frame.

Witherspoon knelt beside the constable.

"You're not getting it." She was looking across the room toward two overturned chairs that had been pulled together to form a barrier. "That gun only has a few more bullets left and you're such a bad shot you'll never hit me." She laughed. "God, you are a fool."

Ted Bruce rose up and fired off another blast, hitting the mirror over the mantelpiece but coming nowhere near his wife.

She cackled with glee. "You're totally incompetent, aren't you? You can't even shoot properly."

He leapt up and fired again, this time hitting a ceramic vase filled with holly boughs. "You cow," he yelled. "I'll kill you if it's the last thing I do."

"It will be the last thing you do, you stupid oaf." She popped up and lifted the case chin high. "You'll never get this. Did you think I didn't know about your little hiding place, you murdering pig?"

"I've done it once, I'm not scared to do it again. And your gun is out of bullets. I should have murdered you years ago." He fired two more times, sending her diving for the floor.

Witherspoon knew they had to do something. "Bruce has his back to the window," he whispered. "Constable Griffiths, have you a decent aim?"

Griffiths nodded. "Yes, sir."

"And I should have left you when Christopher asked me to run away with him, but no, like a fool, I stayed," she shouted. "Well, I'm the one with the briefcase now and you'll never get it."

"I want you to slip outside," Witherspoon ordered, "get to the back of the house, and find some rocks. Do it as quickly as possible and start firing them hard and fast through the window. Aim for Bruce's back, but if he turns, stay out of his line of fire."

Griffiths nodded and hurried down the corridor.

"What are we going to do, sir?" Barnes kept his voice low.

"Once the rocks start flying, we may be able to tackle him. We can't wait for help—he's going to kill her," the inspector said.

"You'll not have it for long." Bruce stood up and fired again.

"I tore up your ticket. The *Tartar Prince* is going to sail without you," she crooned in a singsong voice. "You're not going anywhere."

"You miserable cow. God, I wish I'd never met you." He hurled a china figurine at her. "I wish I'd killed you that night instead of him."

"But you didn't, did you, and now I've got all the money you stole from the company and that's not all. He left me enough to live on for the rest of my life." She cackled, then leapt up and held the briefcase over her head for a second before disappearing. "You've got nothing. You'll never get out of here. They'll hang you for Christopher's murder. Were you that scared of him that you had to shoot him in cold blood?"

He leapt up and fired again. "You cow."

"You're out of bullets now," she called.

"So are you," he yelled.

"Fooled you." She leapt up again, only this time, she was holding a revolver. "I have two and you only had one." She squeezed off a shot as she started toward him.

Suddenly, glass shattered and a huge rock sailed inside, startling both the Bruces. He whirled around just as another projectile crashed through the pane. Surprised, she dropped her gun.

Witherspoon and Barnes flew across the room. The constable grabbed her in a flying tackle just as a third rock came hurling through the window, this time hitting its target. The blow sent Bruce to his knees as the inspector leapt upon his shoulders and dragged him to the floor.

Hazel Bruce screamed, "Let me kill him! My God, let me kill him!"

"No, ma'am." Witherspoon stood up and looked down at Ted Bruce, who'd curled up in a ball and was groaning. "No one is going to kill anyone," he told her. "Mr. Bruce, please get up. You're under arrest for the murder of Christopher Gilhaney and the attempted murder of Hazel Bruce."

"She tried to murder me." He glared at the inspector. "You've got to arrest her as well."

"I don't care if they cart me off to jail." She laughed. "I can afford to hire the best legal help in London. What's more, if they don't hang you, I'm going to divorce you and I won't need my father's help. I can do it with my own money."

"Let's not mention how many bullets was flyin' back and forth," Smythe warned as the three men came through the back door of Upper Edmonton Gardens. "Ruth might get upset if she knows he was standin' so close to harm's way."

"Right, it's best if we let the inspector tell 'er that bit 'imself," Wiggins agreed.

"Good day, ladies," Hatchet cried as they came into the kitchen. He beamed at Mrs. Jeffries. "Once again, you were right. Ted Bruce has been arrested."

Mrs. Jeffries sagged in relief. "I was ninety percent sure it was him, but there was still a bit of doubt. Come sit down and tell us everything."

"I'll make fresh tea." Phyllis got up and grabbed the kettle.

"We can't give you many details." Hatchet took his spot next to Luty. "We did as you instructed. Wiggins found a street lad to take the note into the station and a few moments later the inspector and Constable Barnes appeared."

"They 'ad Constable Griffiths and Constable Evans with 'em," Wiggins added.

"Constable Evans—he's the handsome one, isn't he?" Phyllis put the kettle on the cooker to boil.

The footman gave her a fast, annoyed glance. "He's not *that* handsome. He's just a regular bloke."

"It was a good thing 'e took 'em," Smythe interjected quickly. "There was a bit of a dustup at the Bruce house and . . ." He trailed off, not sure how much he could say without revealing the truth.

Hatchet took up the story. "Unfortunately, as you predicted, Mrs. Jeffries, Mrs. Bruce did confront her husband. It ended with overturned furniture, broken windows, and Ted Bruce being carted off in handcuffs. But what we want to know is how you figured it out."

Luty looked at Mrs. Goodge and the two women exchanged knowing glances. The elderly American knew he was glossing over the details for a reason. "That's right, tell us how ya sussed it out this time."

Mrs. Jeffries clasped her hands together. "Well, I wasn't sure until the inspector made it clear he thought that Mrs. Bruce was the killer. At first I agreed with him, but last night I kept waking up as bits and pieces that we had learned suddenly came together and pointed in a different direction."

The kettle boiled and Phyllis poured the water into the big brown teapot. "It'll be a few more minutes before it's ready." She got their cups down from the cupboard over the counter.

"One of the things that concerned me the most was the motive," Mrs. Jeffries said.

"You told us you thought the motive was fear," Ruth reminded her.

"And it was, but I was completely wrong about why the killer was afraid. Bruce wasn't in the least bothered by what happened to Polly Wakeman, he was afraid of what Gilhaney could do to him now." She shook her head. "I can't believe it took me so long to understand when it was right under my nose, but instead of keeping a clear head, I let myself be distracted by the way Gilhaney acted that one night."

"What do you mean?" Luty demanded.

"Gilhaney was rude and probably had prepared a script once he knew who was going to be present at the Chase home that night. He told his friend he was going to turn down Walker's offer then he abruptly changed his mind. I think that once he thought about it, he realized he could get all those people in the same room and make them see he was the one with power now. I don't know what he planned to do to them in the future, but it was Ted Bruce who was scared of what he could do immediately. That's why Bruce had to kill him that night. Bruce couldn't let him see the books. Gilhaney was brilliant; more importantly, once he saw something, he could remember it perfectly."

"So he killed Gilhaney to keep him from lookin' at the ledgers?" Wiggins asked.

"That's correct. Remember, he only learned that morning that Gilhaney was starting the next day, Friday, and not the following Monday as he'd thought. Newton Walker hadn't just ordered the current financial documents be available the next day, he wanted everything from the past ten years on Gilhaney's desk when he walked in the office."

"You think Ted Bruce has been stickin' his fingers in the company pie that long?" Luty nodded her thanks as Phyllis handed her a cup of tea.

"Longer, I suspect. I think he's been embezzling since he took over." She took the teacup Phyllis handed to her. "I don't know precisely how he did it and I'm not certain it matters now that he's been arrested. What I do know is that he was the one with the real motive. Ann Holter may have hated Gilhaney, but he ruined her chances for marriage years ago. She could have killed him anytime she wanted. Leon Webster, he simply wanted to avoid the man at all costs; the same could be said of Robert Longworth and even Florence Bruce."

"But now that her brother has been arrested, her sister-in-law won't have a reason to keep her in the house," Hatchet said.

"I think she will—remember, it was Hazel Bruce who insisted she come live with them. Her brother was ready to let her go live off the charity of a cousin," Mrs. Jeffries explained.

"Can you explain how you knew specifically it was him?" Phyllis took her own cup and sat down. "I want to understand it better."

"Of course. Let me start at the beginning." She paused, wanting to be certain she presented the facts in the proper order. "Gilhaney coming to the firm wasn't a secret, but everyone thought he would be starting work on Monday, November ninth, but instead, he was going to be there Friday, November sixth. Once I thought about it, I realized it was that change which caused his murder. Look at how Bruce behaved once he found out he didn't have the weekend to either make a run for it or kill Gilhaney. He left the office after specifically telling Gordon Chase that he'd notify the clerks to bring down the old ledgers and documents. He said nothing to them because he knew he was going to murder Gilhaney that night and that was one of his mistakes. If he'd really wanted to appear innocent, he should have made them do it."

"That was a stupid mistake," Betsy said. "Newton Walker was so angry when he saw the empty office, it caused a row between Chase and Bruce that the clerks remembered."

"That's right," Mrs. Jeffries said. "Bruce's second mistake was saying he had an appointment with a Mr. Stowe, but Lloyd Ridgeway, who kept the executive appointment diaries, claimed no such appointment was listed. Then Bruce went home supposedly to pick up some papers he'd left there. But I think he went home to steal his sister's laudanum and an empty perfume bottle from his wife's room."

"Why would he do that?" Ruth asked.

"He needed something to make his wife sleepy," she replied.

"So that's why you had me ask my friend about the effect." Ruth laughed. "Of course! The Bruces watched each other like two jealous old cats. He needed her to be sound asleep. He didn't want her knowing when he came home or what he brought with him."

"Right, his sister would already have been asleep—she took laudanum every night."

"And he dropped the perfume bottle in the front garden," Wiggins added. He thought back to his encounter with the housemaid who'd been afraid to talk to him. "Cor blimey, guess that maid did 'elp a bit. It was Florence Bruce that found it."

"Bruce probably put the laudanum in his wife's wine when the others went outside to look at the fireworks. But the most damning bit of evidence against him was his instructions to the Chase maid to be certain to get a hansom cab for his wife and sister, not a vehicle that could take all three of them home. He needed time to do the deed. I think it happened like this: He overheard Gordon Chase tell Gilhaney about the shortcut through the mews and he got there before Gilhaney did. He shot him, stole the ring and the diamond stickpin, and even took Gilhaney's brass knuckles. Then he went home, accidentally dropping the empty perfume vial in the front garden."

"Another mistake," Luty said.

"He slipped inside and into his study, where he put the items he'd taken off the dead man inside his hiding place under his desk. Then he went up to bed and the next morning went to work as if nothing happened." Mrs. Jeffries took a sip of her tea.

"I'll bet he was tickled pink when that nitwit Nivens showed up." Luty snorted. "Nivens was probably dumb enough to tell the man the crime was a robbery, not a straight-out murder."

"But I'll bet 'e was scared when our inspector showed up six weeks later." Wiggins laughed. "What I don't understand is if Newton Walker suspected Bruce was stealin' from 'em, why didn't he give him the boot? If he was payin' Molly to spy on the Bruces, 'e must have known their marriage was a misery."

"Because he was married to Walker's only child," Mrs. Jeffries explained. "And he didn't want to see her ruined socially. However, I think the reason Bruce was going to flee wasn't just because he was afraid of being arrested, I think he'd realized that Walker was going to help his daughter with a divorce."

"That's right, my source said Walker was tryin' to find out how much a divorce cost." Luty nodded. "Which means that Bruce woulda had nothing. He'd lose his job, his house, and maybe his freedom if Gilhaney was as smart as everyone thought."

"What I don't understand is the relationship between Gilhaney and Hazel Bruce," Phyllis said. "Why would he leave her so much money?"

It was Ruth who answered. "I suspect he genuinely cared for her. My guess is that the first time she told her father she wanted to leave her husband was when she and Gilhaney began their liaison. Her father was adamant that he wouldn't help. She probably felt utterly hopeless."

"She might have even broken it off with Gilhaney so he could move on to someone else," Betsy muttered. "Relationships are never black and white. There's always shades of gray."

"We'll get more details once the inspector comes home."
Mrs. Jeffries smiled broadly. "I'm sure he'll be as pleased as
we are that we all of us will be enjoying the Christmas holiday we planned!"

The inspector did have more details to share when he came
home. He started for his study, but Mrs. Jeffries stopped
him. "Oh no, sir, you must come downstairs. Lady Cannonberry is here—she brought over a bottle of wine for all of us
to enjoy, and everyone's dying to hear about today. We heard
you've arrested Gilhaney's killer."

Mrs. Goodge, Luty, and Ruth had come up with this ruse
earlier.

He grinned in surprise. "Gracious, how did you find out
about it?" Without waiting for her reply, he turned toward
the back stairs and hurried off.

"Lady Cannonberry's butler, Everton, told her and she
told us. I've no idea how he knew." She raced to catch up with
him. They clattered down the stairs and into the kitchen.

The others were sitting around the table, wineglasses at
the ready.

Ruth stood up. "Gerald, I do hope you don't mind, but I
took the liberty of coming over and bringing some holiday
cheer. We're all so proud of you. You've done the impossible—
you've solved the case." She sat back down.

"It wasn't just me. Constable Barnes and many other
policemen did their share." He sat down at the head of the
table next to her. He patted her hand. "It's so kind of you to
bring the wine. Shall we have some?"

"I'll pour, sir," Mrs. Jeffries offered. "You will tell us

about the arrest, won't you?" She moved around the table pouring a small amount into each of their glasses.

"Of course. We arrested Theodore Bruce." He told them what had happened, taking care not to be melodramatic about the events in the Bruce house itself.

Nonetheless, when he'd finished, Ruth grabbed his hand. "Oh, Gerald, you could have been killed."

"We took care to stay down, but Bruce was far more concerned with trying to kill his wife rather than any of us. Luckily, both Mr. and Mrs. Bruce were almost out of ammunition by the time Constable Griffiths started hurling rocks through the window."

"What about Mr. Smalling, sir?" Mrs. Jeffries asked. "Is he going to be alright?"

"He is; it's a minor head wound. Apparently, Bruce coshed him on the side of the head as he was trying to get out the front door." Witherspoon took a sip of the wine. "The poor man happened to arrive just as Ted Bruce realized that Mrs. Bruce had stolen the briefcase from a secret compartment in the floor beneath his desk. Smalling told us he was getting Mrs. Bruce to sign some documents when her husband charged into the drawing room and began shouting. Smalling didn't object to the shouting, but Mrs. Bruce suddenly stood up and pulled a gun out from under the cushions, pointed it at her husband, and called him a murdering pig. At that point, Mr. Smalling decided to retreat. He grabbed his documents and briefcase and ran for the door. Bruce chased him, pulled his own gun out, and bashed him on the side of the head."

"And the rest of the household? What were they doing?" Mrs. Goodge asked.

"Florence Bruce wasn't home, but the servants had realized something was terribly wrong and got out the front and back doors."

"What was in the briefcase, Gerald?" Ruth was still holding his hand.

"Christopher Gilhaney's ring and stickpin and the brass knuckles he always carried, along with ten thousand pounds in cash. Ted Bruce has been stealing from Walker and Company for years."

"Was 'e embezzlin'?" Wiggins looked at the wine bottle and made a face when he saw it was empty.

"Bruce claimed all he did was skim a bit off the top—that's how he referred to it—but stealing is stealing. He kept the money in that hiding place beneath his desk. He killed Gilhaney because he knew the man would spot what he'd done right away and he wasn't ready to leave England until now."

"Why now?"

"I'm not sure how he did it, but he managed to get money out of the company on a monthly basis."

"It probably has something to do with taking a bit off the regular monthly expenditures," Luty muttered. "Skimmin' his cut before the bills got paid to the vendors."

"That's certainly possible, but that's the reason he stayed. He wanted the December money. He'd realized that Newton Walker was serious about getting him out of the company and out of his daughter's life."

"Did you arrest Mrs. Bruce?" Phyllis asked. "She was shooting at him as well."

Witherspoon sighed. "We've not made a decision about charging her as yet. Mr. Walker arrived with his solicitor in tow and pointed out that she was merely defending her life."

"But didn't you say that Mr. Smalling said she pulled her gun out first?" Betsy said.

"I did." Witherspoon smiled skeptically. "But the Walker solicitor pointed out that she probably had the gun because she was terrified he was going to kill her. I'll let Chief Superintendent Barrows make that decision." He looked at Ruth. "Shall I walk you across the garden?"

"Absolutely not. You go upstairs and have a rest. I want to speak to Mrs. Goodge for a moment. We're still coming up with tomorrow night's menu."

"We've got to go," Betsy said as she and Smythe got up. "The little one will be wanting her bath. We've some presents to wrap as well."

"I'll bring the carriage around the front." Hatchet rose to his feet.

"Wiggins, can you move the buckets of sand into the drawing room?" Mrs. Jeffries stood up. "I had them put into the back hall and the tree will be here early tomorrow morning. Oh dear, I've got to get up to the linen cupboard for a floor sheet. I want to make certain it's in place before they bring it into the house. If we don't have something under that tree, it'll scratch the wood."

Within a few moments, the kitchen was empty save for Mrs. Goodge, Ruth, and Luty.

The cook lifted her glass. "Ladies, I do believe we did it. We got them back on the path to justice."

"It wasn't easy. There were moments when I felt awful. I had to say some terrible things," Ruth said.

"Horsefeathers." Luty lifted her glass. "We did what was right and if we hadn't done it, Gilhaney's killer would be on his way to South America tonight."

"True, but I know how Ruth feels. I felt like cryin' at some of the things I said to Wiggins. He looked so hurt. Still, sometimes you've got to be cruel to nudge people in the right direction. I'll toast to us." Mrs. Goodge raised her glass. "Here's to us, we're three very clever ladies."

Ruth lifted her glass. "Oh no, in keeping with the season, here's to us, three very wise women."

They clinked their glasses.

Printed in the United States
by Baker & Taylor Publisher Services